boss level

Three Player Tag-Team Book 6

allyson lindt

acelette press

For every bad ass boss bitch

introduction

Boss levels are the climax points of a section of a game, such as the end of a level, stage, or series, and are specifically guarding a specific objective.

Note from the author: Boss Level takes place in the same timeframe as Dungeon Crawl, in fact it starts one day earlier. If you reach certain points in the book and think *haven't I read this*, you may have. But keep in mind, different people see events in different ways, and I promise that Judith, Xander, and Dominic's story is not the same as Elliot, Link, and Fallyn's.

1 /
judith

M ost days I wanted to be a bad ass bitch, who the world bowed to.

Days like today, I wanted to be submissive and meek and have some imposing man or woman lavish me with cuddles and chocolate covered strawberries and orgasms.

Not necessarily in that order.

Somebody like the man calling me on my personal cell, as I sat in my office taking a precious few minutes of quiet-brain time before my next meeting.

"Hey, you," I answered Xander's call, a smile creeping onto my face. He was my oldest friend. Sure, I'd known a lot of guys in the office for decades, but it wasn't the same. They worked for me. Xander... he was both my best girlfriend and my favorite fuck buddy.

Okay, not the last one anymore. Not since Dominic. But we all stayed close.

"How are you, Judy?" Xander's voice was bright. Warm. Hiding something.

And no one got to call me Judy except him and my ex-husband. Even Cole got a withering look for it. "Yanno. You do know, don't you? You don't really have to ask?"

Seven years ago, a group of us had an insane plan, to build a video game like the world had never seen. Six years ago, we started work. Next week, we'd make it available to the entire world, when we headlined one of the biggest video game shows in the world.

And I had so much work to do before then.

"Conquering the world and devouring their stress as if it fueled you?" Xander teased.

"Not the actual world," I corrected him. "That's on the schedule for three and a half years from now. Only the world of gaming."

"You're going to kill it next week."

"Of course I am." We'd been in early access for a few weeks already, and beta for more than a year before that. I had some nagging doubts, but I'd never let those show. Not even to Xander. Not unless we were behind closed doors and both of us were *really* drunk. "Did you call to tell me what I already know?" I kept my tone light. I did want to talk to him. Friendly chats were something I missed.

"That's exactly why I called." There was that catch in his voice again.

It was subtle. Likely no one but me would hear it. "But?"

"I need to call in a favor. I know the timing isn't great, but I wouldn't ask unless I had to."

Favors were my preferred currency, and I'd handed out IOUs on several occasions since starting this company. I leaned back in my chair and propped my feet up on my desk. It was odd to hear him speak with so much up-front explanation rather than dive right into the core topic. "What's up?" I asked.

"It's for Dom." The way Xander said it, he assumed that would be enough.

Nope.

Xander and I met Dominic seven years ago, almost to the day, when I was trying to decide if this venture was a good idea. Dominic was a lawyer referred to me by a friend, and he, Xander, and I hit it off brilliantly. But Dom and Xander had to ruin it by going and falling in love. They weren't legally married, for their own professional reasons, but they called each other *husband* in our circle of friends.

And Xander would do anything for Dominic. I questioned that on occasion, but it was a good relationship. It was just... immersive. They were *so* into each other.

"You know I adore you," I said. "But I have a

call in two, so I will need the details." I could apologize for pushing for an answer. For not being able to chat longer. But I never apologized.

Xander sighed. "He's got a potential client. A *big* client. The kind that could expand his firm."

"X…" I pushed some warning into the nickname, for him to get to the point.

"This guy is big on family. He's one of those sergeant authorities in that church or something."

General authorities. There was no reason for me to correct him, even though the lingering whispers of indoctrination from the religion I was raised in insisted I do so. Xander knew exactly what he was saying. "And…?" I hated to check my watch when I was talking to him, but I did it anyway. "One minute thirty."

"And this guy was visiting the legal offices, heard someone talking about Dominic's spouse—the employee was good, they played the gender-neutral game—and then Mr. Potential Client saw the photo on Dom's desk.

Oh. Oh, shit. That was the photo that sat on the bookcase behind me. The same one that was in Xander's office as well. It was of all three of us, from the day I signed the paperwork on the building I was in now, and the three of us were toasting champagne in cheap plastic glasses, in the best selfie Xander had ever taken.

If this guy thought Dominic was married, that

explained why Xander was dragging this conversation out. "Thirty seconds," I warned.

"Pretend to be his fiancée through the holidays. That's the favor. Through the holidays and only for his potential client."

The request sent a chill up my spine, and I wasn't sure why. What was I supposed to say? It was a favor, and favors had to be honored, but what he was asking me to do... "I have to walk into this meeting. I'll call you when I'm free. " *I'm sorry.* I swallowed the apology as I disconnected before he could say anything else.

The conversation stuck in my head the rest of the day, and screamed loudly when Xander sent a follow-up text a few hours later.

A fake relationship was a bad idea. If someone found out, it would make things worse than if he'd told the client the truth to start. Then again, I knew Dominic almost as well as I did Xander, and it wasn't like I *couldn't* fake it. Dom was a sexy beast of a man—it wasn't as though I'd have to fake attraction.

And there was a sliver of underlying resentment, like any real couple should have, since he'd stolen my best friend from me. A hint of *how could you* that I'd hidden from him for years.

Right now was possibly the worst time in my career for me to step into something like this, but it would also be a distraction if it didn't interfere with my schedule.

I failed to see how I was the perfect spouse to impress a high-ranking member of any Christian church. I ran a business that was making an X-rated game. There was more nuance than that to what we were doing, but a church man was going to look at me and see a forty-year-old woman who would rather make digital porn than stay at home and raise a family.

Gag me with a spoon.

On the other hand, I wasn't the public face of the company. Yes, I was listed as the owner in trade publications, but if this man wasn't in the industry, it was unlikely he cared who I was.

All the back and forth in my head made me dizzy, but it didn't make a decision any easier.

Around seven in the evening, Ivan, our office manager, made sure I had dinner before leaving for the night. Which was my reminder to send a few employees home. Mostly Adrienne, who was several months pregnant, and looked like she was ready to pop. She'd work all night, like everyone else, if I didn't make one of her boyfriends take her out of here.

But most of us stayed. The developers. Elliot. Nigel. Dustin.

Some days I felt like their mom. I could tell this potential client of Dominic's that. *Of course I chose to raise a family*. A family of kids the same age as me, who worked too hard, didn't eat right, and kept falling in love.

Idiots.

And I adored almost every single one of them.

It was after nine when someone knocked on my office door. I looked up to see Dominic standing in the doorway. He was the kind of man a lot of people would swoon to get a surprise visit from. Taller than six feet, which meant I was always straining my neck to look up at him when he was nearby, short, dark hair, and no hint of the handful of tattoos that lay under his clothes.

He walked in without waiting for an invitation, and closed the door behind himself. His suit was impeccable and expensive, and hugged all the right places to highlight and hint at an incredible physique. The way he strode across the room whispered *power* and *control*.

And I didn't know what I was going to tell him.

Instead of taking the seat across from me, he walked to my side of the desk, and leaned against the wood, less than a foot from me. "Xander said he talked to you earlier."

Having Dominic here intensified the conflict raging in my brain. I wanted to help him. Yes, there was a hint of resentment, but the friendship and admiration were more potent. I wouldn't be here if it weren't for him, and this was exactly where I wanted to be. There were worse people to pretend to be engaged to. "He did."

"And that you've avoided him since," Dom said.

"It's been seven hours, and obviously I'm still working. Hardly avoidance."

Dom smiled. "You know Xander. If there's no drama, the story isn't worth telling."

Not true at all, but fun to pretend. "Uh-huh."

He shifted his weight to bring him closer. It was late, I was tired, and my defenses were down. Which meant that new thoughts could trickle in. There were days when I wondered what would've happened if Dominic and I had hooked up instead of him and Xander. The first time we met, Dom and I jerked each other off under a restaurant table.

Fortunately for me, my first marriage had shown me I wasn't cut out for long-term romantic relationships. I was married to my company, and no one wanted to be the other person in that arrangement.

"It wasn't right of me to have him make that call," Dominic said. "I should've asked you myself and I should've done so in person. Do you have a minute right now, or do you have a meeting?"

The hint of playful sarcasm in his question almost made me smile. "I keep trying, but I haven't found a way to get anyone to agree to meet this late on a Friday." I tried to joke back, but there was a lump in my throat that I didn't want to define.

Dominic knelt at my feet, and pulled a tiny box,

like a ring box, from his jacket pocket.

My heart dropped into my stomach. Thank Goddess he closed the door. "Please don't do this."

Instead of complying with my request, he opened the box. The ring that sat inside was simple but stunning. Low profile, platinum, inlaid with diamonds and rubies. Even in the low light of my office, the light glinted off the gems. "You did *not* buy that for a fake engagement."

"No. It's my grandmother's." He pulled it from the box.

Not *that* ring. Not the one he was supposed to give his wife someday. The one he kept in a safety deposit box instead. He was *not* holding out that same ring and offering it to me.

"This is only for show." Dominic grasped my fingertips. "To get me through holiday parties and negotiations. You don't have to be there all the time, and I'll owe you in return. Fake marry me?"

Not the most eloquent proposal ever, but I didn't want it to be. "Wow, you really know how to romance a girl." I couldn't find my answer. Why was this such a difficult decision to make?

"I can seal the deal with a kiss instead." Dominic searched my face. "Or beg. If you've ever wanted to see me do that, this is your one and only chance."

As tempting as that sounded, I still didn't know what to say.

2 /
dominic

Despite this being a very fake proposal, I held my breath in a very real way as I waited for Judith's answer. This was a stupid idea long-term, but the arrangement didn't have to last more than a few weeks. We'd go to some parties together, I'd land this contract, it would lead to other contracts, and she'd dump me going into next year.

I resisted the urge to drop my hand into my pocket, to run my thumb along the watch I kept there, as I studied the petite woman sitting in front of me. The way wisps of auburn escaped from a low ponytail and teased her cheeks. Her green eyes, dark with thought. The fact that she looked fierce and imposing doing something as simple as thinking, and yet I knew how much kindness lay beneath it all. The lengths she'd go to for her friends and employees.

She was truly beautiful, and I'd be lucky to call

her my fiancée, if only for a short while.

"Yes." At Judith's answer, I let out a long exhale.

I rose to kiss her on the cheek. "Thank you. I will work to make sure you don't regret this."

"You'd better." A hint of teasing slid into her voice, and she tugged me to my feet. "I wouldn't do this for anyone but the two of you, and I want to go on record as saying it's a supremely bad idea."

It was a horrible idea. I was doing it anyway. I grasped her fingers and brushed my lips over her knuckles. "It'll be a laugh. As in, we'll all laugh about it when it's over."

"But you're very limited in when you can have me next week," she warned.

"Of course." I wouldn't expect otherwise. Right as she was making the biggest move of her career? I wouldn't pull her from that. "But tonight?" I plucked a wrinkled cherry tomato from the wilted salad on her desk, and tossed it at her trash can. "Tonight I'm taking you out for a real meal, before you reach the climax of the bedlam."

She moved her food out of my reach, and raised an eyebrow. "Tonight, you're leaving my food alone, regardless of your opinion, and you're letting me finish my work. I'll give you tomorrow night."

I slid the ring on her finger, and it fit perfectly. Did her breath catch?

No. That was the romantic in me. "I'm holding you to that. I'll send you details, don't stand us up."

"I would never." Her shock and offense were exaggerated.

"You would frequently." And I was fine with that. She was as married to her job as Xander and I each were.

She shook her head with a smile. "I'll be there tomorrow. Cross my heart."

I left her to work, and headed home. The traffic was moderate, but I didn't have far to travel. The deeper I got into The Aves, the farther up the side of the mountain, the more the snow lingered. Holiday lights reflected off the patches of white, and seemed to warm the chilly evening with their promises of brightness and warmth.

This was my favorite time of year, and the decorations added to my joy. I might put on a gruff exterior for business and everyday life, but I was a softie when it came to peace on earth, good will toward men.

I wouldn't make this request of Judith for me, the same way I hadn't asked Xander to keep our relationship on the down low for me. Roger, the man who'd started our law firm with my father, was also my father's best friend. Roger had come out to his colleagues in an era where people didn't do that, and it destroyed his career on the other side of the country.

He started over here with my father, but it was hard for Roger to rebuild. I knew the world was different now, but a lot of our clients weren't. They were Roger's age, and to them business still ran that way.

After my father passed away, I decided the best way to honor him was to follow in his footsteps. Roger helped, pushing me through law school, making sure I had this job waiting for me when I graduated. More than a decade ago when he asked me to keep my sexual orientation a secret, for the firm, it was easy to say *yes*. I didn't need the world knowing who I was fucking.

As Xander and I had grown closer, he understood the request. The need for discretion. He had his own reasons it made sense to him. But the longer we'd been doing this, the more it wore on both of us. There were a number of days I felt torn between my loyalty to Roger and my desire to tell the world what Xander meant to me.

I pulled up in front of our house, and our own decorations twinkled at me. Xander had insisted we not go too tacky, so our lights were simple, white lights adorning the boxy house with floor to ceiling front windows.

Inside, the holiday lights from the living room reached into the dimly lit foyer, greeting me. I could hear the TV playing. I found Xander with his laptop in front of the TV. Which meant he was working, but he wanted to see me when I got home.

He looked up as I strode toward him. Unlike

me, he didn't have to hide his ink. The tattoos on his olive skin stretched up under the sleeves of his T-shirt, and seemed to grow from the collar. The tiny silver ring in his right nostril was subtle, glinting occasionally depending on how he turned his head. And his salt and pepper hair screamed *experienced*, which only amplified the whole *mature and wise, but also a bad-boy* look.

Twenty-year-old me would've begged him to teach me all the things he obviously knew.

Who was I kidding? Thirty-five-year-old me had done the same when we first met.

I had his full attention the instant I walked in—he hadn't been getting much work done.

"How'd it go?" His voice was hard to read. He wasn't happy about this entire thing.

Not that I blamed him. Not only did we have to hide *us*, but now I was pretending with *her*.

I also didn't see a way around this that wouldn't destroy my law firm. Roger and I were picky about clients. Having a reputation for being ethical was important to both of us, and we turned down a lot of high-paying work because of it.

Of course, that one big lie both Roger and I told… I hated hiding how much I loved Xander, but the clients I would lose… It would only take two or three of the big ones walking away. It wasn't about the money—not for me anyway. If the firm crumbled, a lot of people would be out of work.

I wouldn't throw away all of Roger's hard work for selfish reasons like love.

Besides, another thing I loved about Xander—career was as important as love. Something we had in common with Judith. Speaking of, "She said *yes*."

Xander let out a ridiculously high-pitched squeal of fake excitement. "*Oh-em-gee*." He squealed again.

"Rein it in." I rolled my eyes, but let my amusement peek through in a smile.

He leaned forward to set his laptop on the coffee table. "Seriously though? Good. I'm glad. But don't think I want to stretch this out for any point of time."

I crouched in front of him so we were eye-to-eye. "I know. Less than a month, and I'm all yours again."

Xander gripped my chin tightly and his fingers dug into flesh. His touch both ached and enticed, and it sent a shiver of desire through me. He held my gaze. "You're always mine."

"Yes, I am." And I always would be. I rose to crush my mouth to his, pushing devotion and need through the connection. Having Xander in my life was one of those things I'd never surrender. I'd remind him again and again how much I wanted and needed him.

And tonight, that meant driving home the physical.

I lowered myself to my knees as I glided my fingers down his torso. When I reached his waist, I undid his belt and trousers, never breaking eye contact with him.

He watched me impassively, expression blank except for the challenge in his single raised eyebrow.

Fine with me. The way his dick jerked when I brushed it through fabric, the sharp intake of breath he tried to hide, told me all I needed to know.

I slipped my hand inside his boxers to grip his half-hard cock. A low groan rumbled from his chest. I worked him free and stroked, pausing occasionally to draw my thumb over the head, smearing precum over the sensitive tip and bringing him to fully erect.

Never looking away from Xander's face, I leaned in and drew him into my mouth. The flutter of his eyelids, the way he tilted his head back and let out a long groan, was something I felt through my entire body.

Now we could play. I traced my tongue along his shaft as I held him in my mouth. Pumping faster, squeezing tighter, and sucking harder in response to his movements and the intoxicating sounds he made. We'd been together long enough that I recognized his cues, but I still got hard from getting my husband off.

Our connection flowed between us, drawing my own cock to fully hard until it dug into my zipper.

Should I work myself free and stroke both of us at the same time.

I ached at the thought. Would waiting be worth the reward?

"Stop." Xander's command was rough.

I gave him a wide-eyed look, but I'd never pulled off *innocent puppy dog* very well.

He chuckled and reached past me to slap the lid of his laptop shut. He turned off the TV.

Though I'd pulled my mouth away from him, I kept my hand wrapped around his cock.

Xander tugged me to my feet. "Let's go to bed."

I might be disappointed, if I didn't recognize the heavy need in his tone, in his movements, and how it matched and fed my own.

We moved into the bedroom, and spent whole seconds stripping each other down. I was desperate to be close to him, to feel his skin on mine, and more than one button went flying in the flurry of tugging at clothing.

Then we stood body to body, heat flowing freely between us. Xander gripped my cock, and a sharp spike of desire drove into me. "I need you to come when I do." His voice was gravel. "I need to feel it. To see your face when you come."

Fuck. "Me too." I wrapped my hand around his shaft again.

We watched each other while we jerked each other's cocks. He'd been close in the living room, but I was peak-turned-on by bringing him to that point. The pain-plus-pleasure on his face told me he was holding back, and that he ached for release.

But he pushed me past my limits, stroking me harder and faster, drawing orgasm from me first. I groaned as I came, covering his hand, and when he hit that point shortly after, it drew out my climax.

We both kept tugging until our bodies shuddered from too much pleasure, then half-collapsed against each other, half-supported each other.

When we found the energy to pull apart, we cleaned up and climbed into bed. *Our* bed.

Xander gripped the base of my neck as we lay face to face, and pressed his forehead to mine. "I hate this," he said with resignation in his voice. "But I love you, and I wouldn't trust anyone else with either of you than each other."

"That almost made sense," I teased.

He stroked a thumb along my skin. "You know what I mean."

I did, and I wished he hadn't brought Judith into the statement. He meant the one thing he never said, or even admitted to himself, and that was about where Judith lived in his heart.

Not that she was competition, but I'd never had any delusions about how I shared him.

Sleep didn't come that night, as I lay there thinking about what was coming. What we'd put into motion with this entire fake engagement.

3 /
xander

My best friend was engaged to my husband. So apparently that was a thing I could check off my *I never thought I'd say…* list.

Around us, the world carried on as if this was an everyday occurrence. Just another blip in the weirdness that was reality. Christmas lights lined the streets, tinsel-lined shapes decorated poles, and traffic lit up the roads with row after row of taillights.

When I pulled my '69 Impala into the restaurant parking lot, I swore Dom sighed, but I couldn't tell if it was in disappointment or relief. Us being here wasn't a surprise, and the three of us met here on a regular basis.

But this time of year, it felt different. We'd met here, as in Judith and I met Dominic here, seven years ago, almost to the day. Had I picked this place on purpose, to *celebrate* this sham of an engagement?

Absolutely.

Was it petty of me?

Very probably.

I wanted him to remember the night he came into my life. To be reminded of it myself. And yes, it was true, that first night he and Judith had also gotten each other off under the table, and I wanted him to remember that was only sex that became friendship. Not romance.

Judith was already waiting for us inside, in almost the exact same spot Dominic had waited for her and me years ago. Exhaustion lined her face and drooped her shoulders, but when she saw us, the tiredness faded behind sunshine.

Always one of my favorite sights.

I gave her a tight hug. "You didn't stand us up," I teased.

"*You* did the standing-up most recently." She squeezed back. "Yes, I'm keeping score." She always was.

So was I. "Touché."

Dom gave her a hug too, but it hit me differently than usual when the soft lighting in the room glinted off her engagement ring.

I hated hiding my relationship with Dom, though I understood why he asked me to. In my not-so-humble opinion, he should go tell Roger to own who he was, and remind him that this was the twenty-first century, not the eighties, and men were open about loving other men.

I understood, I did. My Aunt Rosie was a lesbian, and had faced a lot of shit when she was younger, even before she figured it out for herself. But even though she wasn't *loud and proud*, she didn't pretend to be something she wasn't.

I also saw how much Roger meant to Dominic, and I was willing to bend to make my man happy. There were few things that lit up my world more than knowing Dominic was content.

Besides, I'd known what this was going to be from the start. He'd never hidden from me that he required a certain amount of discretion in his position.

The host showed us to our table, and the waiter was already there to tell us about the specials and take our drink orders. Not our regular, and in a way I was grateful for that. The small talk would be less personal.

I was in a *drink until I can't think* mood. Was it a good thing or a bad thing I'd driven? "Coke for me." Fuck it. "Champagne for the happy couple." I pointed at Judith and Dominic.

The look Judith shot me could've stripped the lacquer off the table, and it was meant for my eyes only, since it vanished behind a painfully bright smile a heartbeat later.

"What are we celebrating?" The waiter—Percy —asked.

Judith showed him her ring, and Dominic rested his hand under hers, holding both up.

Disgustingly synchronized. The two of them probably knew each other better than most actually engaged couples.

"Congratulations." Percy clapped twice. "I'll grab that bubbly for you, while you think about your dinner."

The instant his back was turned, Dominic and Judith dropped their hands, and she blew out a long puff of air, knocking a loose strand of auburn hair from her face.

"Actually having to do that hits differently than thinking about it," she said.

No kidding.

Under the right circumstances, I liked to watch the two of them together. This was very much *not* right. "Might as well face it now. In fact, it's as good a time as any to figure out what's on the itinerary for this engagement of the century."

"Not a lot." Was that a hint of tension in Dominic's voice? "Office Christmas party. Client's office Christmas party."

Judith wrinkled her nose. "Those haven't already happened? Damn, I was hoping to miss at least one."

"What? You'd skip out on the best part of any

relationship?" I tried to let playfulness slide into my question.

Dominic rolled his eyes. "Since when do you hate office parties?"

"I don't. I said *best part*." I wasn't going to ruin this evening. I wasn't going to be a total ass, especially since I'd agreed I was okay with this. "But they're not the same when you can't be yourself."

For instance, I'd loved the office Christmas party Judith's company threw last week. She had good people working for her. Talented, fun, non-judgmental. Dom and I got to be out. Open.

The atmosphere had been laced with stress, they were releasing the biggest game of their careers on Monday, but they were all this huge, friendly bunch. Basically family. It had almost made me wish I was more a part of things at AcesPlayed. I'd been an investor from the start, but I'd always stayed hands off. Cheered from the sidelines.

I shook the rambling thoughts away.

"Wait. I didn't realize I couldn't be me," Judith said.

I raised an eyebrow and pursed my lips.

Dominic sighed. "They're conservative, but we all know how to act in a business environment. It won't be that much of a stretch."

It sounded like a painful front to me.

"We're newly engaged. We probably need to sell the *I love you so much the rest of the world doesn't exist*."

Judith leaned into Dominic, head on his shoulder and dopey expression on her face.

He kissed her on the forehead. "I'm sure we can manage."

I clenched my fist under the table. "Maybe you're marrying for money. These people should be into that."

"Technically, that's absolutely what we're doing." Judith straightened up again. "But I don't think we want to tell them that."

Percy returned with a bottle of champagne on ice, and three fluted glasses. He made a proper show of popping the cork, and topping all of us off. I'd have been more grateful for the presentation if I was as happy about this as I pretended to be.

"Do you all know what you want?" Percy asked.

"We'll both have the scallop and chicken special." The instant I said the words, I knew I'd fucked up. I was so used to ordering for both Dom and I... "I mean, that's what I'll have."

"Same for me," Dominic said.

Judith shrugged. "Make that three."

Some habits were going to be harder to break than others, but Percy either didn't notice or was too well trained to say anything. He asked if we needed anything else, and was on his way again.

But speaking of expectations, "You know they'll expect Judith to be prim and proper and reserved. A timid little housewife."

Judith snorted in disbelief, and Dominic failed to hide his smirk behind his water glass.

"Yeah, that's not going to work for me," Judith said.

Dom set his drink down. "You can't tell them you make a smutty game for a living." His words were almost apologetic.

The way Judith bristled, it didn't matter. "I get that." An edge crept into her voice.

I might not want to see them together, but I also didn't want them to fight. They both needed to be in my life when this was over. "As long as you get your stories straight"—I suppressed a cough—"and agree what topics you'll steer away from when possible, you'll be great. The two of you already know each other, so that won't be a problem. For instance, where did you meet?"

"Here." Dom gestured. "A friend introduced us seven years ago."

This was our story, and I didn't know how I felt about that.

"The sparks were there from the start." Judith picked up the tale without pause.

Dominic nodded. "I couldn't stop thinking about her after that first night."

"Could've fooled me. I thought for sure he was more interested in my friend who was with us," Judith said.

"But I had to call her."

No. I didn't like this at all. Not the way Judith got to play two parts in this twisted version of my past, and not the way she and Dominic slid so easily into writing me out of the story. The voice growling *mine* in my skull nearly drowned out my thoughts. "Her friend, huh? That must've been awkward."

"Not as much as you'd think." Judith was so cool and casual, as if this was really about her. "She realized the chemistry wasn't there, making room for me."

This was a mindfuck.

Dom cupped her cheek and gazed into her eyes. "The rest is history. I could go on forever about my Judy."

Mistake. Only I could call her Judy and not piss her off. Like that I felt better.

Before he could brush his lips over hers, Judith had her hand on his chest and was pushing him back. "Call me anything but that." Her tone was flat.

"J-bird?" Dominic asked.

Uh... *no*.

"It's not bad." Judith looked unfazed. "It might grow on me."

"I'll keep trying," Dominic said.

I wanted to see that kiss for real. Why? Because I was a sadist, even when it came to myself. Besides, I might be conflicted about tonight, but the memory of the two of them together our first time here...

That never failed to light my skin on fire. "That kiss didn't sell me."

Judith shook her head. "What kiss?"

Dom rested a palm on her cheek, and forced her gaze to his. She froze, eyes wide, when he dipped his head toward hers. The kiss was soft. Subtle. No tongue, just lips pressed to lips. But the way Dom's mouth lingered on Judith's, I swore I felt what she did, and speaking of sparks...

Egging this on was a bad idea. Jealousy muted desire, and that roar of *mine* was louder than ever.

Yeah, Judith and I had fucked each other plenty over the years, but we'd never kissed. Not like that. It was one of those agreements we made when we were younger. *No kisses on the lips.* Because when you're twenty and think you know everything, that's the kind of thing you think keeps you from falling in love. So, yeah. I'd had my mouth pretty much everywhere on her body except her mouth.

If this was me on Engagement Day One, I was in trouble for the next few weeks.

Why hadn't they pulled apart yet?

I summoned every ounce of self-control that I had, and forced it through my veins, until my blood ran colder than the melting snow outside. "I'm sold, and if you can convince me, you can convince any stodgy old colonel authority."

"General authority." Judith broke away to correct me.

It was impossible to miss the breathiness in her reply, or the way she had her fingers halfway to her mouth before she paused and dropped her hand into her lap.

Dominic gave a short, sharp jerk of his head. "We'll be fine, and we'll be done by Christmas and broken up by New Year's."

Percy returned with our food, but the interruption didn't lift the heavy cloud at the table.

When he was gone again, I focused on Judith. "You ready for Monday?" I asked.

"I will *never* be ready. But of course I am. We've also never been more ready."

This was better. Talking shop. Diving into our jobs. Being the forty-year-old workaholics we all were. This was more like it.

It didn't erase the memory of that kiss from my mind, or the possessive, chanting voice roaring for me to remind Dom he was mine.

But it made both easier for me to ignore. At least a little bit.

4 /
judith

All around the world, kids—and adults—were counting down the days until Christmas.

Ever since I was in my late teens, Christmas had haunted me. My ex-husband had tried to help. Xander got close, but he hadn't quite pulled me back to being able to tolerate the holiday.

But for me, *today* was Christmas morning. A Christmas I'd been waiting on for more than half a decade. I didn't remember the last time I'd felt this kind of anticipation. Not even on my wedding day.

Then again, that ended in divorce a few years later. This was far more important. At ten in the morning, noon on the East Coast, our game would go live. It had been in early access for a short while, but we were officially opening the servers to the world in a few hours.

I had no idea how I was going to focus until then, but I didn't have a choice. The rest of my work didn't become any less important because this was the most significant Monday of my life. As I sat down at my desk, a message came in from Dom.

Stepping into a day of meetings. Wanted to tell you congratulations. No one deserves today more.

The words warmed me. I needed to remember that yes, I was doing him a favor, but there were worse things he could've asked than for me to pretend to be in love with him, and he'd done a lot for me and my people, especially over the last few years.

Muddling my way through any of my work proved to be as effective as the kids trying to stay quiet and not wake up Mom and Dad while they waited to open the presents from Santa.

About ten minutes before our go-live, I walked down the hall of the old, converted community college that was our offices. Everyone was at their desks, in Art, Music, QA, Story, Security, and my stop—Development—but I doubted any of them was getting any more done than I had.

I headed straight for the Director of Development's office, and knocked on Eliot's door.

He motioned me in without pause. I liked Elliot. Of course, I liked most of my people, but I'd been working with him the longest. He was smart and driven. Not the same kind of driven as me. Or Xander or Dom. But he knew what he wanted, and a lot of it had to do with this game.

As one of our office grumps, he looked brighter today than normal. Was that an actual smile?

Good. He should be proud of what he and his team had built.

We didn't make any small talk, and instead got right down to our final checklist. I was grateful he was a business partner, an investor, and so much more than a manager. Eliot had been by my side through all of this, and it was reassuring having people around who believed in what we were doing.

And then we were done with that final list of items. "It feels like there should be something else," he said.

"There's not. We're done." Were we really? No. There would be work to do on this game for years. Bugs we didn't catch in QA, new content, marketing pushes, good and bad press… "But I get what you mean." There was nothing else we could do in the next seven minutes that would matter.

He shrugged. "Well, you know my motto."

I didn't. Not at all. I was pretty sure there was nothing I heard him say over and over, and the only rule he lived his life by was *don't get attached*. That was a good one. Still, I would give it a shot. "Always expect trouble?"

"That's *your* motto." Elliot laughed. "Mine is *if you can't fuck it, eat it, or kill it, play with it*."

Uh…. No. "I've *never* heard you say that. And by the way, it's time."

Like that, Elliot's mood shifted. He gestured to his desk phone. "Would you like to do the honors?"

Damn right. I dialed everyone in the office, and put the call on speaker. If they were all doing the same, the noise out there must be a myriad of echoes.

Maybe I should've prepared a speech. Fuck it, I'd wing it. "I'm going to make this short." I hoped. "It doesn't matter if you've been here since the Cord days, if you've come on in the last year, or somewhere in between. If you're here today, be proud of yourself. Regardless of what happens next, we've already set records, broken barriers, and told the industry they're a bunch of stodgy old fucks and we know where the future is."

"Of course, what happens next is going to be even more incredible than what we've already seen." Elliot stepped in.

That made me smile, and he was completely right. We might not be creating world peace or solving the world's problems, but we were definitely about to change *something*. "Last chance to tell us *no go* before we pull the trigger."

I went through the entire list of departments, asking each of the heads if they were ready for this game to launch, and one after another they assured the office they were a go. Though the goofballs over in security stretched out their answer to a round of giggles.

So much better than the last guy over there. The one who was currently suing me for wrongful termination.

When everyone else had given their blessing, I looked at Elliot, whose broad smile was as out of place as my own. "Last, but never least. Development?"

He gave me a thumbs-up, though I was the only one who would see it. "Go."

It was time. Metaphorical Mom and Dad—me and him, I supposed—had woken up. Now the countdown began. I gave him a look, and he started a literal count toward Go Live. I moved to his side of his desk, to watch him put the final pieces into place.

Fuck me, this was real.

When he hit *Two*, every muscle in my body tensed. This was almost better than an orgasm.

Or maybe I wouldn't go that far. But it was pretty good.

On *one* he hovered his finger over his mouse, and on his own *Go* he launched the page that would let people log in.

I should focus on breathing, but I was too fascinated by the sudden silence that rolled through the office. I swore even on nights and weekends, it hadn't been this quiet in here since we moved in.

And then status reports started rolling in from everyone who was monitoring. Not only were we launching a new game, that was adult in its nature, more controversial than anything out there, and we were sending it into the world a few days before one of the biggest gaming conventions. A huge convention that we were headlining, because most of us had come from the company who hosted it.

So it was crucial that we work out the bad kinks, while keeping the good ones intact, before RinCon started.

And we were doing it. People were playing. So many people wanted in that the servers were maxed out and the login queues were full. But our game was running and not crashing.

"We did it." I mouthed to Elliot.

His grin was as stupid broad as mine. "I know, right?"

We exchanged a high five. I listened to the status reports a little longer, before I was comfortable saying I'd done all I could. "I'll be in my office, and I'm here for anything you need," I said. "Make sure your guys eat."

Elliot scoffed. "I know how to take care of my team."

"I know." I was reluctant to leave and go back to my desk, but now that the kids had opened the presents, someone needed to clean up the wrapping paper strewn about the living room.

On my way back to my office, I checked my

phone. In the last little bit, I'd been inundated with *Congratulations* messages, including another from Dominic that said *I snuck out of a presentation to see you go live. It looks incredible.* You're *incredible.* The note warmed me, but there was one absent in the bunch. I didn't want to notice, but it was impossible to ignore.

Especially since I'd seen Xander's mood on Saturday night. I knew him well enough to tell this fake engagement bothered him, despite what he said, and I got it.

But for him to not send me any sort of *Go Team Judy* hurt.

There could be a dozen reasons for why I hadn't heard from him yet. No reason to let my imagination run away from me.

When I stepped into my office, and saw that someone had moved my keyboard and spelled out *Congras* in colored paper clips on my desk, the creeping cloud of disappointment evaporated. My grin was back full-force. So where was he?

"You did it." Xander pressed into my back. "Not that I ever had any doubt."

I stepped into the room, and let him follow me. Turning to face him, I leaned against my desk. "My team did it."

"*Your* team. Exactly." He leaned against the door to close it, and crossed his arms. His biceps stretched the limits of his long-sleeved T-shirt, as he dragged his gaze over me. "God, you're one hell of a bad ass bitch."

"Thank you." I was more warmed by his words than any series of stats about usage, and I shouldn't be. This was an emotional reaction, and I tried to be above that kind of thing. "I couldn't have done it without you."

"You would've found a way."

"Fine. I wouldn't have wanted to do it without you."

Xander opened his arms wide. "Come on."

I stepped in without hesitation for a hug. The way he held me was comfort and assurance and safety. It was years of friendship and support.

I'm engaged to the wrong man.

The thought struck me hard, carried on the swell of an emotional day, and I struck it down without hesitation. I wasn't engaged to anyone, and Xander was all-but married. That was enough of that.

"You spelled *Congrats* wrong," I murmured against his chest.

"I ran out of paperclips." He rested his forehead on the top of my head, and the heat from his breath brushed my scalp. "But don't worry—I asked Ivan to order a *lot* more for next time. You're not wearing your ring."

I freed one arm to slide a thumb under the chain around my neck. "I am." I couldn't fathom setting the ring down somewhere and risk misplacing Dominic's priceless heirloom, but I wasn't ready to answer questions in the office about why it looked a lot like an engagement or wedding ring.

Xander dipped a finger under the delicate titanium rope, and glided along my neck, down my collarbone, and to my chest, where the ring rested. "So you are."

Like that, the hug was over.

Disappointing, but expected. And with some distance between us, I could pretend the heat spilling through me was nothing. "Did you come down here to check up on me?"

"I came to congratulate you." Xander sounded offended. "You know that."

"I do." My smile was back, and there was no reason to get stuck in another loop of *thanks to you. No, thanks to* you. But I couldn't help snapping a picture of the paper clip art before I cleared it away and sat at my desk. "How are things at the office?"

Xander sucked his teeth and settled into the chair across from me. "You sure you don't want to linger in the bliss a little longer? My answer won't change between today and tomorrow."

Well, fuck. "I'm gonna need you to tell me now, when you phrase it that way."

Xander was a partner in an angel investor firm. He personally had backed AcesPlayed, but he'd also sold his firm on supporting us. One of their partners had decided over time that they didn't like their name being associated with the kind of game Aces-Played was producing.

Rather than pulling their personal approval and moving on, like an adult, they'd been working to undermine The Raphael Group's entire interest, and convince the other partners to pull out.

"I'm dealing with it," Xander said.

"You're keeping me in the loop, so I'm not blindsided." Technically, I shouldn't ask for that, but I had to know.

He pinched the bridge of his nose. "He's compiled an entire brief detailing how you've *wasted* our capital to date. It's bullshit, but he thinks the numbers tell the story he wants."

My insides curdled at the thought. The contract we had with our investors allowed us to buy them out if we felt they were no longer a good fit, and let them demand the same of us. I wasn't in a position to buy out our biggest wallet.

"I'm dealing with it," Xander repeated. "I promise you."

There was no one I trusted more, so his insistence would have to do for now.

Xander pushed to his feet with a sigh. "I'm gonna let you get back to work, but before I go, check your top drawer."

"Why?" I was already sliding said drawer open,

rather than waiting for an answer. A white box, the kind that came from a bakery, sat inside. I extracted it and opened the lid, to find a chocolate cream puff inside that was twice as big as any single-serving pastry should be. On top, in wobbly frosting, it said *Bad Ass Boss Bitch*.

Now I was swallowed by warm fuzzies again. "Thank you."

Xander reached across the desk to squeeze my hand. "Talk soon."

After he left, I spent the rest of the day working, monitoring the game's status obsessively, and picking at the cream puff.

We were all working late tonight, like we had most nights for the last few months, and I was at my desk when I got a notification of a video going up on one of the channels I followed. A lot of our developers didn't care for Fallyn's Phallusies—Elliot had declared her his arch nemesis—but I was grateful for her content. Every one of her videos gave us a bump in traffic, and to have one launch on release day…?

Supposedly she was in town this week. I had no idea if I'd have a chance to meet her, but I hoped so.

Watching the video would have to wait. I had other tasks that were far more pressing.

A few hours later, I was still working on said tasks, when I got a text from Dom.

Dinner tomorrow night? Client facing?

As long as the game doesn't break, I can be there, I replied.

His message came through within seconds. *I owe you. Really.*

I sank back in my seat with a sigh, *and so it begins,* echoed in my mind with an ominousness I didn't care for.

5 /
dominic

I parked in front of the AcesPlayed building, sent Judith a text to let her know I was here, and stepped around to the passenger side to wait for her. The air was crisp, the hint of stars hanging in the inky dark blue overhead. I hated taking her away from the game as much as I hated doing dinner with a client and leaving Xander at home.

I'd expected her to tell me *no* tonight. She'd never had an issue saying work called, and it was important.

A couple strolled along the sidewalk, walking a beagle, who stopped to sniff my shoes. "Hey there, little guy." I wanted to ask if I could pet him, but then I'd get fur on my suit.

"Hi." The woman gave me a shy smile, and studied me through her lashes.

"Come on, let's go." The man tugged both dog leash and woman's arm, moving away from me.

Not too many years ago, I would've flirted with her—or him—just a little to see him react.

"Sorry to keep you waiting." Judith's smooth, confident tone penetrated my thoughts, and I looked up to find her strolling toward me. Her pale sweater hugged her torso, showing off every curve without looking like she was trying, and the deep burgundy color complimented her rosy cheeks, even in the dim lighting.

"I'm here for you. I don't mind waiting." I couldn't help but look her over as I opened the car door for her and she climbed in. In the heels, she was still a few inches shorter than me, and her dark slacks made her ass look incredible. "Especially if it means I get to check you out." I let out a low whistle.

She took her seat and twisted to give me a look of disbelief, but her pursed lips didn't hide the amusement crinkling at the corners of her eyes. "You don't look so bad yourself."

"Of course I don't." I grasped her fingers playfully, and dipped my head to brush my lips over the back of her knuckles, and paused mid-kiss. No ring.

Judith sighed. "I forgot to put it back on."

Xander had told me where she was wearing it when she was in the office. I hooked my finger under the exposed hint of chain and tugged the ring free from where it hid, nestled under her top and between her breasts. Following the metal rope back to the clasp, I forced myself to ignore the sparks that leaped between us, twisted the contraception loose, and caught the ring with my other hand.

"Only until dinner is over." I slipped the band onto her finger, and hooked her necklace into place again.

With her settled, I hurried to my side of the vehicle, and a moment later we were heading toward the restaurant. "How's the game launch going?" I'd gotten updates from both her and Xander, but with this being release week, I assumed the status changed constantly.

"Really good," she said. "Enough that I could walk away for a couple of hours for this." Fair point. "How's work?"

I discovered one of our clients was pushing for a contract we weren't comfortable with, and pushed back. Roger agreed with the decision, but it was a financial hit we weren't in a good place to take. The truth died in the back of my throat—not because I thought Judith didn't want to hear it, but I didn't want it in her head before we had dinner with a prospective client.

I'd already applied pressure to get her here, and I wasn't going to add guilt on top of that.

"What?" Judith prompted.

"We've got hiccups, but we're dealing with them." That was as good a way as any to phrase things.

"I can respect that. As your future wife, I'm here if you need to talk anything out." Her amusement was cut with a more serious tone.

"You're joking, but I know you mean it."

We arrived at our destination before the rest of our party, and Judith and I moved inside to avoid the chill. Though we were five minutes early, Roger showed up a moment later. He introduced his wife, Grace, to Judith, and polite smiles and handshakes were exchanged.

Grace was another reason I was willing to stick to Roger's requests for discretion. She knew who her husband was, and the two of them had been close friends for almost as long as I'd been alive. I didn't want to put any undue attention on her by pushing him into being more open about who he was. Their life was good as far as I knew.

Dale Monson, the prospective client, showed at least five minutes late. He was about twenty years older than me, and the woman on his arm had to be at least ten years my junior. He introduced her as Claire. She held onto his arm like he was a security blanket, only letting go to greet everyone.

The way Judith wrapped her hands around my bicep as we were shown to our table told me she'd noticed too.

We were seated and the waiter took our drink orders. I let the rest of the table go first, to follow cues. I was disappointed, but not surprised, at a round of *I'll have water*, with the exception of Claire's, "Do you have Dr. Pepper?" as if she was asking for something wicked.

So much for a good stiff drink to get me through the night. I stuck with Coke, and was surprised that Judith got a strawberry lemonade.

Claire instantly perked up. "Ooh, that sounds good. I'll have that instead."

The instant the waiter was gone, Judith leaned in, smile too bright. "Claire. My Dom has told me so much about everyone else, but I don't know anything about you. Who are you? What do you do? Spill."

The posture was bullshit, but Judith sold it so hard she almost had me fooled. Impressive, but also suspicious.

"Oh, I'm a housewife," Claire said with enthusiasm. "And I'm going to have babies."

"There's a woman who knows what she wants." Roger chuckled. "Good for you."

Judith settled a hand on my knee the instant my jaw moved.

"What about you? At your age, you must already have kids. How many? Did you lose your husband? I'm so sorry." Claire strung her questions together with the enthusiasm of a Dallas Cowboys cheerleader.

Why did I think this was a good idea?

But Judith's facade never faltered. "I was

married once before, but…" She dropped her head with a frown. "No children. It's so hard to talk about."

"Oh my gosh, I'm so sorry." There was nothing but sympathy in Claire's reply. "But at least you found someone again before it was too late."

Judith's fingers dug into my thigh, but she looked pleasant. Sweet. "I am *so* lucky I haven't run out of time to give my Dom all the babies he wants."

I didn't know whether to laugh or cry. I didn't have any issues with people who chose family over career, but assuming the rest of the world felt the same as the person who'd made that choice…

Fortunately, the conversation didn't really go downhill from there. It was more of a sideways shift into no-intermission awkwardness.

I was doing this for Roger, who had been like a father to me since I lost my own. Who had mentored me. Who made sure I came up in this industry. I was doing this for the people who worked for us, so we could keep giving them good jobs and opportunities.

It was only for a few weeks.

Despite telling myself those simple things over and over, when we reached dessert, I insisted I had an early meeting, and bowed out as forcefully as I could while being polite and resisting the urge to bolt for the door.

I pulled out Judith's chair for her, helped her into her coat, and offered my arm, so we could stroll sedately from the building.

Neither of us spoke in the car. I got a few blocks before I pulled into an empty park, picked a spot away from the road, and shut off the engine. I flopped against my seat with a loud sigh. "One night down."

"And we survived." Judith's tone was impossible to read.

"This was a mistake."

She gasped loudly and her hand flew to her chest. "But I thought we meant something to each other." Apparently she was still in bullshit mode. "I thought we had a future together. I thought you wanted me to have a dozen of your babies, until my womb was too withered and old to be useful to you, and then I could... I don't know... make you dinner a lot?"

I didn't know if I should laugh or... "I do *not* want you making me dinner." Might as well try to float some humor.

"You really don't." She snorted, and her mask finally slipped. "But you act like you expected tonight to be something else."

"I didn't expect his wife to be less than half his age."

Judith slid her hand under mine, where it rested on the gear shift. "Tonight was nothing. You know that, don't you?" She spoke with the resignation of someone who had seen things.

"Do you want to break it off now?" I wouldn't blame her.

"No." She turned her hand upside-down and squeezed mine. "I was her once. Granted, I was about half *her* age, but I know how deep the indoctrination runs, and if this is the life the two of them want…" Her tone faltered, and when I glanced at her, it was in time to see a shadow pass over her face. "I said I'd do this, I owe you, and I'll see it through."

I really did adore her friendship. The thought hit me hard. Despite the way her relationship had changed with Xander, despite her drifting away, she was such an integral part of our lives.

"This'll help you feel better," Judith said. "Do you know what would've horrified every other person at that table?"

I was about to ask *what's that*, but the answer came to me. "Hearing the actual story of how we met?"

"That was a dinner I'll never forget." The wistfulness in her voice floated on heat.

And now the vivid images were flashing into my mind, and I was eager to let them replace less pleasant thoughts. "Why have we never done that again?"

"Because you hooked up with my best friend. Don't you remember your own origin story?

And now I was picturing her in a bodysuit. How much fun would it be to strip that off her? "Like we're a couple of superheroes?"

"Just mutants."

"Come home with me tonight." The offer tumbled out easily. The three of us, Judith, Xander and I, had played around and fucked for a while after I met them. When Xander and I started dating, the rest tapered off, but tonight that part of my past was clamoring for attention.

Judith fluttered her hand to her chest once again, her exaggerated gasp filling the car again. "Why, future husband, are you suggesting what I think you are?"

I turned in my seat, rested a finger under her chin, and tilted her head up to meet her gaze. "I believe I am, future wife."

"Should we warn Xander we're coming?" She licked her lips.

"Not until you actually are, but maybe let him know I'm bringing home a treat."

The way one corner of Judith's mouth tugged up was dangerously seductive. "Is that what I am now? A treat?"

"The best kind."

"I'm sold. Take us back to your place, future husband."

She didn't have to tell me twice.

As I drove, she texted Xander. "I told him you were bringing me with you, and he said *and*?"

"Maybe he doesn't understand the significance of the situation."

Judith clucked. "Maybe I should show him."

"You're going to send my husband dirty pictures?" That was an alluring and distracting thought.

"You said it, not me."

Out of the corner of my eye, I caught her moving in her seat, and when she pulled her sweater up over her breasts, I had to fight to keep my eyes on the road. Especially when she started snapping pictures with her phone.

Thank fuck we weren't far from home.

Judith had straightened her clothes again by the time I pulled into the driveway. When we stepped into the house, Xander was waiting for us.

"What the fuck was that?" he asked.

"An outlet?" Judith offered.

I added, "fun?"

"No. That was painful." Xander took both our hands and led us deeper into the house. "Fortunately, I can give as good as I get, and now the actual fun starts."

He spun Judith in the living room, stripping off her coat in the process, and settled his hands on her hips when her back was to him.

The two of them together were fire. They always had been. I was torn between *why did we ever stop doing this* and *is it a mistake to start again?*

Heat and desire were winning out, but they didn't erase the whispers of doubt.

6 /
xander

I didn't need this—a night with all three of us—until Judith texted me. We'd barely made it past verbal foreplay, and already the ache inside me roared for this to not be the last time.

Tonight things were going to be the way they used to. Not *way* back, but after Dominic.

I turned Judith with me so we faced Dom. "I think you helped instigate this," I said to him.

"I did. And I don't feel bad about it."

Good. "Sit. Watch. Your turn to keep your hands to yourself."

He sank into a chair with a faint smirk and folded his hands into his lap.

I led Judith into the center of the room. It was probably a good thing we weren't in front of street-facing windows, because I wouldn't hesitate to take her in front of the entire neighborhood. I stripped off her sweater and paused to trace light lines along the spade tattoo on her shoulder blade.

Dom had one in the same place. I had one too, but mine was on my bicep. A lot of Judith's people had the ink now, but the three of us, plus Elliot and Link, did it first. This was how we rang in a new era. How we sold our souls to each other and this path Judith was on.

I had a lot of tattoos, but the spade was one of the most significant.

"You took those pictures in the car, in the middle of traffic." I glided my fingers under her bra straps, and followed a path down her back. "Did you have an audience besides Dominic and me?"

"I hope so." She sounded smug.

This woman and the things she did to me… "Step out of the heels."

She complied. The way she shrank was deceptive. She looked tiny, but she was terrifying when she needed to be. Tonight, I'd make sure the only thing she had to be was here.

I undid her slacks with a flick of my wrist and shoved those to the ground, leaving her in nothing but her bra and panties. *Fuck* she was tasty.

It had been too long. Or given the ache from my fingers to my cock, not long enough. I walked around her, drinking in the sight. "Where should we start with you?"

"Rhetorical question?" The way she glanced over her shoulder at me was alluring and playful.

"I'm open to suggestions. I may not take them, but I'll hear them."

Dominic raised a few fingers, grabbing my attention. "She's already shown she's in the mood for teasing."

Judith opened her mouth—to protest?—but snapped her jaw shut again without saying a word.

I pressed two fingers to her lips and past, shoving into her mouth. She let me in, sucking and licking. Dragging her tongue along the pads.

My cock was hard in an instant as the images of her doing the same lower down teased me. I pushed my fingers deeper, toward her throat, and she relaxed. Sucking. Watching me. Letting me do what I wanted.

When I pulled out, drool dribbled between us. Experience said if I dropped my hand now, her pussy would be as wet as my hand.

"You remember how to play, after all this time." My tone was thicker than I intended.

Her shy smile was something she reserved for the bedroom. "Only for you."

I dipped my slick fingers under her panties, between her folds. As predicted, she was wet. A spark of jealousy flickered inside that her arousal may have as much to do with half-undressing in front of Dom as it did with my touch, and I shoved the reaction aside.

When I plunged my fingers inside her, her gasp was intoxicating. I worked my fingers in her, sliding, pumping, watching her expression shift through degrees of pleasure and loving the sounds she made.

"How does it feel?" I nipped her ear.

"So good."

Yeah, she did. "How close are you?" I dragged my tongue along the curve of her neck.

"I won't come this way."

"No?" I wasn't surprised at her answer. I knew her body and I could make her sing.

She licked her lips. "But I want to. I'll beg. *Please?*"

I pretended to consider it, but I'd already made up my mind. "Not yet." When I drew my fingers out of her, she made a sound that was half-grunt, half pout.

Apparently that could be a noise.

I was slick with her juices. I pulled Dom to his feet for a kiss and to share. Hunger flowed between us when we crushed our mouths together. Our tongues tangled with each other. With my hand. Licking Judith's taste from my skin.

Dominic and I tugged each other's clothes off, shirts, pants, boxers, until we were naked and pressed together. I smirked as I pressed a palm to his chest, and nudged him playfully to fall into his chair again. "No touching yourself while I'm with her," I warned.

I returned to Judith. "No condoms?" I asked, as I finished stripping off her clothes as well.

"No condoms."

I'd been *fixed* years ago, and neither one of us lived the lifestyle we used to, so infections weren't a concern. I teased my fingers along her slit again, this time sliding up to her clit. When I brushed the swollen nub, her gasp was fuel on the raging fire of my need. I homed in on the spot, circling, nudging, coaxing her until her breath came in short pants and her legs wobbled.

She dug her fingers into my arm when she came in a chorus of gasps and cries.

But I wasn't done. I had to feel her wrapped around me. *Now.*

Hands on her hips, I guided us both to the couch, and tugged her to straddle my lap. She hovered over my cock, and I thrust up inside her in a single push. Her warm heat enveloped me. Cradled me.

When I pressed against her clit again, a shudder ran through her, and her body spasmed and clenched around my cock.

She was a goddess as she rode me. A thin sheen of sweat on her skin, pink glistening underneath, and that faint smile that said she was lost in the bliss of this moment. I couldn't help but slam inside her, hammering hard, fucking her with abandon as I coaxed another orgasm from her.

The world fell away, nothing existed but the three of us. My body tightened, and the sensation focused into my balls. I loved the way it felt, spilling inside her.

Silence blanketed the room as we slowed to a stop. I needed to catch my breath. I need this night to go on forever. I needed it all.

I looked past Judith to Dom, who watched us with lust in his eyes and his cock standing at attention. "Clean her up," I said as I helped Judith shift onto the leather, and moved aside. "If you do a good job, if you give her another orgasm, you can fuck her."

Her laugh was light and his was hungry. He fell to his knees and crawled across the throw rug, like a lion stalking his prey. When he reached us, he kissed up the inside of Judith's leg, his hand following the same path on the other thigh.

When he reached her pussy, he dragged his tongue along the cream, licking up his dessert. Her whimper was incredible when he dove into her, devouring everything that clung to her skin.

Fuck I loved watching this. I was spent, but I was already hard again. Seeing the two of them move together. Seeing Dom pleasure Judith, until her body shook with orgasm again, then him pulling her into his lap, back to him, and fucking her.

Pounding her hard and fast. Both of them lost in the bliss.

I leaned past her to kiss him. To taste everything on his lips. To devour and memorize the flavor of our passion.

When Dom came, I swore I felt it in my own dick. He and Judith sat there, silent and glowing, as the seconds ticked away.

I finally nudged her to her feet, supporting most of her weight. "Clean up, and bed."

She nodded with a tired, silly smile.

A few moments later, with all three of us plus the couch wiped down, I pulled them into bed. I placed myself between them, needing to feel both of their bodies against mine.

I remembered now why we stopped doing this. There was an ambivalence inside I refused to examine

And tonight wouldn't change that.

But I was happy to have Dom back in our bed, even though he'd technically never be gone.

It had been too long since Judith was here. Watching her lay against my chest, her hair splayed out around her, and knowing how relaxed she was at this moment... This made it easy to remember the girl I used to know. She hadn't really changed since we were teenagers, so much as realized her potential, and I adored who she was now.

I'd move the world for either of them.

But sometimes, every once in a while, I wished she still needed me to protect her.

Or maybe thinking that she ever had was delusion on my part.

Wednesday morning, the rhythm in the house didn't feel disrupted. Judith flowed with our routine as easily as if she was there every day. It was tempting to stay and add another round of play to go with the memories of last night, but she and I both had packed schedules.

Dominic got to take his time, not having to be in the office until nine.

"Fucking lawyer hours," I teased him.

He blew me a kiss, and patted his ass.

Judith dressed in the same outfit she'd arrived in. No one in her office cared if she showed up to work in yesterday's clothes, and she said she had something more casual to change into when she got there.

I couldn't help the sliver of satisfaction that ran through me watching her put the engagement ring back on its chain.

I dropped her off on the way to the office, and promised to give her a call in a few hours, to see what she needed my help with during RinCon.

When I reached the Raphael Group offices, the

buzz of excitement in the air was tangible. Aces-Played wasn't our only big property—we were tech investors, and we had half a dozen companies launching titles at RinCon this week.

The partners were taking last minute calls, taking friendly bets on who would get the most buzz, and taking large gulps of caffeine, to get them through the day.

While Aces wasn't the only company having a big week, theirs was the only one that mattered to me, regardless of which of the others I had invested in. They had been one of our first buy-ins as a firm, and one of the longest to reach this point, and I was proud of every single second and cent spent.

With the memories of last night lingering in my head, and a week of incredible releases stretching out in front of us, it really did feel like I could own the world.

The instant I had the thought, I knew it was a mistake.

But it was a good thing I wasn't superstitious and didn't believe in jinxing things by challenging the universe.

7 /
judith

I'd helped make RinCon. Planned the very first year along with my then-colleagues. Watched our little few-hundred-person event grow into a global phenomenon. And I hadn't been this anxious, this excited, about walking through the convention center doors, since that first year.

They wouldn't be letting attendees in for a few more hours, but people had been buzzing here and there for a few days. Vendors setting up their booths. Rinslet employees setting up everything else.

Being here again was soothing. Familiar. It almost made me forget what an important week this was. So far the game launch had gone smoothly, so that was great. This was our next hurdle, though. We were the headliners of the show, since Scott McAllister, one of the owners of Rinslet, was also one of our primary investors.

It was good to know people at the top.

It was great to be one of the people at the top.

A splash of vibrant color caught my attention. A woman in red and black, bright amid the muddy mix of the carpet, approached Link—one of our developers. They were too far away for me to hear anything, and her back was to me, but her body language was guarded. Shy.

Link was defensive, which was the most disconcerting thing about the exchange. He wasn't defensive with anyone.

The two talked for a moment, and then he led her into a side room.

I raised an eyebrow. I didn't care who my people fucked, but I'd rather they didn't do it where we did business. And despite their insistence to the contrary, it was an open secret that Link and Elliot were at least a little together.

But they also hooked up with other people, and new company rules said they weren't supposed to be fucking each other since Elliot was Link's boss, so if this was Link's way of obeying then non-fraternization rule, then good for him.

Or, he and the woman were just friends, and I should save my limited imagination for more important things.

I moved on to my next stop—the main hall where the biggest panels would be held.

Dustin had this entire setup thing under control, but I had to see it all for myself. I needed to know.

I found Reese—the lead singer from Plaid Peanut Butter—in the back of the room, pacing and inspecting. She was with Alys, another of our developers and her drummer. The band was performing at the opening ceremonies tonight, and while they couldn't finish setting up in here until the day's panels had run, there were some things they could put in place now.

They didn't look up when I walked in. Reese finished what she was doing, beckoned Alys closer, and they talked in low voices with their heads bent together.

"And she thinks we haven't seen her," Reese said with a smirk, and looked up at me.

I shook my head. "I did think that, yes. How's pre-setup going?" There was no need for small talk, not with everything going on, and Reese would understand that.

She shrugged. "Not bad." She turned toward the stage. "It would be going better if Dustin could get the sound check right." She raised her voice and it carried beautifully through the room, without the help of a mic.

"Sound is great." Dustin's voice crackled to life over the PA system, and he was cut off by a feedback whine that made all three of us wince. "Never mind. I'm on it."

I should leave them to work.

"Is that a ring?" The awe in Alys's voice

stopped me.

As the words caught up to my brain, my heart sank. I looked down at my left hand and the engagement ring I'd forgotten to take off. Fuck. I shoved my hands in my pockets. "Do you need anything from me?"

"Uh-uh." Reese grabbed my wrist and tugged my hand into the open again. "That's definitely a ring."

If anyone else did that to me except maybe Xander or Dom, I'd fix them with a deadly glare until they backed away in fear. Not that any of my people would dare. But Reese was a different breed of woman. "It's only a ring, and I'd appreciate if you forgot you saw it," I said coolly.

Dustin couldn't hear us from here, could he? No. He was backstage with sound equipment and wouldn't hear anything not shouted.

"What ring?" Alys picked up on my less-than subtle request easily.

Reese scrunched up her nose. "Uh, no. Because one, it's stunning, and two it looks a lot like an engagement ring, and three I love knowing secrets."

It's not an engagement ring. I should've said that immediately. The denial should've been there the instant she said the word, but my retort lodged in my throat. "I can't tell you. If I tell you, then by the end of the day, the entire office will know."

Reese didn't work for me, but she was best

friends with one of my artists, she was dating my security guy and my composer, and they were all good friends with other people at the company. It was great that we were all so close, unless there was a secret to keep.

"I swear, no gossip." Reese made an X over her heart. "I won't tell a soul until you're ready."

"I won't ever be ready." I had to give her something, so it would be as much of the truth as I felt like I could get away with. "There's no engagement. I'm doing a favor for a friend, and when it's over, we're going to pretend it never happened."

"Hmm." Reese seemed to consider this. "Boring for such a pretty ring. Okay."

Alys shifted her weight from one foot to the other. "So I should probably not point out that a fake engagement never works in the books?" Her voice was soft. Meek.

"You should probably not point that out, no. And I said it wasn't an engagement. It's a favor." As I talked, I slipped the ring from my finger, and re-affixed it to the chain around my neck. I never should've had it on today anyway. Wanting to remember what it looked like on my finger was a bad reason to risk conversations like this. "And you never saw anything."

"What ring?" Alys repeated, a tiny smile on her face.

Forcing my neck to unknot, I returned the look.

"Don't tell the guys, but you've always been my favorite."

"I never even saw you this morning." A hint of confidence worked into her voice.

"Hey." Dustin's voice over the speakers was much smoother this time. "We working or plotting world domination, ladies?"

Reese looked up. "There's a difference? Much better," she shouted. "We need to do a mic check," she said to me in a normal voice, and grabbed Alys's wrist to tug her toward the stage. "Your secret is safe. Promise."

I spent the next few hours checking on every-thing, and by the time the con opened, that *little girl on Christmas* anticipation was back.

Actually, scratch that. This time, I was the momma on Christmas morning. Watching people flood to our booth, seeing their reactions to the game, was like seeing the kids unwrap the perfect present.

I stood with my back to the closest pillar, and took a few minutes to enjoy the view and let the crowds rush past. A group of cosplayers stopped near the booth, several of them in X costumers— the lead character from Rinslet's most popular game franchise.

And no one knew but a few of us, but I'd gotten Chloe to name him after Xander, all those years ago.

I squinted as a woman joined them. She was wearing red and black... Yup, she was the same person I'd seen with Link this morning. I focused on her face.

And she was Fallyn. *Oh.* What would Elliot say about that?

"Hey, little lady, did you get lost?" The voice was closer than was polite from a stranger.

And I would've ground my heel into his toe if I didn't know him, but Xander's comment made me smirk. "Nope. I'm exactly where I'm supposed to be."

"You really are." He nudged me over to share my pillar, and his arm pressed into mine.

We stood there in silence for a few minutes, absorbing the ambiance and chaos.

"It must be nice," I finally said, teasing in my voice.

"What's that?"

"To be an all-important investor who can skip work and play all day."

Xander chuckled. "It's incredible. I'm meeting the Queen of Hearts later for mimosas and golf."

"As if. I hear she takes off your head if you offer her mimosas after lunchtime."

"Busted." The way he slumped put him a few inches closer to my height. "Seriously, though. I told the other partners I was coming to peek in on our investment. Really I'm here to help you with security so you don't have to spread your devs' time too thin."

The consideration warmed me, and having him here with me felt right. It was a shame Dominic couldn't join us until tonight. I may not have embarked on this adventure if it wasn't for his advice. "Too bad I can't stick around and watch," I said.

"Watch me be fierce and imposing?" Xander dipped his head to rest his mouth near my ear. "Kinky girl."

"Judith?" A new voice cut through the playfulness, and my gut sank when my brain caught up to my ears.

My fear was confirmed when I looked up to see Claire standing a few feet away, watching us with a weak smile and a furrowed brow.

Fuck me. "Claire, *hi.*" I could play the chameleon if I needed to, but here? Now? The last person I wanted to be was someone's sweet, naive bride-to-be. "Xander, this is Claire. Dale Monson's wife." *You know—Dominic's potential new client?* I didn't have to say the last part aloud. He'd know.

Xander stepped closer to her. "Pleasure to meet you."

Claire ducked her head. "Hi." Her voice was instantly soft.

Yeah, the tattoos and salt and pepper hair did

that to a lot of women. The muscles didn't hurt either.

Xander squeezed my arm. "I'm going to leave you two to talk. I need to get to work."

"Ah— Good luck." I cursed his name in my mind, and let him walk into *my* booth. "So, Claire, what are you doing here?" I turned back to my unexpected companion, for at least the next minute or two.

With Xander gone, she was back to her smiley self. "I love video games. Like, so many of them. So I had to come. There's some stuff I'm not quite cool with"—she glanced at the AcesPlayed booth—"But I had to see the rest of it." She frowned suddenly. "Where's your ring? Did you lose it?"

Fucking— Take the ring off. Put the ring on. I showed her the chain, with my ring at the end. "I didn't want something happening to it."

"Like, it getting stolen? Does that happen here?" Claire looked horrified.

"Like it getting damaged or lost."

"Oh. Right. Of course. So what brings you here?" Claire asked.

Mother-fucking, God damn, son of a— "More or less the same as you. I've come every single year since they started. I love this show." Sometimes truth was the best deception.

"Oh. Does that mean you know the best places to check out?"

"All of them." I had no idea what kind of an answer she was looking for. "Go to as many panels as you can, visit all the booths. Why would you pass up any of it?"

She grabbed my arm, and I resisted the urge to jerk away. "Are you here alone?" she asked. "We should go see it all together."

I can't. I have to oversee my billion-dollar porn game. It killed me to swallow the retort. *For Dominic.* "I'm actually meeting some friends soon. But we'll catch up later." Only a tiny mistruth. My day would be spent in meetings with investors, vendors, and other industry professionals.

"Oh. Okay." Claire's expression fell.

"Will you be at opening ceremonies tonight? The concert?" What was I doing?

She shook her head. "The one featuring the smutty smut? No thank you."

Like that, any twinge of conscience I'd had about abandoning her evaporated. "I guess I'll see you around." I spun away. She only had to believe I was marrying Dominic and not tarnishing whatever bullshit image he supposedly had. She didn't have to be my new BFF.

But Claire's being here was going to cause some serious issues, if I couldn't let her see me doing my job.

8 /
dominic

I decided to walk the half mile or so from the office to the convention center, to meet Xander and Judith after work. I had a perfectly good parking spot in our lot, and it was unlikely I'd find anything closer.

There was a chill in the air with the sun down, but that helped brush away the stress of the day. I loved my work, but most days I ached for the people who came to us who had been taken advantage of.

Reese, for instance. Who we were watching sing tonight, because when she came to me a year ago with a shitty deal and a shittier band manager, I'd broken her free.

Knowing that one less person was bound to a bad deal was nice, but free Plaid Peanut Butter tickets for life was even better. Besides, we were negotiating a sweet rights deal for her that would catapult the band.

Traffic slogged along downtown streets, backing up two or three lights, and crossing the road was a bit like playing Frogger.

I had nothing but respect for Roger, but the last few years, my sympathy for his *discretion* request became more like frustration mixed with pity that he couldn't live his life as himself, and that kept me from doing the same.

But I owed Roger a lot. He'd made sure every step of the way that I had the help and resources I needed, and I had never regretted following this career path. I owed that to him, and if he wasn't comfortable doing something like coming out, the least I could do was respect that.

When I stepped inside the convention center, it was like moving into a different world. Bright warmth and a cheerful mood washed away the dreary cold of outside.

It wasn't as crowded in here as earlier, which I knew from the handful of pictures Xander sent me of the crowds. He'd spent most of his day here.

Speaking of, I sent him a text, letting him know I was here. He replied with a note telling me where to find them, followed by *be prepared to perform*.

Weird thing to say.

I walked past the line outside the main hall that was waiting to get into opening ceremonies, and found Judith and Xander a short distance further into the building, waiting away from the crowds.

She was wearing a flannel shirt open over a Nirvana T-shirt and jeans. The way the T-shirt was tied off at the waist, and how faded and baggy it was, said it had probably been Xander's once upon a time. Her hair was in a ponytail that was perfect for pulling, and she looked like a different person.

As sexy as ever, though.

Xander was in the same Henley he'd left the house in this morning, and he looked as good as he had twelve hours ago.

I was the guy out of place in a suit and tie. Fine with me. I was drawing stares and murmurs about being *a normal*, and I knew I looked great.

When I reached Xander and Judith, she pulled me into a tight hug. "I missed you, my Dom."

Ah. This kind of performance. I shifted the hug to tilt her head up and brush my lips over hers. The kiss was sweet. Chaste. But the longer I drew it out, the more intense the sparks were that flowed between us.

There was an odd kind of ambivalence doing this in front of Xander. The fact that it wasn't real made it feel wrong, but knowing people were enjoying the show, that he was at least partly enjoying the show, made the kiss hotter.

"Who's this for?" I murmured against her mouth as we broke apart.

She rested her head against my shoulder. "Claire is here," she whispered.

73

Well, fuck.

At least Judith's people didn't care who she kissed.

I looked between them. "I feel like you could've mentioned that before I got here."

"Busy day." Xander shrugged.

Judith worked a finger into the knot of my tie, loosening it. "Claire says she's not going to the concert, *because smutty smut*." She undid the top button of my shirt and brushed her nails over my skin in a light tease. "So the main hall is safe."

Safe enough to push her against a wall and give her a real kiss? Or let Xander do the same to me?

Judith let us in through a side door—no line for us—and we found three seats in the front section reserved for the AcesPlayed crew. She left us so she could go play her part in the opening ceremonies.

The noise level in the room was too high for any real conversation with Xander, but his fingers tangled with mine conveyed what they needed to.

The stage show was all hype and energy, and the crowd loved it. Over the years, Judith's team had learned so much more than how to make an incredible game. When everyone in the room was worked into a frenzy, Dustin announced the band.

The reaction was deafening. Amazing.

Judith joined us as the music started. Was this what it was like for her and Xander when they were younger? Cons weren't like this twenty years ago, but concerts, late nights after work, and feeding off each other's passions...

There were times when I was jealous of their past together. That they shared so much history.

I'd rather ignore that and enjoy the electricity in the air. The raw sexual tension that spilled from the stage and radiated from my companions. Seeing Judith enjoy herself tonight, her smile even as she restrained herself at the opening notes of *Glass Slipper*, was intoxicating.

There had been a draw to her from the first night we met, to both of them, but most of the time I could focus it all on Xander. But the *pretend* kisses, and the sex with all three of us the other night made it harder to ignore Judith. Not that I wanted Xander any less.

Instead, intense need swelled inside as the band moved into the song. This particular one had always hit close to home for me, not just because it was the first song they released after I started representing them, but the Cinderella-like story sounded too much like one I was witnessing.

Xander let loose the easiest to the music, like he always did. As if he knew how heavily it weighed on my heart, he grabbed me and pulled me into a spin.

Two grown men twirling in an aisle of chairs, trying not to knock anything or anyone over, should look ridiculous, but fuck how it looked.

As he let me go, and the next song started, I

spun to face Judith, who was glancing at us with a smirk, but not doing more than tapping her feet.

I'd never stopped wanting her, so a fake engagement was easy to play along with. The reason I was with Xander, and neither of us was with her, had everything to do with Xander and Judith themselves. She wasn't interested in a committed relationship. She made that clear again and again, and pulled away from anything that implied attachment.

And Xander wasn't interested in a committed relationship with Judith.

I used to wonder why, but I'd figured it out over the years. He was her black knight in tarnished armor. Friendship was great, fucking was fine, but he wouldn't let himself take more from her.

I pulled her into me, though Xander's touch never left me, and I rested my hands on her hips as I pressed into her back. The more I swayed to the music, the more she did the same.

We'd all grown a lot in our time as friends. What if this was a chance for all three of us? The notion hit me hard, and the desire to make it real even harder. Would Xander and Judith fight it? Probably, since they had for longer than I'd been in the picture, but we were all so good together. If she was a part of *us*...

She turned to face me with the next song, and draped her arms around my neck. As the concert rocked on, we lost ourselves in the music. Heat spilled between us as the three of us effortlessly slid from one partner to another, with Judith grinding against me sometimes, and Xander stepping in at others.

Could this be the right time to nudge the walls both of them had put up, until they crumbled?

After the third encore, when Reese finally walked off stage and didn't return, I was grinning like an idiot. Pretty sure we were too old for shit like late night concerts and dancing in the aisles, and maybe I'd regret it in the morning, but I doubted it. How could I regret anything this easy and fun?

As most of the room made their way into the convention center, we headed backstage, to where the band was packing up before heading out to meet their fans.

"You were brilliant," I said to Reese.

She scoffed. "Of course I was."

"Good job." Xander pulled his brother, Maddox, into a quick hug.

As they broke away, Maddox snorted. "You sure you noticed? I had a great view of you three from the stage."

"Which was thanks to the music." I was too happy riding this buzz to let him bring me down.

Reese clapped once, loudly. "Come on, all. Our actual fans await."

We chatted with the entire band for a few more minutes before they headed out. That didn't mean we were done. So many people approached the instant we walked into the halls, to congratulate Judith. She glowed as she accepted each and every bit of praise with grace.

She deserved it, and I didn't care that we were there until most everyone else was gone.

When it was the three of us again, more than an hour later, I knew I had to make a quick decision. Let the night end, or ride this buzz a little longer. Spend more time with a Part Two from the other night.

"I think we," I pointed to Xander and me, "should make sure you get to your room safely."

Judith had gotten a hotel room across the street, so she didn't have to deal with commuting this week. I had no idea when she'd found time to check in between spending the night with us and work, but I assumed she was capable of making any schedule work. She could probably will a time-turner into existence if that was what it took.

Her mouth twisted in amusement. "It can be pretty scary out there for a woman on her own. I wouldn't complain about the help of two big, strong guardians." She traced a finger down my chest, then spun away. "Keep up."

"Given the view, what choice do we have?" Xander focused on her ass as she took a few steps forward.

The view would've been even better if it weren't

for the flannel shirt, but I did like the sway in her hips and the confidence in her step as she walked away.

All three of us headed outside, and the icy blast of reality slammed into us. This time it tasted more like magic and less like rush hour traffic. A lot of the cars were gone, and the holiday lights twinkled from trees and lamp posts.

The hotel was across the street from the convention center, so we crossed at the light with a block of people, and let the crowd provide the pace. When we moved into the Howard, the pack split apart.

Judith stopped, a look of horror splashed across her face. "What if Claire sees us?" Her expression faded into a giggle.

I pulled her closer. "I'm having a quiet, sexy night with my wife-to-be."

"Nope." Xander gave a single shake of his head. "Not before you're married, you're not. Naughty boy."

"Hmm..." Judith grabbed both our hands and tugged us toward the elevator. "I guess we have to make sure we're not being followed."

I made a show of looking around us as we packed into a waiting elevator car. "I think we're safe." My whisper was exaggerated.

"Are you su— *Fuck.*" Judith scowled, left the elevator right before doors closed, and reached into her pocket in a single fluid motion.

Xander and I hurried to follow.

"Yeah." She was already answering the call as she moved toward a quieter corner of the lobby. Her brow furrowed deeper. "Fuck. Keep me posted. I'll be on my laptop in a few minutes."

She disconnected with a heavy growl, and looked at us.

"What's going on?" I asked.

"Game crashed. We're offline."

Such a simple statement that could mean so much disaster. "Fuck."

9 /
xander

When I was sixteen, I had one of those teachers who cared. The ones they make movies about, who try to make a difference in kids' lives. She decided I had untapped potential, and wanted to see it tapped.

Unlike the movies, I wasn't an underprivileged kid, I was a rich kid with the same last name as the town we lived in. And the only thing I wanted to tap was the cutie redhead my teacher assigned me to work with on a team project.

And then I got to know Judith. Smart. Driven. Commanding. She walked into the library, and she was in control of our presentation about female serial killers.

Fucking annoying. I wasn't going to have anything to do with that, especially since she was one of those goody-two-shoes who didn't put out.

The first night I saw the cracks in her armor, the

first time she broke up with a boyfriend, and I found her trying like hell to keep from losing her shit, I realized my heart was in trouble.

And the first time she sobbed all over my shirt until she was cried out, cleaned herself up, and pronounced without any prompting that he wasn't worth it and she was moving on...

That was the night I swore no one would hurt her on my watch. Ever. Including me.

Yeah, idealism was a bitch, and I was an idiot for thinking I had that kind of control over the world, but I'd done my best anyway. For twenty-five years.

As I watched her talk through the game crash with Elliot, on one of the worst nights imaginable for things to be offline, I felt an old, familiar twinge of *I failed to keep her safe*, despite this being something I couldn't have prevented.

"Okay. Keep me in the loop." Judith hung up the phone and set it on the dresser next to the TV. She stood there, palms pressed to the polished wood and eyes closed, breathing through her nose.

The tension was too much. "How bad is it?" I asked.

"They know what caused it but not how it happened." She never looked up. "Elliot and Luna are working on putting up some new fences."

Fences...? Ah, to keep people out.

"So it's not all hands on deck?" The concern Dominic watched her with matched my own.

She shook her head. "Just the two of them. And presumably Link."

Inspiration struck. "I know the perfect distraction."

"If you say *sex*, I'm kicking you out." Judith looked one-hundred percent serious.

"Give me some credit. The last thing you want is to be mid-orgasm when your phone rings."

She finally looked at me, and rolled her eyes. "Sure. That's my only reservation."

If she had the excess energy to be sarcastic, then her mind wasn't completely occupied with the problem, but odds were she'd work herself up until it was.

"Let's go to Denny's," I said. "Grab your laptop, in case, and we'll go drink coffee and eat French fries."

"We don't do shit like hang out at Denny's at eleven on a Thursday night. We're not teenagers."

Dominic trailed his gaze over her in a way that sent heat rushing through me. "You sure?" There was a softness in his teasing. "What else are you going to do while you wait? Watch TV? Doomscroll social media and read the thoughts of all the people bitching about how your game is down?"

I loved when he and I were on the same page.

With a huff, Judith crossed her arms. "Maybe. I

hadn't thought about it, but you say that like it's a bad thing."

There was no way she didn't know what she wanted to do next. Judith's plans had plans.

"It is a bad thing." I grabbed her hand and her phone, and Dominic grabbed her laptop bag.

When we made it downstairs and saw that the hotel's twenty-four-hour diner was open, we decided to stop there instead. "Bring us three coffees, lots of those little flavored creamers," I told the waiter as he showed us to one of many empty tables.

"You got it, boss." He set our menus on the table and left.

Judith snagged her computer from Dominic, slid into one side of the booth, and managed to take up the entire seat between her and the bag. Dom and I sat across from her, as she set up her laptop.

I didn't expect any different. I grabbed the menu. "What are we having?"

"There was mention of fries." Leaning in, Dominic read over my shoulder.

Under the table, I nudged Judith's foot with mine. "They have mozzarella sticks. Sampler platter with potato skins."

She raised her eyebrows but didn't look up from her work. "I'm not really hungry."

Yeah, I'd heard that *many* times before. At least a couple today. "You can help pick, or I can pin you down and force you to eat."

That got her attention, and she met my gaze with an even stare. "You wouldn't."

I might. I arched an eyebrow and otherwise let silence be my answer.

"Sampler platter sounds good.." One corner of her mouth tugged up. "This crash is already giving me heartburn, might as well embrace it."

"Way to be positive," Dominic teased.

The waiter returned with our coffee and to take our order. He hesitated for a moment when Dominic told him to leave the pot, then shrugged and set it on the table.

When he left again, Dominic dumped a packet of sugar into Judith's drink, and I followed with three of the little vanilla creamers, before I stirred it all together.

All while she muttered, "but why this? Why now?" and scanned her computer.

"Elliot's working on it. Luna's working on it." Not that I blamed her. I'd be doing the same thing in her shoes, and because she was doing it, I'd have answers for the other investment partners in the morning when they inevitably asked me what happened.

As if my thoughts had summoned a response, my phone chimed with a new text. This time of night, it had to be a concerned partner. Oliver, maybe.

I extracted the device from my pocket.

I'll be out for the next week. My father-in-law passed away. Break a leg with AP.

The text from Wade made me frown. Poor guy. He was the founder of the entire company. This thing had been his dream, and he brought us all on. *Take as much time as you need. Let me know what we can do.*

Though I didn't know Wade's father-in-law, I knew Wade and what a good guy he was. The news tugged loose an old memory. Judith had been working for Cord for a little while, months maybe. And I was off to college. Notre Dame. Dad's alma mater.

At the time I hated it, but now I was grateful I'd gone.

Judith lost her mother, and she blamed herself for leaving the older woman behind when she got out. I wasn't there for her while she dealt with grief and guilt.

Cole was, though. I didn't know how she managed to find the most stoic, reserved person in that company, and decide he was the guy whose shoulder she needed to cry on, but in a way it made sense. She wanted someone who wouldn't amplify her pain, so she could let it all out and move on.

The way I'd done for her in high school.

I shook the random thought aside. No reason to tumble into the past.

"Everything all right?" Dominic asked.

86

"Wade's wife's father passed away," I said somberly.

Dominic and Judith voiced their sympathy and the news set a somber tone at the table when added to the existing stress.

We ate, we watched the servers, we cheered when the game came back online and again when Elliot confirmed a few hours later that the hole that allowed the issue had been patched.

It was nearly two when Judith closed her laptop. We sent her up to her room, and Dominic and I drove home in tired-but-comfortable silence.

In the morning, I emailed my assistant to make sure Wade's family got flowers, emailed the other interested partners to assure them Judith had everything under control, and dropped Dominic off at his car before I headed to the convention center.

The doors opened at eight today, and the place was already packed to the gills with people. Fortunately, Judith would either be at the booth, in the meeting room she had reserved for the next three days, or walking between the two. I'd start with the booth.

It wasn't difficult to navigate the crowds; for the most part people moved out of my way without question. I was almost to the vendor hall entrance when a familiar flash of auburn caught my attention, and I turned.

Judith was standing near the elevator talking to

someone in what almost looked like a cape. Except it barely reached their waist.

It was Claire, in a T-shirt with a Batman logo on the front, like a cheap costume top from a store. At least it was Batman instead of Superman. I was more about the dark and brooding anti-hero than the slippery-clean savior.

In this case, though, I'd go see if my Wonder Woman needed backup. Judith didn't look distressed, but she was also a master of blending into uncomfortable social situations, when business was involved in any way.

"Xander, *hi*," Judith grinned as I approached. It was one of those bright, sunshiny smiles that lit up the entire area around her, until she was the only thing that mattered.

Yup, the smile was fake and she was not into the conversation.

"Ladies." I gave a short nod.

Claire's *hi* was quiet.

"We were discussing the finer points of *Batman Beyond*," Judith said.

We loved that show when we were younger. Judith and I would watch after school cartoons at my house, with the excuse of keeping Maddox company. She hated going home to an empty house when her parents were working late, because her new neighbors were dealing.

So we'd study, we'd watch TV, the cook would

make us snacks, and we'd all discuss the finer real-world points of a retired, crime-fighting billionaire training his protege in a comic book world.

I had to know, "What are we discussing, specifically?"

Even back then, I'd sided with the jaded, old Batman who had seen his efforts thrown back in his face time and again, and was tired. But Judith took up Terry's defense. She insisted even if there were bad apples, the cause was righteous.

Looking back, the subtext of her relationship with her faith at the time was obvious. She was at a point where she was starting to waver, which made her dig in and defend it even harder. Trying to convince herself as much as anyone else.

"I love that Terry was so unswayed by fear and the opinions of those around him," Claire said. "He knew what was right and he pursued a way to make the world better."

"And Bruce Wayne had learned that focusing his efforts was better than attacking everything that moved." Apparently sometime in the last few decades, Judith had started to see this my way.

Claire shrugged. "Or you could say Bruce decided his shortcomings weren't worth overcoming."

Ouch. Wrong thing to say. I could interject, but this was fascinating to watch.

"I absolutely could not say that. It's not true."

The flash in Judith's eyes was at the challenge. She was excited, rather than frustrated. "If a feature proves to be more expensive to build than the ROI, there's no reason to pursue it. That's not a short-coming, that's a strategic decision."

She was sexy when she talked about things she was passionate about.

The way Claire wrinkled her nose, she disagreed. "You sound like Dale. *You play the game or the game plays you.*"

"Yeah, no." I couldn't help but interject. "I guarantee, she's nothing like Dale."

Judith's smile was strained for the first time since I arrived. "If that's how he feels about *the game*, he's playing the wrong one."

"Dale's super smart. He knows what he's doing." Defensiveness bled into Claire's voice.

I'd heard that before, but under different circumstances. Judith wouldn't use those exact words, but she had similar defenses about her father knowing what he was doing. Being smart and expe-rienced. Usually right after her parents fought, and she never sounded like she believed it any more than Claire did now.

That was definitely a bit of the past I didn't need to dwell in. It was done and gone, like my memories of it needed to be.

10 /
judith

I wanted this conversation to go well. Talking to Claire wasn't bad as long as we stayed away from topics like family and work. But if I heard *Dale says...* one more time, the mental calming breaths were going to stop working.

"Dale says—"

"What about what you say?" I was done with this.

Claire furrowed her brow. "What?"

She'd heard me. I had no doubt. "If I wanted Dale's opinion, I'd be talking to Dale. What about what you think?" I asked.

The quick shake of Claire's head was frustrating. "I think he's right, of course."

"Because he *is* right, or because he's your husband?" I should be tucking boss-me away, and embracing docile, wife-to-be me. Or, fuck that, because no.

Her hesitation told me everything I needed to know. "Because he's right," she said.

Uh-huh.

"You agree with a lot of things Dom says, right?" Claire asked.

I bristled hearing the nickname come from her mouth, but I hid the reaction. "Dominic. Only Dom for his spouse to be." Apparently I'd been helping Dom and Xander play the pronoun game for so long that I defaulted to it. "And yes, I do. I wouldn't be engaged to him if we didn't see eye to eye on a lot of things. But I don't agree with all of it."

For instance, fake engagements to trick real people into thinking we were a perfect little church going family.

"I don't agree with everything Dale does, either." Now Claire sounded defensive.

I didn't want that. She'd stop listening, she'd resent me at future meetings, and worst, she may double down on the behavior that was keeping her trapped—

Stop. It wasn't my place to decide if her relationship was wrong or right, as long as she was happy.

"Okay." That seemed like the least confrontational thing I could say. "Good."

Deep creases appeared in Claire's forehead, and she twisted her mouth. "Good."

This was when I needed to make my exit.

"Like when he ordered dinner for me the other night. I don't even like steak," she said.

I didn't blame her for being bothered by that. Would saying so make her more or less open to the conversation?

Claire dropped her chin. "I didn't mean that. Ignore me."

I couldn't let it drop. That nagging voice inside said *remember being there?* With a controlling father. Not only me, but my mother. "We can talk about it. I'm here to listen."

"I'm fine. Nothing to talk about." The way her smile stretched her face was painful to look at. "I need to go. Catch you around." Claire stepped into the crowd and it carried her away before I could say anything else.

I shouldn't keep nudging her. We would've been fine if the conversation stayed on Batman. If we'd kept talking about geeky things and video games. But no, I had to poke and prod someone I only knew because I was lying about getting married. A woman I wouldn't see ever again in a few weeks.

The impulse to lean into Xander surged through me. To use him to steady myself. The flash of weakness dragged a whisper of self-loathing behind it. I didn't *need* anyone to make me stronger. I was fine. Especially after a simple conversation.

Instead, I settled for swaying to bump his arm with my shoulder. "Morning," I said.

"So I hear." His tone was light. "You get any sleep?"

"After I convinced myself that the game was really back online? Like a baby."

Xander moved to face me. "Waking up every few hours screaming?"

This was better. This was normal. Casual. Real. "Something a lot like that. You?"

"Like I had your fiancé to keep me warm." He winked.

I let out a short laugh. "Lucky bastard."

"You know it. You want me on security?"

I want you on me.

Down girl. Release week stress was no reason to lose control. Of my libido or anything. "That'd be amazing."

"What are the odds you have a break around lunch? Dom says he's going to try to get free from the office early, and come visit."

I was bummed we'd missed out on sexy fun times last night. I shouldn't care—work needed me, and I didn't regret for a moment that I'd been available. Besides, I'd gone for years without fucking Xander or Dom, and now after a single night, I couldn't stop thinking about more.

No reason to drop my panties every time one of them smiled at me, though really I would. As long as the game wasn't crashing. "I'll make time. A little after one?"

"Text me, we'll find you. Until then." Xander kissed me on the forehead, and headed toward the exhibitor hall.

If I were younger, more innocent, more like Claire, that would make me swoon. But it was the way Xander and I had always been. It was nothing special.

I spent the next few hours in meetings. When one of the bigger MMOs wanted to talk about crossover possibilities, I was all over the idea. When the adult novelty website spent the first ten minutes ignoring me and talking only to Dustin, I shut the conversation down.

Some things in this industry hadn't changed at all over the decades. Others had, and one of my favorites was that instead of being required to sit through that bullshit and let Dustin do all the talking, I got to remind the other party I was the boss, and show them to the door.

The early end to the meeting meant I had time to kill. How weird was that? I wandered through the exhibitors' hall, taking in the atmosphere. I'd seen all the booths before the show opened, and talked to a lot of old friends about what they were up to, but seeing it all with the fans around was a different experience.

I caught snippets of talk about AcesPlayed, and had to stop and listen every time. There were the vocal people upset that the game had been down at all, and most of them were convinced it was solely Elliot's fault. As if he were a magical game god who was responsible for every single thing that happened at AcesPlayed.

But most people were surprised that it was the only real downtime we'd had this week, and they were loving the game.

A little before one, I headed toward the front of the hall, toward the AcesPlayed booth. I wasn't surprised to see Dominic had arrived, and was talking to Xander and Phillip.

Phillip saw me approach, but the other two had their backs to me. He didn't say anything.

"Excuse me." Satisfaction flitted inside me when Xander and Dominic both jumped a little. "I don't pay you guys to stand around."

"Pretty sure that's exactly what you're paying me for," Xander said.

Dominic scowled. "Wait. You're getting paid? I'm not getting paid."

I stared at him in mock disbelief. "You're not working."

"You're paying him to stand around. I'm standing around."

Phillip raised his hand. "Can confirm."

"Are you getting *actual* money?" Dominic sounded genuinely surprised.

"Actual money, yes," Phillip said. "Not even Monopoly money or bottle caps."

"Don't tell them." I pretended to growl. "They'll want the same."

Xander moved to stand next to me. "Nah. I'm cheap. Let me buy you lunch, and I'll keep doing the job."

The way Phillip rolled his eyes, I was surprised they didn't pop out of his head. "Not how jobs work. Should I be concerned that you're one of our money guys?"

"Shhh." Xander pressed a finger to Phillip's lips. "Don't talk. Don't think. It's better that way."

"Come on. Let the man work." I was laughing as I grabbed Xander's and Dominic's arms and tugged the men toward the outer wall of the room.

We weren't leaving, but traffic was lightest here. This way we could loop around to one of the mini food courts without much obstruction.

As we wove our way through people, something caught my attention out of the corner of my eye. I turned to see what it was, and almost missed it. There it was—Link was sitting on the ground against a far wall, next to Fallyn. Second time in as many days I'd seen them together.

It shouldn't strike me as odd, and if it were anyone else besides the two of them, I probably wouldn't notice. But I couldn't help but draw parallels between Xander, me, and Dominic. Big difference—Dominic and I didn't have a history before that night, seven years ago, and we were never enemies.

I needed to stop. Who Link spent his time with had nothing to do with my past, and was none of my business until it impacted his work. Which he wouldn't let it do.

We grabbed our food, and I led Xander and Dominic toward a quieter part of the convention center. "Great thing about knowing the people in charge," I said, as I unlocked a generic door with no label, "is keys to all the secret places."

I let us into a room where the tables were stored when they weren't in use. The vast space spread out in front of us, empty aside from the broken tables shoved against the walls.

"This reminds me of sneaking into the janitor's closet at school." Xander's voice was light.

Dominic raised an eyebrow. "You do that a lot?"

"Not after a point."

"That's not what I heard. Xander had a *reputation*." The teasing came easily, and I wasn't worried about this being a surprise to Dominic. They knew each other, including their pasts.

What did surprise me was the shadow that crossed Xander's face. But it vanished again before I could process it further.

"Busted. Which I never was back then." Xander winked.

That was more like it. "I was thinking this was

more like a picnic than a closet," I said. "And me without my blanket." I frowned. "That came out wrong."

Xander offered me a hand as I lowered myself to sit. "Did it?"

"When I was younger, I thought a picnic was one of the most romantic dates a girl could be taken on." I decided it was best to move on.

Dominic settled next to me. "This isn't making you think otherwise, is it? This is romantic. Only the best for my girl."

The entire setup was actually not bad. Better than that—it was nice. Sitting. Taking a break with the people I trusted most in this world. The people I wanted most.

Where did *that* come from? I shook the errant thought aside. "I have to admit, it's pretty dope."

"I can't believe you just said *dope*." The amusement in Xander's voice was audible.

I pretended to be surprised. "You'd prefer *fly? Epic? Extreme?*"

Before either of them could reply, a phone rang and we all reached for our own.

"Mine." Dominic held his up. "It's Roger." He answered. The conversation was mostly Dominic listening, but he kept glancing at me.

That put me on edge.

"We can't, she's got plans," he said. "I told you when you—"

"Hang on." I talked over him.

Covering the mouthpiece, Dominic looked at me.

"I have plans for when?" It wasn't that I had a problem with Dom turning down events on my behalf, but I was in this specifically for that reason. If we were going to do this engagement thing, we might as well do it, and if he was risking something by me not being available, I could at least try.

"Dinner. Last minute invite from one of Dale's partners. I told Roger we're not—"

The feeling of *I shirked my responsibility* would haunt me if I made Dom miss this. "I'll do it."

"It's tomorrow night."

"I said I'll do it." I wouldn't leave him hanging.

The way he stared at me, the challenge in his expression, it looked like he was ready to argue. Why was this suddenly so important to me?

I didn't have words to say beyond *I promised to be there for him*, and that was important anyway, but suddenly it meant so much more.

11 /
dominic

I was pretty sure I knew why Judith was insisting we make it to dinner—because she felt like she owed it to me. But I'd promised her not during RinCon and Roger had promised me.

I also knew why Roger was asking—he was pulling out all the stops for Dale's company—but if we weren't going to draw the line now, before they signed, we were going to have a hell of a time working with them when they were actually clients.

"No." I told Roger again. "We will not be attending last minute, especially during the holidays, but even if it were the middle of May. I suggest you tell them the same."

Roger let out a short huff. "I'll talk to you next week."

Really? He was going to try to make me feel guilty about this? No. I shoved my phone into my pocket with a scowl.

"So, we're not going." Judith's tone was hard to read.

"No. I'm willing to jump when it's reasonable, but this... No." There shouldn't be a need to say more. They both heard what I told Roger.

The light smile that played on Xander's face helped unsour my mood. "Fully agree with you," he said.

I didn't know if I was more bothered that Roger asked me to begin with, or that I wasn't more surprised he'd made the request.

We finished lunch quickly, so we could send Judith to her next meeting, and Xander and I decided to actually see the show.

The two of us wandered the exhibitors' hall, pausing with each thing that caught our eye. The event was more than new game announcements, it was a celebration of fandom. There were comics, collectables, and more.

The booths weren't the only thing that caught my eye though. There was a tangible energy in the air, from being surrounded by so many people enjoying this thing they were passionate about. And with me being next to the man I was intensely and madly in love with, I wanted to let that same vibe flow through me. I wanted to tangle my fingers with his. Steal random kisses. Enjoy everything about Xander's company.

And I couldn't. Claire was here. Who knew who else?

I hated it.

The thought gripped me hard, and refused to let go as we wandered from one row to the next.

"You went quiet all of a sudden," Xander said. "What's up?"

The one thing we'd rehashed dozens of times before. Too much, but never enough. "After all this time, why do you put up with it?"

"Why do *you*?" Xander seemed to know exactly what I meant.

Because I was the one who asked for it. Because how could I expect him to play along if I didn't? Because I loved him, but loyalty, and a promise to my father's best friend and my mentor that was older than my relationship with Xander, got in the way. "You know why."

"I hate it. You know that." Xander slipped his hands into his pockets, but the gesture didn't hide his balled-up fists. "But I love you, and I know how this town, these businesses, treat people with relationships like ours. You made the decision before me, and you do it for family."

He leaned closer, mouth near my ear, in a way that was far too intimate to be innocent. "And if I left you, I'd lose the chance to rail that tight fucking ass whenever I wanted."

Always the romantic. "I'm pretty fond of that too."

"Of course you are."

There was so much to do and see that it took us the rest of the afternoon to make our way through it all. As the clock ticked closer to closing time in the hall, Xander and I left to change for the big event tonight. Several of the larger companies had courtesy suite activities happening in a few hours, and AcesPlayed was hosting a costume masquerade and karaoke ball.

It was a mishmash of concepts, and I didn't expect anything less from Judith's crew.

Xander and I changed into pinstriped suits and fedoras, donned sunglasses as masks, and headed as the Blues Brothers to Judith's room.

When she opened the door, my jaw fell open. She wore a shimmery red evening gown that hugged every one of her curves, and showed off one leg with the nearly hip-high slit. Her heels made her four inches taller, and the way she let her hair frame her face in soft waves turned her into a real-life Jessica Rabbit. The delicate mask she wore added to the entire look and did nothing to hide who she was.

She placed a finger under my chin and pushed up. "Mouth shut, Wolfy."

"Besides, everyone knows Red goes home with the dog," Xander said.

I raked my gaze over him, truly appreciating the

way the suit accentuated every muscle. "You are *not* Droopy Dog."

"I'm not droopy anything while she's wearing that dress." The way Xander adjusted himself was anything but subtle.

Judith looked between us, her raised eyebrows not hiding her faint smirk. "Do you have this out of your systems?"

"Not until later, I assume," Xander said.

"You're not going to ask us to behave are you?" Because that sounded dull. "No one else down there will be."

Judith twisted her mouth. "My people will be."

"Since when?" Xander snorted.

"Since most of them are attached to each other and in love." It was impossible to tell if that sigh at the end of Judith's statement, the one that landed on *in love*, was sincere or sarcastic.

Xander rolled his eyes. "No fun."

"You're attached and in love too," Judith said.

With one key exception. "We're still fun."

"That's debatable." That time Judith was definitely teasing.

Stepping behind her, Xander slid a finger up her bare back. She shivered as visible goosebumps rose on her arms above her gloves.

"No fun, huh?" His voice was a low growl.

"A little fun." She relented.

I stepped closer, needing to feel their heat. "A lot of fun."

"Not until later. I was promised." She almost sounded disappointed.

The wait would be worth it.

We headed down to the AcesPlayed suite, whose theme was masquerade and karaoke. Despite being early, the line was already around the corner to get in, and there were almost as many people waiting to sign up to sing. I liked seeing this for Judith. She's worked so hard and she deserved it.

Within the hour, the room was packed, the music was loud, and the mood was incredible. Everything felt so open. These were all fans of the game, or mostly, and that meant they were at least a little all right with open discussions of consensual sex.

No one here cared who danced with whom. Who made out with whom. I could dance with Judith and Xander and 8-bit Sephiroth and no one batted an eye.

Dancing with Xander—close, dirty, carefree— felt *good*. When Judith joined us, it was even better. A twinge of doubt sparked in my chest that I should want them both the way I did, but the desire wasn't anything new. I'd decided to embrace it, to see if I could get the two of them to agree, and there was no reason to let what others said influence that.

As the night flowed on, some of the singers were

incredible and some of them were painful to hear, and all of them got their turn on stage. When Reese-as-Joan-Jett stepped to the front of the room, I expected a throaty, seductive rendition of... Well, anything.

"Hey, all." That was her *are you ready to rock* voice, but she wasn't singing. "I promised my guys I wouldn't hog the stage tonight, and as much as that kills me, a promise is a promise. *But* our list for karaoke is empty, so this is an open call. Who wants to come up and sing?"

A few hands shot up. All from people who had already taken their turn, but I was pretty sure no one cared.

Reese must, because she looked past them at our group. "What about the lovely lady in red, Jessica Rabbit?"

"No." Judith didn't hesitate. "I promise, you do *not* want me singing, unless you like the sounds of strangled dolls."

Come to think of it, I'd never heard her sing.

"Come on."

"It can't be that bad."

A wave of encouraging cries rippled through the room.

Judith held up her hands. "You all know I don't have any fear of public performance. But I know where my strengths are."

"We'll go," a voice called from the crowd, and a

heartbeat later, Maddox was tugging Alys with him onto the stage. They'd come as the Mad Hatter and Alice in Wonderland. Because of course they had.

Reese clapped along with everyone else, but held onto the mic. "The rest of you better be signing up to go again, because I don't want to break a promise, but I will if the stage stays empty."

Reese promising to sing if no one else did seemed like a good way to keep the sign-ups low, but she was probably banking on that. Regardless, she handed off the stage to Maddox and Alys. Both of whom sang back-up vocals for Plaid Peanut Butter, in addition to playing, so we were in for a treat.

I was surprised and amused when *Girls on Film* started playing.

"This is in honor of the game that brought us here tonight, and the most awesome people in the world who built it." Maddox's words coaxed a loud cheer from the room, and he and Alys flowed into the song. Like so many singers tonight, they switched up the lyrics. Sometimes it was girls on film, sometimes boys, and sometimes orcs.

Later, as the energy in the room faded, and people drifted out to head home or up to their rooms, excitement crackled in my veins. I wanted this feeling to last. I wanted the night with Xander and Judith to last.

I pressed into Judith's back as someone on stage sang a tortured rendition of *Truly Madly Deeply*, and

I made sure Xander was paying attention. "If I make you laugh, can we take you back to your room?" I asked.

She leaned her weight into me, pulling Xander with her, until the three of us were sandwiched together. "Depends." Her voice was low and seductive. "Is that rabbit in your pocket or are you just happy to see me?" Slipping a hand behind her, she brushed the front of my trousers.

Xander cleared his throat. "I get what you're going for, but not sure it works. A rabbit? Like a vibrator? An actual bunny?"

"Like Roger Rabbit." If I had to explain the reference, was it even funny?

Xander wrinkled his nose. "He's not joining us, is he? Because I'm not sharing either of you."

"Except with each other," I said.

The way Xander twisted his face, he looked deep in thought. "Maybe. Haven't decided yet."

Judith grabbed both our hands and spun away from between us. "If you stop, the answer is *yes*."

I could ask *stop what* but why ruin a good thing? Instead, I made a show of snapping my mouth shut.

The three of us walked hand in hand toward the elevators. We were halfway across the lobby when a familiar voice said, "Judith? Dominic?"

And that was Claire. Fuck.

12 /
judith

No. Really. Where did this woman keep coming from? And now that she was staring at the three of us, what did she think she was looking at? Because if this was completely innocent to her, there was no reason for me to try to explain.

"You're here late." I kept my tone friendly. Casual. The feeling that swelled inside that I'd been caught doing something naughty didn't sit well with me, and yanked on a past of indoctrination I hadn't touched in years.

Claire shrugged. "Dale's out of town for a few days and I don't like being home in the empty house, so I was in the Digital Media suite. They're holding a cart racer competition." She was staring at me. Why was she staring at me? "You look really pretty."

She sounded so sincere.

"We were at the masquerade party," Xander

said before I could decide if honesty was the best path here.

"Oh."

If she followed that up with a comment about smutty smut, I wasn't sure I was in the mood to behave tonight.

"So, I guess I should get going." Claire turned her gaze to her feet. "Could this maybe stay between us?"

One of the last things I expected her to ask, but I was happy to let it be her idea. "Sure. If that's best for you, of course."

"Thank you." She didn't look at us again as she turned and walked quickly toward the parking garage.

"What was that?" I muttered, as much to myself as my companions.

Xander wrapped an arm around my waist. "Right at this moment? Don't know, don't care, given how well it ended."

Dominic kissed the back of my knuckles. "He's got a point."

"A big hard one," Xander said.

"Let's see what we can do about that." I let them finish leading the way up to my room.

The instant we stepped inside, and the door closed behind us, Xander was at my back, his hands on my hips. "The only thing better than seeing you in this dress is going to be taking you out of it." His low, heated words rolled through me.

"Cheesy, but the way you say it is so sexy."

Dominic was in front of me, and he draped his arms over my shoulders. Gliding his fingertips along my neck, he untied the straps of my dress.

The top slipped down, but the rest stayed in place. Xander huffed at my back. "Your dress is stuck to you."

I stepped away from both of them. "I'm good, but I'm not *nothing slips out of place because I willed it not to* good. Strategically placed tape." Slipping my fingers under the fabric, I glided my touch along my body, peeling dress from skin as I moved past my breasts, down my stomach, and along my lower back.

As I moved, the dress fell away, but Xander's and Dominic's gazes never did. Shimmery red fabric landed like water pooled around my feet, leaving me in panties, stockings, and heels. I was exposed. More vulnerable than anyone else would ever see me.

And yet, my tension had fallen away with the dress. This sense of safety was something I felt so rarely that it ached in my chest.

Dominic grasped my hand again, raised it to his lips, and kissed each fingertip one at a time. The gesture was so gentle and *real* that it washed away my lingering hesitation. For tonight, I was theirs.

Xander took my other hand, and each of them peeled off a glove. Dominic gently removed my mask while Xander stepped behind me. A moment later, my world went dark when one of my own gloves covered my eyes. He had to stretch the fabric to tie it, but it was a soothing feeling rather than uncomfortable.

When Xander used the other glove to bind my hands behind my back, my pulse skipped and a fresh need throbbed between my thighs. "Don't move," he whispered in my ear.

Where was I going to go, mostly naked, blind-folded, and restrained?

The sound of the door opening and closing reached me. Did they just leave? Anyone else and I'd panic, but I trusted both men.

Wait, one of them was still here. Heat brushed my back and warm breath teased my neck. It was probably Dom, because his cologne smelled the strongest, but they were both on my skin, making it hard for me to be certain.

I was good with that.

After what felt like an eternity, but had probably only been a minute or two, I heard the door again, followed by a soft *thunk*, something being set down, and a rattle.

I knew that sound. Why couldn't I place it?

Cold touched my lips. Ice, that was it. I parted my mouth in a gasp and the singular point of chill raced through me. A mouth followed, claiming mine in a hot, hungry kiss. That was definitely Dom.

And the contrast was delicious.

Was it odd that I was both sad and relieved it wasn't Xander? I wanted to know what he tasted like. How he kissed. But I wanted to look him in the eye that first time his lips met mine.

Ice, one piece on my earlobe and one on a nipple, shattered any other thoughts. The touches from two different directions lingered, slipping along a tiny area of my skin. Just as each became too much, it was replaced with a hot mouth wrapping around the area.

Ice then sucking, ice then sucking, until my mind spun and the rest of the world had vanished.

Dominic focused on bathing my nipples with his tongue, and the other touch fell away, replaced with Xander pushing my panties to the ground.

When cool fingers parted my slick folds, I gasped and pressed into Dominic's mouth. When Xander brushed ice over my clit, I whimpered. He glided along my skin, never lingering too long in one place, but it was almost too much.

Almost.

Xander slipped the ice toward my opening and pushed it inside me. My entire body tensed at the delicious ache, and I felt the melted water roll down my skin. He followed by slipping fingers inside me.

The slow, steady pumping warmed me quickly now that the ice was gone.

Dominic moved his fingers to my clit, and both men pressed their bodies into mine. They'd shed their clothing too, and their hot, bare skin against mine was delicious. I loved this feeling of being sandwiched between them.

With Xander finger-fucking me and Dom circling my clit, both pressing in when my gasps grew louder, I fell quickly toward orgasm. They kept pushing, coaxing, as the pressure built inside, until climax overtook me.

They eased their touches away as my body shuddered from pleasure, but they kept holding me up.

I'd loved the other night, but when it was done, I hadn't been sure I ever wanted half a dozen orgasms again. Right now, I was considering it.

The tension on my wrists and head vanished, and the restraints and blindfold fell away. Combined with the lingering bliss, I felt light. Not quite here. Heavenly mixed with just a little bit of wickedness.

Dom drew my gaze with a finger under my chin. The way his jaw worked, it looked like he was going to say something, but he brushed his lips over mine instead. "On the bed."

The state of mind I was in, I only wanted to comply. I lay in the middle of the mattress, and watched his tight, sleek frame as he crawled up my legs. The hunger in his eyes sent a brand-new kind of chill racing over me.

When he gripped my hips and rolled us both, I squealed in surprise. I landed on top of him with a soft grunt, and a laugh escaped as I righted myself so I was straddling his legs.

Dominic reached up to cup my face. "You looked incredible tonight. But, you always do."

My breath caught at the intensity that flowed between us, and I caught my bottom lip between my teeth. "You looked pretty good too."

"Sexiest three people in the room." Reaching between us, Dom glided the head of his cock along my skin.

When he penetrated me, I moaned. The sound blended into a gasp when he thrust up, spreading me open and pushing inside me. We sat there for a moment, as if the world had paused except for his cock twitching against my inner walls.

Xander pressed into my back, and nudged me forward until my chest met Dom's. Gliding slick fingers up my ass, Xander applied a cool, slick layer of lube to my rear entrance. That first nudge, when he wanted in, my body tensed.

I breathed through it, relaxing. Enjoying the strain of almost-too-much. Letting Xander inside me until he and Dom both rested in place, my body sheathing them.

The way the three of us rocked together was a

slow build. Gentle waves carrying us. Dominic cupped my breasts to tease my nipples, and Xander reached between us, seeking out my clit.

After the ice and the orgasm, bits of me were overstimulated and numb, but the two of them coaxed me past that edge of *too much* and drew me back toward mounting pleasure. Our rhythm together increased and so did their touches, until fresh pleasure built inside me.

I wasn't sure I could climax again, but then it was rushing through me, yanking me into orgasm and tearing cries from my throat.

As if that were a sign, both men increased the pace, slipping in me, pounding harder and faster, their grunts and groans filling their air as our bodies moved together.

I lost track of where my orgasm trailed off and theirs flowed in. I wasn't sure who came first or last or of much of anything except that this all felt so fucking good. Even after their grunts had faded along with my screams, the pounding continued a little longer.

Until we all slowed to a stop, and fell into a tangled mess of limbs.

Was it overstating things to think this was one of the best nights of my life?

I didn't think so.

I didn't remember the last time I'd slept until eight, but it felt incredible. Even better was being wrapped up in Xander, Dominic curled around us.

I'd need to get down to the show soon, but right now, I was going to stay here and luxuriate in warm fuzzies for a few more minutes.

My phone rang, and I untangled myself to reach for it without having to leave safety completely behind. When I saw the name on the screen, my gut gave a half twist. This was one of our on-call developers. "Hello?"

"Hey. The game is down." No fanfare. No small talk.

Exactly the way I preferred.

Reality was back, full-force, and I jerked upright in bed. Tension cranked through me. "Did you call Elliot?"

"Tyler is on with him now. He's on his way in."

Exactly what I expected, and good news. Elliot would handle this, but our game was down. *My* game. "I'll be there in fifteen."

"What's wrong?" Xander asked as soon as I disconnected.

I was already on my feet, tugging clothes out. "Game's down."

"Go." He bit off the word. "We've got the rest."

That could mean a million different things, but I didn't have to ask which ones he specifically meant. I trusted him to handle anything I couldn't focus on right now. I brushed my hair into a ponytail, showered and dressed in record time, and was out the door six minutes later. The keycard I left on the dresser by the TV would let Xander and Dominic do whatever they needed to in order to dress, come and go, etcetera.

I got to the office and did one of my least favorite things—waited.

Elliot checked in with me when he was done talking to his developers, and introduced me to a puppy. I could've oohed and ahhed, or asked why his dog had been in Fallyn's livestream a week ago. I didn't have the bandwidth to give a fuck about either right now.

We still didn't have answers when Xander stopped by an hour later with breakfast and coffee for me.

"I can't eat." I told him.

He unwrapped the egg sandwich and sat it in front of me. "You can. Don't test me."

I complied because I didn't have anything to do besides wait for news. Feeling useless was the worst feeling.

Xander tapped a foot rather than sitting. "I'll run interference for you with the other partners. You do what you need to here, and don't worry about anything else."

I gave him the closest thing to a grateful smile

that I could manage, and it came out more like a grimace. "Thank you."

Over the years, I'd kept my basic coding skills intact, but I wasn't up to the level they needed to bring the game back online. Instead, I stayed on site. Helped them test things as they fixed them. Did for my devs what Xander had done for me and made sure they ate.

I'd be here until my game—our game—came back online.

When it did, sometime after midnight, exhaustion tempered my relief.

When I got back to my hotel, of course I was the only one in my room, but that didn't stop disappointment from joining the tiredness that penetrated every inch of me. Housekeeping had been here while I worked, and the sheets smelled clean instead of like a mix of Xander and Dominic's colognes.

Not that I had the energy to ponder any of it. I curled up, silenced the ache at the loss of that feeling of safety from a day ago, and passed out.

In the morning, I was up as early as ever. I was too old for late nights and early mornings, but knowing that didn't make it any easier to fall back asleep.

A quick check of my messages showed the game was online. I needed coffee. A lot of it. A short while later, I returned from my journey of retrieving massive amounts of caffeine.

Now what?

I was zombie-ing my way through the lower priority emails I'd ignored for the last few days, when the alerts I had associated with the company name, with Elliot's and Link's names, started coming in hard and fast. Clicking through the links, I pulled up pictures of the two of them with Fallyn, in the hotel parking garage, Friday night after the masquerade.

"What have you done, Elliot?" I muttered at a room that wouldn't reply.

Fortunately the photos weren't damning. The three of them were talking. Industry professionals having a conversation in the same place an industry event was happening. When Dustin's official statement from our company came through, it said pretty much the same.

Good. Crisis averted.

I had time to breathe and finish my first coffee when my phone started having fits again.

Oh. Fuck me. These were chat logs from our game. The anonymous leaker claimed they were between Elliot, Link, and Fallyn.

I had no idea if she was Demon Kittie, but I knew their characters.

Fuck, Elliot. These conversations were explicit. And they were pretty irrefutable proof that he was hitting on someone who worked for him. My lead developer. One of our key investors. Breaking some serious non-fraternization rules, and possibly worse.

I knew this was coming, and I chose to look the other way. It was easier to pretend they'd stopped. I couldn't ignore it now.

When Xander called, I answered immediately.

"Is this what it looks like?" he asked.

I so desperately wanted to say *no. It's nothing.* "Yes."

"All of the partners are freaking out over the legal implications of this."

Of course they were. They didn't care that the game had a potential massive security flaw. They cared about their image. Before I could give him an answer, one call tried to ring through and then another. From Scott McAllister and Grant Lent— our other two big investors and board members.

Dustin was incredible at PR. He could deal with almost any disruption, but this...

I had to get ahead of this. "I'm calling a board meeting for tomorrow," I said to Xander. "Aces-Played offices. I'll call the others."

"What's the goal?" Xander asked.

"To keep my game funded. To keep my Director of Development from bringing down our company without losing him. To cover our asses." But none of those answers carried a solution.

"Elliot's one of us."

Something I didn't need to be reminded of. He

wasn't just an AcesPlayed employee, he was as much a part of the beginning as I was. As much as Xander. "I'm not planning on hanging him out to dry."

No one was taking my people from me.

13 /
xander

I told Judith to wrap up what she was doing, check out, and head over so we could make a plan. There was no doubt in my mind she already had something brewing, but I needed her here. I needed to know she was…

Safe? A bit.

Not going out of her mind? That was more like it.

Dominic was sympathetic and ready to help as well, and I loved him for it.

Most of what I was doing involved answering calls from the other partners, from associates, that stemmed from texts and messages. Most started along the lines of, "I know this isn't on your side, but if you have any information…"

I started on the easy end of the spectrum, and worked my way toward the calls that had the potential to be more frustrating.

"How's everyone holding up?" Liz asked when I called her back.

"About as well as can be expected. Judith has a plan, and she's adding details now."

The sound Liz made was somewhere between a cluck and a sigh. "I expected that. I mean have you started climbing the walls yet because it's not resolved? It was more of an emotional question."

"She's good. As far as I know the people involved are too." I actually doubted that was true. Elliot was probably real close to climbing the walls.

"Hmm. Well, send them my sympathy. Via proper channels and all that." Liz had been through this kind of fire-by-social-media before, and so had her boyfriend and girlfriend. She probably knew better than a lot of people what Elliot was dealing with.

I remembered the day Rinslet let Jordan go. Judith had been furious. Though she'd never said, I suspected that was one of those moments that pushed her closer to spinning off her own gaming company "Thanks. I will," I said.

There wasn't time for much small talk, because I had a list to work my way through. Jonathan and Kandace were sympathetic to the bad publicity, but wanted to remind me this was an investment, not something I could make personal.

Fuck them. This was most definitely personal,

and their warnings made me want to publicly announce I was the one fucking Elliot.

Or simply tell the truth about how I felt about J—

A call rang through before I could pick whose to return next, and I decided now was as good a time as any to talk to Grant Lent.

I knew the older man through multiple channels. First meeting had been decades ago, when my father introduced me. Grant was the reason I'd accepted Wade's proposal when he wanted to start The Raphael Group. I saw the impact Grant's companies—the companies he'd supported—were making on technology, and I wanted to be a part of that.

There was no friendly banter where I answered. No *how are you holding up?* Or *How's your Sunday?*

"Don't go down with this ship," Grant said.

Ah, yes. One of his long-standing pieces of advice. Don't go down with any ship. Grant believed if the captain couldn't steer the boat away from icebergs, it was best to be on the first lifeboat.

Once upon a time, I thought that was brilliant advice. Today, it made me want to deck him. "I'm good with the decisions I'm making."

He let out one of those *I'm very disappointed in you* sighs. "Your changing direction now doesn't mean the investment was a bad one. No company stays on top forever, and some never quite make it there."

He wasn't only talking about punishing Elliot. This was about me pulling my money.

Fuck that. "I'm good with my current decisions," I repeated. "If I need your input, you'll hear from me, but otherwise assume I don't."

"Ah. I'll see you in the offices tomorrow," Grant said, and hung up.

I dropped my phone onto the couch next to me, and met Dominic's gaze.

"That sounded exceptionally non-productive," he said with a sympathetic smile.

The nerve twitch behind one of my eyelids agreed with him. I scrubbed my face. "Any luck?"

"No." Dominic was reviewing the company contracts, looking for a cut and dried way to pronounce this matter no big deal and move on. "Remind me next time I review a contract to build in a few loopholes only I know about." He'd been another set of eyes on the existing AcesPlayed employment agreements, both the originals, and the non-fraternization amendments from earlier this year.

When Judith arrived, laptop bag slung over her shoulder and lines etched in her brow, she joined us in the living room. This was mostly brainstorming, so we could keep the setting casual. She sat cross legged in a chair, computer in her lap, and Dom and I took spots next to each other on the couch.

"How are Elliot and Link coping?" I asked.

She blew out a puff of air, ruffling the hair that hung at the side of her face. "Link is in the office making sure the issue isn't widespread. I made Elliot sit on his hands until at least after the meeting tomorrow."

"I bet he loves that." Sarcasm dripped from Dominic's retort.

Judith gave him a dry smile. "So, so much."

I understood why she'd done things this way, and I would've made the same call, but it sucked that it was necessary. In order to save Elliot, she and he had to play by the rules up to a point, so there were no additional reasons to say *he has to go*.

"Is it really Fallyn?" I asked. In the pictures, there was little doubt. But in the chat logs…

Judith fixed me with a neutral stare. "As far as any of us know, no. And I'm being honest when I say I didn't ask. On purpose."

Smart. Plausible deniability.

"The problem is, it really is Elliot and Link." Dominic stood and strode to stand behind her. "And your chat logs show him telling a female presenting player, and one of his employees, that he's going to"—He leaned in to read over her shoulder—"Pin them to the bed and by the throat and fuck them like the whores they are."

"I mean…" I let the unfinished thought hang in the air.

Judith's smile was tired. "Yeah. Hot. In context."

"I should've pegged Elliot as having a degradation kink." My preference was praise, but to each their own, as long as it was consensual. "It is Fallyn, though."

"I assume. I wouldn't have thought so before this week, but…" Another sigh. Judith was going to work her way through a lifetime's supply today. "Even if it's not, people think it is."

Judith and I grew up in a small town, and in some ways internet gossip was almost identical to what spread like wildfire along Main Street whenever anyone did anything. Biggest difference was that back home, the rumors meant everyone looked and whispered when you walked by, but on the internet, it could tear down entire corporations.

"What are the odds the board will buy-out-slash-kick-out Elliot?" Dominic asked.

He knew what the base plan was, because he'd already heard enough of my conversations to figure it out, and I would've told him anyway. Grant was flying in from California, and the entire board, minus Elliot, would vote on whether or not Elliot got to keep his seat.

I shook my head, both to clear the dark clouds and in answer to Dominic's question. "Oliver will vote for him to stay." Oliver was our representative from The Raphael Group, and our partners weren't ready to threaten this relationship.

"Scott will vote *stay*. So will I," Judith added.

Grant wouldn't, but at this point it was three against one and it wouldn't matter.

"And what if Grant pulls his investment when you all vote against him?" Dominic grabbed the possibility we hadn't discussed yet.

Then Grant was a bigger child than I thought possible. "We can deal with that if he does that." *We* being the other investors.

"We have all our bases covered," Judith said. "We've made plans on plans for this, for years. Not specifically Elliot"—because the only other person in a position like his, being both an investor and employee, was Judith—"but we've accounted for so much. I want to do more, but I don't know what else we can do besides double check the safeguards. We have to ride this out until tomorrow."

It had to kill her to say that as much as I hated hearing it. *We have to wait.*

"So… this waiting. Does it involve pacing and wearing holes in our throw rugs?" Dominic sounded less than pleased with that idea.

It wouldn't be that bad. "Neither of us is wearing shoes. I'm sure there won't be any holes worn down." *Phrasing.*

"That's what she— No, wait, that doesn't work." Judith laugh-sighed.

Hearing her make the joke was nice, though. It meant she didn't think all was lost. Because it wasn't. I looked at Dom. "I assume you have a suggestion for what we could be doing instead?"

"I do." He moved to stand between us.

"We're listening," Judith closed her laptop and set it on the coffee table.

"Pizza. Pool."

The list felt incomplete. All lists needed at least three things. "Porn?"

"If you want it. I'm not sure we need it." Dominic offered Judith a hand, and pulled her to her feet.

She twisted her face in consideration. "I was kind of loving the *wear holes in carpets* idea, but this sounds okay too."

"He's right." And I wasn't only saying that because he was my husband. "We need to distract ourselves." We headed toward the game room in the basement.

"By proving we're all fairly equally matched at something?" As we descended the stairs, Judith's skeptical question pinged off our surroundings.

It was a good point. We were all good at pool, and our balance of wins to losses was fairly even against each other.

"We'll play for fun. For the distraction of it." When he reached the landing, Dom turned to face us.

Judith and I exchanged glances.

"No winners?" I asked.

"I don't understand," Judith said.

Dominic rolled his eyes. "Right. Of course. I'm sure we'll figure something out."

Our game room had started as a more traditional space, in an open basement. We had a pool table and a dart board.

We also had half the room dedicated to large screens hooked up to computers and gaming consoles. Because what kind of game room didn't have a place to play video games?

Each of us had our favorite cues and different ways of playing, but the first several games were as evenly matched as predicted.

"When does this get distracting?" Judith bent over the table to rack the balls. The arch of her back led to the perfect curve of her ass, and followed shapely legs down to the ground.

Amazing view. "I think it just did."

She glanced over her shoulder at me, and a slow smirk spread across her face. "So that's what we're playing."

"We don't have to *play* anything." Dominic's words were less than compelling.

I brushed my lips over his. "You can watch, if you don't want to participate." Because the new game *was* distraction.

"Oh, I'm in." Dominic gave a dry chuckle. "But only if we have rules."

"Pft." In a single sound, Judith conveyed *unimpressed*. "Fine. What are the rules?"

"No bumping the table or the person taking the shot. Easy enough?" Dominic's question was full of challenge.

This was going to be fun. "Game on."

14 /
dominic

As Xander stepped up to take his shot, he pushed up the long sleeves of his Henley to almost his elbows, leaving tattooed forearms corded with muscle on perfect display. The way his body flexed with each movement felt more exaggerated than last turn.

Not that I minded.

And he made his shot.

My turn.

I almost felt ridiculous, fondling a pool cue. Taking my time gliding my hand along the shaft, brushing my thumb over the tip before chalking it. I stopped short of fellating the damn thing, but I had Xander's attention regardless.

Judith didn't look quite as captivated.

I'd need a better gimmick for the next round.

Judith strolled up to the table, her fingers sliding along the long chain that hung around her neck.

The one with my ring on the end. She slipped her touch smoothly to undo one more button on her top and angled herself so that when she bent to take her shot, she offered a perfect view of her cleavage.

It was also a horrible angle to approach the balls from. "You're never going to win that way," I said.

She glided her tongue along her bottom lip and met my gaze without straightening up. "Aren't I?"

When she knocked the cue ball, she probably barely struck her target, but I wasn't paying attention to the balls on the table.

This would gnaw at the two of them. I wasn't fond of losing, but they both hated it. Xander slid closer to me, until his arm pressed into mine. "I had a thought," his voice was so low I barely heard it.

"Hey." Judith stared at us. "Conspiring is against the rules."

"It's not," I said.

Xander's chuckle was low. "You know, if we redefine *winning*, then it becomes easier," he murmured in that same quiet voice. "Especially if she keeps taking off her clothes."

Winning was winning, so I wasn't sure his logic was sound, but I liked the desired outcome. "I'm in."

"Are we playing, boys?" Judith stepped back from the table, eyeing us with suspicion.

Xander smirked. "We're playing. My turn." There was nothing unique or out of the ordinary about the way he approached to take his shot, except that he bent over *much* deeper than he needed to, to sight the balls.

And then it was my turn. I felt a lot less peculiar *not* having to make out with the stick while I used it.

Judith studied us, brow furrowed, looking back and forth. "I don't think either of you is trying."

"We most certainly are." The indignation in Xander's voice was distinct.

"To win?" She asked in disbelief.

He nodded. "Without question."

Cue in hand, Judith approached the table. She paused. "Are you still playing the same game I am?"

That didn't take long.

"We are absolutely still playing with you," I said.

She scoffed and rested her stick on the table. "Spoken like a top-notch attorney. That's not what I asked."

"Are you saying you'd like to make a plea bargain?" Hmm… That didn't quite fit the conversation. I could take it back or leave it out there anyway.

She crossed her arms, exaggerating the curve of her breasts and the fact that she had extra buttons undone. "Pretty sure I'm not saying that. Positive you don't practice that kind of law."

"Really?" Xander crossed the room to stand behind her. He glided his finger along the curve of her neck. "You're positive you don't want to plead?"

The part of her lips in a silent gasp was as alluring as the flutter of her eyelids. "No touching the person taking the shot."

"You set your stick down." Xander's voice was a deep, seductive growl.

Should I be jealous that they fell into this so easily? I wasn't. The exchange between them radiated more heat than a raging fire. I could imagine what she was feeling each time he touched her, and it was as easy to put myself in his shoes.

Judith snagged his hand before he could move higher, to brush her ear. She pulled his arm around her as she pressed her ass back into him. "That means I can pick yours up. Is that what you're saying?"

In a blink, Xander twisted his wrist, freeing himself and grabbing her instead. He tugged her arm behind her, restraining her and eliciting a gasp. "Seems like a good place to start."

An unwelcome sliver of reality wormed into my thoughts. Would this all end when the *engagement* was over? When the current stress from work had been dealt with?

I wasn't going to dwell on that today. As long as things kept up like this, with no one denying how much we really wanted each other, I wouldn't have to think about it ending later either. And I wasn't going to sabotage the good by overthinking it.

Xander pulled Judith into him. "What are we

going to do with you?" His voice was rough and peppered with need.

"Whatever you want, I assume." Sass dripped from her reply. "I hope." And there was a lilt of submission.

I strode toward them. The pair looked incredible together—the ownership in Xander's stance, and in Judith the perfect blend of defiance and yielding that would be impossible for anyone else to pull off.

I brushed my lips over hers. Did Xander just grunt? Judith definitely whimpered.

It was a good thing I didn't have to keep my hands or anything else to myself. The electricity in the room wrapped around all of us, charging the air until I couldn't help but press into her. With Xander restraining her hands, she couldn't touch, but there was no way she could miss my erection digging into her stomach.

"Look what you did to us." I tilted her chin to look her in the eye.

A smirk greeted me in response. "That was the point. Job well done. Go me."

I dropped my hand to slide a finger under the waistband of her jeans. "Really? This was just an item on your to-do list? Turning us on?"

"What else would it be?" Judith shrugged.

I pushed my hand lower without warning, under

her panties. Her gasp was intoxicating and her skin was slick.

Xander reached his free hand around to undo her jeans, giving me more room to move. I dipped my fingers toward her opening, teasing the edges enough to draw a moan from her. "It feels like you enjoyed it," I said.

"A job well done always turns me on." Judith was in prime form this afternoon.

Fantastic.

Xander leaned his head forward, mouth near her ear. "Is that so?" he asked. "You walk around all the time with a wet pussy, eager to be fucked?"

"As far as you know."

"I don't buy it." I glided to her clit, and she grunted, thrusting toward my touch. I slipped away again. "This is for us." I pushed my fingers deeper inside her this time. "You don't get wet like this for anyone else." As I pumped into her, slowly, deliberately, her lips parted in a silent gasp.

Snatching the edge of her ear in his teeth, Xander nipped the tender skin hard. "Because no one but us can keep up with you," he growled out the words. "No one else fucks you the way we do."

Judith didn't say anything, but the way her chest heaved with each breath, the way she swayed her hips with my touch, spoke volumes. I moved back to her clit to tease and stroke. To draw out the pleasure until she was on the edge of orgasm.

"Is he right?" I asked. "This is only for us?"

Her smirk was defiance and desire. "Maybe."

"Fair enough." I pulled my hand free, holding her gaze as I sucked the first finger clean of her juices.

Judith visibly deflated. "What was that?"

"If you can get this kind of orgasm from anyone…" *Fuck* I loved the way she tasted on my skin.

When Xander let go of her as well, her frown settled in.

"That is…" Her scowl deepened.

Xander spun her so her back was to the pool table and she was facing us. He pressed a hand to her throat.

I knew what that grip felt like, having been on the receiving end of it many times. Seeing Xander touch Judith that way would make me instantly hard if I wasn't already.

"It's a simple question, Judy." Xander's voice was playful. "Does anyone get you off the way we do?" He pressed his free hand to her pussy, through her jeans, and rubbed.

The way she tilted her head back, eyes half-lidded and breath jagged, while she ground into his touch, was a good answer.

"Please." The hint of her begging was so sweet.

I was rubbing my own erection through my slacks with still-damp fingers, imagining myself on either side of that exchange, and enjoying the fuck out of the power struggle.

"Do they?" Xander asked again.

"No." Judith's whimper didn't mute her playful smirk. "No one fucks me the way the two of you do. Please. *Please* let me come."

Xander pressed his touch harder into her cunt, and she ground back with intensity. I stroked myself with the same fervor. I didn't care if I was watching the two of them or touching them, as long as I was a part of this bond the three of us shared.

Judith dug her fingers into Xander's forearm hard enough that pale marks blossomed around her touch, on top of his corded muscle. She made the most delicious sounds when she came, her entire body shuddering.

I was going to do the same if I didn't stop, so I dropped my hand from my cock, and stepped in as Xander eased up. Tilting Judith's chin up, it was obvious her gaze wasn't quite focused. I kissed her on the forehead, then pressed my lips to the hollow in her neck, under her ear. "Do you want more?" I asked.

She nodded. "Yes, please."

We moved into the bedroom, and Xander and I helped Judith out of her clothes. We were gentle, teasing fingers over her bare skin every chance we got, but we were also rushed. I wanted to be closer to her, and it was clear Xander wasn't feeling patient either.

Not that he was known for his patience, and not that I minded.

"Get comfortable on the bed." I nudged Judith in that direction.

Xander and I stripped out of our clothes as well, and then I knelt between Judith's legs. I kissed up her torso, teasing her nipples with my tongue, while my cock rested at her opening.

I sucked and licked, never entering her, until she was squirming under me and my balls were aching. When I finally slid inside her, a long *Fuuuuuck* tore from my throat.

Before I could fuck her hard and fast, Xander knelt behind me and yanked me upright. He bit my shoulder then my neck, each time hard enough to leave a mark. "Don't move," he said.

The familiar sensation of him applying liberal amounts of lube made my pulse spike, and my anticipation built, my cock twitching inside Judith.

When Xander inched his shaft into me, I almost burst from the pleasure. The connection that flowed between all three of us, being intertwined this way.

And then the three of us were moving together and against each other in a kind of synchronization that should've been impossible. I pressed into Judith, teasing another orgasm from her, and when she clenched around me, I couldn't hold back anymore.

I let go of the restraints and came hard, spilling inside her, hammering for all I was worth.

When Xander made those familiar grunts of climax, I knew he'd found that spot as well. He dug his teeth into my shoulder blade and his fingers into my hips when he climaxed.

I swore a shudder of release and pleasure rolled through the entire room.

The world slowed to a stop as we did, and in that moment, everything else fell away but the three of us. I wasn't sure how long we lay there, pressed together and unmoving, but it was enough time that I softened and slipped out of her.

This was a good time to pull apart. Clean up. But after that, we were back in bed again, naked and wrapped up together.

We hadn't been laying there long this time when Judith pushed herself into a sitting position. "I should get home."

Are you sure you can't stay? I forced the question back. Of course she couldn't. With the weight of tomorrow looming, she needed to be rested and so did Xander.

He stood and tugged her to her feet. "Are you set?"

"As set as I'm going to be." Judith dressed quickly.

Until today I never would've described the act of putting on clothing as *efficient* but she managed it.

Within a few minutes, we were all clothed again, and she was on her way.

"Do you ever wish she could stay? Have you ever wanted that?" My question to Xander wasn't subtle, but I needed a direct answer.

He gave a quick shake of his head. "For me? Yes. For her? No. Never."

I wasn't sure what he meant, and I wasn't sure I wanted him to explain it.

15 /
judith

Last night, I wanted to stay with Xander and Dominic, and at the same time I hated the weakness in that thought. I didn't have a problem admitting the sex was great, and so were the friendships I had with both men, but I never wavered on spending the night alone when I needed to.

Not that I'd slept. The idea of this meeting haunted me, and so did the fact that I couldn't simply tell everyone *Elliot is the best at what he does. Fuck the rules.*

I was the boss. I was also far too well versed in the politics of investment and business and how letting one person slide meant consequences in other places.

In this case for instance, we'd let one person go about two years ago, for sexual harassment. We were probably about to fire a second for the same thing, and worse, they were friends, and Bryce was suing us for wrongful termination.

Letting Elliot stay could set a precedent and weaken our cases for firing both the assholes.

I'd do it anyway. I'd find a way. But if the board voted him out, what I wanted only went so far.

So much for being the boss.

When I got to the office, Ivan, our office manager, was already in. He was setting up coffee and bagels for our board members.

I was glad he'd gotten my message. "Elliot's not here, is he?" I asked.

Ivan shook his head.

"Good. He'll show up early. He's not allowed anywhere but my office and the small conference room."

"Ouch. Is it really that bad?"

I adopted the impassive face I'd need to wear the rest of the day, to survive. "With any luck, it's nowhere near that bad."

If I could sit at my desk and pick at my nails until everyone showed up, I would. The world was going on regardless of this drama, so instead I spent the next few hours immersing myself in work.

When Elliot walked into my office and dropped into the seat across from my desk, I didn't look up. "I shouldn't be seeing you."

"Definitely not. I'm already in trouble for fucking one person in the office."

Seeing. Dating. Fucking. Funny.

Not. I gave him a withering look. "Do you have that out of your system now?" Most days I didn't care. Given what he was here for? The nature of the joke mattered. "You knew this was a rule. You said you understood."

"You knew I was doing it."

Fuck, he was right.

"That better not be your defense for the board," I said.

Elliot scrubbed his face. "It's not. You know I can't give this place up any more than you can."

I did. This would be a lot easier if I believed otherwise. "If you stayed, would you stop seeing Link?" I already knew the answer, but if I was wrong, if I had that to go into the meeting with, it would be an angle to negotiate from.

Elliot's lack of an answer was all the confirmation I needed. He loved the job, but even if he hadn't admitted it to himself, he loved Link more. I couldn't imagine, but I'd be glad he had that if it wasn't threatening to cost him so much.

I had other meetings to be in before the big one, so I pushed back from my desk. "Stay here until it's time. I'll see you in the meeting."

The mood in the office was somber and oppressive. A week ago, we'd all been riding the high of a game launch, and now everyone was wondering if we were about to lose one of our own. By the time the board meeting rolled around, I needed a resolution. *Now*.

As I was heading toward the small conference room, my phone rang. "This is Judith." I paused in the hallway as I answered.

"Hi, it's Claire. Dale's wife?"

What? "I remember you." And I didn't have the time or patience for small talk. "I'm sorry, I'm about to walk into an appointment."

"That's okay, it won't take long. I was wondering if maybe you and Dom— Dominic want to have dinner with us tonight."

Double what? I really didn't have the bandwidth for this. "I don't know. I'll have to call you back."

"Yeah. Okay. Talk to you in a little bit. Good luck in your meeting. Appointment."

"Thanks." I'd wonder more about the call, but I was walking into a shark tank.

There was no need for introductions. Elliot, Scott, Grant, Oliver and I were the board, and Ivan would take notes.

"So there are no misunderstandings, we need to state why we're here, and what we need to accomplish by the end of the meeting." Grant had been an investor in Rinslet since its early days, and was happy to fund AcesPlayed when we branched off to do our own thing. He was typically a silent partner, unless he thought his money was at stake.

And I didn't like him stepping in and taking

control. This was my meeting. "The chat logs from our game that were recently made public involve Elliot Howard, one of our board members and one of the more public faces of the company. While this exposure wasn't his doing, the content contained within puts us at a serious legal risk."

"But does it really?" Elliot asked. "Nothing contained in those chat logs violates the rules of the game—a game that exists specifically to allow this kind of interaction, among other things. Anyone who supports the game can't find fault with what I did."

I was torn between wanting to gag him and agreeing completely. The problem here was that we could only govern ourselves until we had to mingle with the outside world. Then we were subject to their perceptions.

"It's not about what you did, it's about who you did it with," Oliver said.

The edge in his voice added to the one slicing through me. Xander was positive he'd vote to keep Elliot. That Oliver was here to represent the majority interest at The Raphael Group.

I wasn't sure I trusted that.

"Who I did it with? A woman whose face I never saw and whose real name I never asked for or wanted? Who, the chat logs will show, consented to and appeared to enjoy everything we did."

I already hated that Fallyn had been sucked into

this. A woman I really only knew through videos, but whom I had the utmost respect for. She wouldn't be his shield in this meeting. "Do you want to bring her into this? Because that's one more name—one more person you benefit from influencing—and things are already bad for you. And her."

Elliot snapped his jaw shut.

"We're talking about a man who works for you," Scott said. "Whose career you hold in your hands. Who you have power over and who you have the ability to fire in a blink or destroy his career."

"But I wouldn't." The force of Elliot's retort came fast and hard.

Scott frowned. "It doesn't matter." Did his tone soften? "You could."

"You're going to look me in the eye and tell me you would've done things differently with Kenzie? With—"

"Watch it." The warning leaked into Scott's tone.

What I was doing with Xander—was it the same thing we were talking about stringing Elliot up for?

The thought hit me hard.

It wasn't quite the same. Neither of us worked for the other.

"Would you have?" Elliot asked Scott.

Scott clenched his fists. "They don't work for me anymore, and your situation is different."

Just like mine.

"You can't fire Link for this." Elliot might be an ass sometimes, but he was loyal.

Grant scoffed. "That's the last thing we want to do. It's your job on the line."

The arguments went back and forth, but in the end it came down to one thing—we all had our opinions and no amount of discussion would change how we were going to vote.

"So we're all on the same page?" Grant asked. "As far as why we're here?"

Unfortunately. "Let's make this official." I needed to say the next words, but I couldn't.

"Do we allow Elliot Howard to stay in this position, or is it time for him to go?" Scott sounded reluctant to speak as well.

Time for him to go. I hated the sound of that. "We're voting on two things." I forced down my hesitation. "If we buy out his investment and if he can stay on as a head developer."

"We can't waver on things like this," Grant said. "My votes are that he goes. Both places."

"I vote that he stays. Both places." And everyone else had better do the same.

Scott nodded. "As do I. Blanket rules with no room to consider the circumstances don't do anyone any good. We know Elliot—*I* know Elliot—and this organization is stronger with him."

Two to one. I knew from Xander that The Raphael Group didn't want out of this deal, and relief hovered at the edge of my thoughts.

"Grant's right," Oliver said.

Elliot's expression fell and an ache of betrayal pinged inside me. "About what?" I couldn't let it go at that.

"About all of it. My vote is that Elliot goes. From the position. And if we don't buy him out, be prepared to buy us out instead."

It took all of my restraint to not stare at Oliver in dumbfounded shock. If I so much as twitched, the mask I'd frozen in place would crack. I looked at Elliot. "Take the rest of the week off, while we resolve this. I'll tell your team you're out. I won't say more until we know more." As I spoke, my fingers curled tighter and tighter into balled up fists, until my nails cut into my palms.

Elliot's smile looked more like a grimace, and he left. Ivan went with him, under the guise of returning to his desk, but more likely to make sure he was following my request from this morning to not let Elliot wander the office.

When they were gone and the door closed behind them, I directed my anger at Oliver. "That's not how Raphael Group votes."

"Really?" He didn't look unimpressed. "Last I checked, I speak for them, not you."

When I talk to Xander—

Everything kept me from saying those words, no matter how badly I wanted to. I didn't fall back on anyone to make my point, and even if I didn't hate the thought, using his name this way put me in a similar position to Elliot. Favoritism. Blurred lines.

Fuck. "We'll see. We need a tie-breaking vote and until we have that, it doesn't matter."

I was grateful no one wanted to sit around and chat. Normally I liked Scott's company, but today...

At least he hadn't left a knife in anyone's back, though.

I got back to my office to find three text messages that came in at oddly spaced intervals.

First one was from Dominic, about ten minutes ago. *How'd it go?*

Next was Xander. *WTF. Looking into it now.*

Anyone who said tone of voice didn't carry over text had never gotten an angry one from Xander. I'd be assured if I wasn't upset about the same thing —Oliver's vote.

Dominic sent another a moment ago. *I'm sorry.*

I could call Xander, but he had more pull to get answers and talking to me wouldn't provide them. No matter how much part of me...

Wanted to hear his voice.

The same part of me hated that indulging that

impulse would make me look weak. Scott didn't have to worry about that perception. Elliot didn't.

Enough of that. I called Dominic instead.

"Hey." He managed sympathy and strength in a single syllable when he answered. "I know about the vote, but nothing else. How are you holding up?"

I hate this. Why can't we let people fuck who they want, and trust that the people we trust won't be assholes about it? "I've had better days."

"Yeah. Anything I can do?"

A random thought popped into my head and I was almost grateful for the distraction. "Did you give Claire my phone number?"

"No. Why would I do that?"

"You wouldn't." But she'd gotten it somewhere. "But she called me and invited us to dinner."

I expected surprise from Dominic, so his sigh, followed by *fuck*, caught me off-guard. "I already told him no," Dominic said.

"Without asking me?"

"If I'd had the kind of day you 're having, if I was dealing with this shit, the last thing I'd want would be to field dinner invites with people I don't like. You would've done the same."

True. But admitting that didn't make it any easier for me to swallow the fact that he was making decisions on my behalf. "Doesn't matter. She called me anyway."

"What did you tell her?"

I barely remembered. It seemed like a lifetime ago. "Something about I'd let her know."

"I'll call Dale again and tell him *no* again."

That was smart. I shouldn't protest because that was what I wanted. "Don't." What was I doing?

I needed something to go my way today, even if it was just convincing some asshole that Dom's firm was the perfect firm to put on retainer. "I'm up for it if you are."

16 /
xander

Barely suppressed rage thrummed inside my skull.

Oliver had represented us, every Raphael Group investor in AcesPlayed, in that meeting, and instead of voting our wishes, he went off and picked exactly the opposite. Which was why all of the investing partners were gathered in a room, and I was telling myself violence probably wasn't the answer.

Normally Jonathan would join us remotely, since he was based out of L.A., but he'd been in town for RinCon and stuck around with this news. Liz and Kandace were also here, in addition to me and Oliver.

We'd picked him to sit on the board at Aces-Played specifically because he didn't have any connection to the company outside of his investment.

But also because he was the boss's brother. Every partner owned a stake in The Raphael Group, but Oliver and Wade sat at the top of the pyramid.

I didn't care. I was going to string Oliver up regardless. He could explain, and then—

"We need to understand why you did this." Kandace's tone was cool. Professional.

Oliver leaned back in his chair and crossed one ankle over the other knee. "This investment was a mistake, and we all need to recognize that. It was iffy before, but since launch it's crashed multiple times, and the press keeps getting worse. Our name is associated with that, and so is our money."

Red danced at the edges of my vision.

"Most games crash multiple times at launch time. Every game—every app—we've ever backed has had an issue or two." Jonathan sounded rational. Reasonable.

I wouldn't be so level headed when I opened my mouth. The only reason I stayed silent was because violence was a bad career move.

"The vote won't go through until Wade is back to cast a tie-breaker vote," Liz said. "We reverse our decision now, and this goes back to fine."

Oliver let out a barking laugh. "Why would we do that? This is our chance to be done with AcesPlayed."

"We'd do that, because it's an incredible

company worth what we've put into it." I could do this. I could be as surface-calm as everyone else. "Getting rid of their management means disrupting the things that make it good. Look at the numbers for anyone else we're backing, and the data isn't as promising as it is here. AcesPlayed has industry veterans who are high profile and known for excelling at their craft. MMOs don't run on servers in garages, and having people in charge who know their jobs is a bonus for us. Elliot knows what he's doing. Judith knows—"

"How you feel fucking her?" Oliver jumped so far over the line of appropriate, it vanished.

Nope. I'm done. I was on my feet in a flash, crossing the room and hauling him to his feet.

"Enough." It was rare for Liz to take center stage, but her tone implied she'd step between us if she had to. "You." She pointed at Oliver. "Walk away. From the office. And you." She turned to me. "Don't do something you're going to regret."

Like putting my fist through a wall? Through Oliver?

I wouldn't help anyone by Hulking out, as much as I'd love to believe otherwise. "I'm good. And if he wants out, I'll buy him out."

"No." Oliver paused in the doorway. "You won't reverse the vote, and this is an all or nothing proposition. Either we pull out as a company, or Elliot Howard does."

I was ready to lunge again when Kandace rested a hand on my arm.

The pause let a sliver of reason leak into my thoughts. If Oliver was doing this, he was playing the Boss's Brother card. I hated this situation, but I loved this company we'd built.

Oliver wiggled his fingers in a wave, and walked out of the room, leaving me furious that he'd gotten the last word in.

And in a way he had. Wade was off the grid until next week, but when he got back, when he cast his vote, odds were nearly nothing that he'd vote against his brother.

"What now?" Liz asked.

I leaned against the nearest wall and crossed my arms. "Anyone know someone who breaks knees?"

"Not funny." Kandace glared at me.

Liz shrugged. "Kind of funny."

"We spend the week keeping you away from Oliver, and trying to change his mind," Jonathan said. "The data is there, and he's doing the one thing he's not supposed to—making this decision personal."

Swell. I both loved and hated the solution.

When I got back to my office, I closed the door and called Judith.

"Hey." She sounded stressed.

I got that. "Hey. How're you doing?"

"Eh. You know."

I did. "I wish I could give you good news."

"I know." She sighed.

Damn it. Of all the things I could do for her, this one wasn't on the list. While the decision impacted Elliot, it took choices away from Judith. It stopped her from running her company her way. That was one of the things she'd wanted more than anything—to show the world she could do this.

And Oliver was stripping her of that, because...

Because I didn't know why. "So…"

"So." Judith mimicked me.

My phone beeped with a call from Grant. I ignored it. "I'll call you if I hear any news. Good or bad."

"Sounds good. Xander?"

My breath hitched at the change in her tone. The softening. "Yeah?"

Her pause was longer than I cared for. "Thank you," she finally said. "Talk to you soon."

That was less than satisfactory. Shit on a shitty day.

Might as well top it off by listening to Grant's voicemail. "Wondered if you want to get lunch while I'm in town. And by the way, you all did the right thing by voting the way you did today."

I wouldn't throw my phone across the room; it hadn't done anything wrong. But if I called Grant back, I'd say things I'd regret.

Or maybe not. Maybe I'd enjoy every single

thing that came out of my mouth. Would I burn bridges for this? Destroy my career?

Interesting question. I'd kept my mouth shut about my relationship with Dominic for years, despite hating it. But that was for him, not me.

And this would be for Judith.

Except it wouldn't help the situation any, so telling myself that was bullshit.

I settled for sending Grant a text telling him my calendar was full. Any sort of meet-up was a no-go.

It wasn't a lie. The rest of my day was full of cramming in last minute meetings before the holidays and new calendar year, including catching up with everyone besides AcesPlayed who debuted games at RinCon. I made it home around six-thirty, which wasn't bad for me.

Dominic's car was in the garage, and I parked next to him and headed inside.

An ache bloomed in my chest at the sight of a simple bouquet with a single sunflower in the middle, the entire thing wrapped in green tissue paper. The flower sat on the kitchen table, and even if Dom hadn't told me about his dinner plans, I would've known it was for Judith.

"Hello?" I called.

"Bedroom." Dominic's reply carried to me from the other room.

I found him exactly where he said he'd be, in the walk-in closet, putting on cufflinks. He held out his right wrist and the link, and I stepped in without a word to help slip it on. He'd always had trouble with the mechanics when he used his left hand.

"Thanks, handsome." He kissed me on the cheek and took a few steps back.

I leaned against the doorframe and watched both him and his reflection as he finished dressing.

For a night out with the woman he was calling his fiancée.

With Judith.

The gnawing in my thoughts grew, chewing holes through me with the kind of jealousy that could devour a soul. Not because Dominic and Judith were going out tonight, but because they didn't have to hide it. Their engagement wasn't even fucking real, and they were going out to dinner as a couple. Telling the world they were in love. Dining with his business associates and not hiding a thing.

"Saw the flower." Maybe if I climbed out of my own head, pulled it out of my ass, and talked through this, I'd be okay.

Dominic gave me a faint smile while he straightened his tie. "So Judith can brag about the sweetheart she's marrying."

Unlikely it would come up. Judith almost certainly wouldn't mention it to near-strangers.

"And with the day she's had, she needs it," Dominic added.

My jaw tried to tighten, and I forced myself to relax. He didn't know the story behind *why* it was Judith's favorite flower, and passive-aggressive digs weren't his style. I wouldn't get upset about Dominic being the man I loved.

It would be nice if I could block out the whispers of the past, though. I'd been walking her home from school, and she was in a foul mood. One of our teachers, one of the women she looked up to, had told Judith that she should be prepared for the reality she'd be stuck in that small town forever. Judith was furious.

"We won't." I'd offered the only reassurance I had. The only truth I knew. "You'll get out of here and so will I."

"How do you know?" Even then, the doubt was unlike her.

My answer came easily. "Because you won't let that happen. You can will reality into existence."

"If only."

We'd been nearing a sunflower field, and inspiration struck. "I'll prove it."

Judith hadn't looked convinced. "How?"

"You need something to cheer you up, right?" I reached over the fence and grabbed one of the closest flowers. Pulling a knife from my pocket, I sliced through the stem, then tucked the flower behind her ear.

Her smile had been brighter than the yellow of

the petals. After that, she always said sunflowers were her favorite.

I tucked the past back into the safe box in the back of my mind, and gave my focus on Dominic.

"I'm off." He looked incredible, no surprise there.

Impulse snaked through me. I rested my hand at the base of his neck, pulled him close, and crushed my mouth to his in a long, desperate kiss. His groan when I finally let go was delicious.

"Never forget who you belong to." My voice came out thicker than I intended.

"I never do."

"And at the end of the night? Don't bring her back here." Fuck it hurt to say that.

17 /
dominic

When Xander asked me not to bring Judith home, I was dumbfounded. I didn't know which bothered me more—his reaction or the fact that I couldn't let go of that single moment of the conversation.

I needed to put it out of my head so Judith and I could make it through dinner without incident. And speaking of surprised, I couldn't believe she'd agreed to do this tonight. Insisted on it.

We met Claire and Dale outside the restaurant and exchanged polite *hellos*, before the host showed us to a table. This was the kind of steakhouse made to look high-end, but wasn't quite, and I was fine with that. I was also fine with a perfectly neutral start to our double date.

The waiter took our drink orders—a wonderfully dull round of *water for me*—and left us to consider the specials.

"I was happy to hear from Claire that the two of you are friendly, Judith. When did you have time to chat?" Dale's tone was casual.

"I was shopping and we ran into each other." Claire jumped in before Judith had a chance.

Not technically untrue, if she counted the exhibitors' hall at RinCon as *shopping*. Would Dale see it that way?

His shrug and *okay* were dismissive and struck me as odd. I couldn't imagine not asking Xander for details about his day. Not to be nosey, but because I cared.

But Dale's level of interest in Claire's life was between them.

The waiter returned with drinks and bread, and to take our orders. Good service meant one more reason to make this a fast night and I was fine with that.

"We'll have the filet special," Dale rested a hand on Claire's. "Two. Rare."

"Really? The steak?" The surprise in Judith's voice was undercut with something more subtle, though I doubted anyone but me heard it. "I was looking at the chicken. Doesn't that look good." She focused her attention on Claire.

In return, she got a tight smile. "I suppose it sounds all right. I'm good with what we're getting, though," Claire said.

The waiter wrote down Judith's order then

turned to me for mine, as Dale let out a quiet sound that was something like a grunt of disbelief.

Did he really expect me to treat my partner like a mindless creature? I had to tell myself not to roll my eyes.

Judith was the embodiment of poise as she draped her napkin over her knee, and sipped her water. "How was your trip, Dale?"

Was that panic on Claire's face? Despite the calm start to the evening, and us only being a few minutes in, the tension in the air was already dense.

"Beg pardon?" Dale asked.

"When I ran into Claire, she mentioned you were traveling for business."

Dale raised an eyebrow. "It was fine."

Odd answer. "I don't know if I've ever described a business trip as *fine.*" I was happy to listen if it kept me from saying the wrong thing about Judith's or Claire's story, but I was also more pleased than maybe I should be to subtly call Dale on some of this shifty behavior. "There's always something that comes up. You'll have to tell me who your travel agent is, that you didn't even have bumps in your flight plans."

Dale's chuckle was flat. "I'll get you her name."

Thank God for awkward silence. Though the way Claire was dissecting her bread, pulling tiny pieces off and letting as many fall on the plate as she ate, I felt sorry for the poor piece of multi-grain.

"Any interesting new clients, Dominic?"

I couldn't believe Dale asked that. I did an imitation of his unamused laugh from a few minutes ago. "You know I can't tell you that."

"Really?" Dale had the audacity to sound shocked, as if he hadn't had a dozen lawyers explain attorney-client-privilege to him during his career. "Not even client names? Privilege extends that far."

I gave a brief shake of my head. "Not even client names. Put yourself in their shoes."

"You're a contract lawyer, not a defense attorney. I wouldn't think people would be ashamed to associate themselves with you."

If he was trying to get under my skin, it wasn't working. I was amused. Curious about how this helped him exert dominance. "They're not ashamed, but people have other reasons for keeping things to themselves, and that's their decision to make." Like how their business trips went, or the fact that they'd spent their week at a gaming convention and didn't want their spouse to know.

Judith nudged my foot with hers, and I wondered what I'd missed, until my gaze fell on three people walking toward us. At the sight of Cole, Graham, and Luna, both my tension and amusement leapt.

Especially when Cole looked toward us, and smiled.

This ought to be interesting.

He had redirected his partners, and all three were walking toward us.

Double interesting. Triple, even.

"Judith, Dominic, great to see you." The warmth in Cole's voice was genuine as he approached.

Judith gave him a well-rehearsed smile. Was she as darkly amused by this as I was? I should be concerned about what one of the new arrivals might say, but this was a train wreck and I couldn't look away. "Same," she said.

"I'm Dale." He injected himself into the conversation before anyone else could speak. "An associate of Dominic's. And this is my wife, Claire."

"Cole is my ex-husband." Judith wasn't going to hide that. Okay.

Probably smart if she didn't know how much Cole would play along. He'd never been much for putting on airs, so it seemed unlikely he'd be willing to fall into a scripted part for this.

"Oh." Claire's mouth formed a shocked circle. "*Oh*. I was under the impression her first husband was... Dang it."

Cole's smile grew. "Did she tell you I was dead? Judy is such a joker."

The nickname might be taking things a step too far.

"It's true. I'm known for my bouts of hilarity." The way Judith delivered the line would've made a flat plane jealous. "But seriously, we were married so long ago, there's no animosity."

"Very progressive of you." Dale managed to beat Judith out for static, level delivery.

Claire frowned. "Being friends with an ex is?"

"Who are your companions, Cole?"

I didn't like the way Dale brushed off Claire's question, but I was very much looking forward, in a sick, twisted way, to how Cole would answer Dale's.

"My girlfriend, Luna." Cole nodded at her.

The way Dale looked her over, his gaze lingering on every curve, pushed away my twisted amusement, making my skin crawl and my fury rise. "Pleasure."

I was surprised he didn't hiss on the *s*.

Claire scowled, Judith pursed her lips, and Cole wrapped an arm around Luna's waist, pulling her closer.

Graham took Luna's other hand, tangling their fingers together.

"And our boyfriend, Graham," Cole said.

I almost fist bumped, especially at Dale's shock. Should I be more upset at how messy this was getting?

"Progressive." Was Claire mimicking Dale on purpose?

Dale clenched his jaw. "Not the word I would've used." He hadn't had any problem speaking his mind up to this point. What was stopping him now?

Judith held up her left hand back toward Cole and the others, and wiggled her ring finger. "Since you're here, it's as good a time as any to let you know—Dominic and I are making things official."

"Well it's about time." Cole didn't so much as flinch, though Luna raised her eyebrows. "Congrats to both of you." He clapped me on the shoulder. "Do her better than I did." He leaned in to give Judith a kiss on the cheek, lingering to whisper something I couldn't hear.

Luna and Graham offered their congratulations again, and the three were on their way. I almost asked them to stay, to see what would happen, but if I were going to sabotage this entire charade, I could tell Dale the truth about my relationships.

I'm actually committed to an incredible man, who's put up with keeping our love quiet for years and deserves better. As I thought the words, they pushed to be heard.

I was doing this for Roger. For the firm.

"Dodged a bullet divorcing that one." Derision dripped from Dale's voice. At least he waited until Cole was a reasonable distance away.

"I did." Judith's tone was more thoughtful.

I was familiar with Judith and Cole's past. The fact that even the divorce was so long ago that they were friends now. How Xander felt about it all. Her response was for very different reasons than Dale's. "He's not all bad. He won your heart at one point." I squeezed her hand gently.

"But he's a disgusting deviant," Dale said.

So much for subtlety. I swore I heard Judith thinking *you have no idea*, but with amusement and affection instead of disgust. The twitch of one corner of her mouth reinforced my assumption.

"The church used to practice polygamy." Claire's voice was soft, and she clamped her jaw shut with a frown when Dale looked at her.

His scowl deepened. "Do you want me to take another wife?"

"Can we introduce her as *our girlfriend?*"

At Claire's question, Dale clenched his fist.

And this was where the train crash I'd been waiting for happened, but not at all in the way I expected.

She cast her gaze toward her lap. "I'm sorry. It was a joke. A bad joke."

Her reaction was more than submissive. She almost sounded terrified.

I didn't like this at all, and the way Judith tugged at a loose strand of hair said she didn't either.

"I just remembered this is a bad night for this." Dale's tone was tightly controlled, but the way his eyes flashed said anger lay under the mask. He grabbed the attention of a nearby waiter. "Tell the kitchen to wrap our order to go." He handed him a credit card. "And run my payment. We're not staying."

"Claire is welcome to keep us company. We can drop her off later," Judith said.

Claire shook her head "No. I'll go home with my husband."

I didn't like this at all. The awkward silence that settled in was bad. When the waiter returned with the check and our food, the way Dale grabbed Claire's arm and yanked her to her feet was worse.

"I'm sure Claire can stand on her own." Tension coiled through me. I had no idea what I was going to do, but it would be something.

"It's okay. We're okay." Claire sounded anything but.

Judith covered my hand with hers. To stop me or encourage me, I wasn't sure. "Are you sure you don't want us to drop you off later, Claire?" she asked.

"I'm positive. Stop asking." The tightness in Claire's voice wasn't reassuring.

Dale wrapped an arm around her waist, and forcefully steered her from the restaurant.

Judith grabbed my arm when I took a step after them.

"Being an asshole isn't illegal." Judith sounded as angry as I felt.

I sank back into my chair with reluctance. "We can't just…"

"What? We can't just grab Claire and shove her in your car. She all but told you to back off, and he's a top-of-the-food-chain religious leader. What are we going to do that won't make the situation worse for her?"

Something. Anything. Sitting here and ignoring the problem wasn't right.

"You can tell Roger tomorrow to stop pursuing this contract," Judith said.

Sure. And I would. But that didn't make letting this encounter go feel any more right.

18 /
judith

Dominic dropped me off at home, and I squelched the tiny voice that was disappointed he hadn't invited me back to their place. I was getting too comfortable with the fake parts of this relationship, and backing off was a good idea.

Besides, coming home early, by myself, meant time to get some work done before bed. Dive deep —again—into how to keep Elliot. Focus on getting some ideas down for the future of the company.

Worry about Claire's situation. Think about how AcesPlayed would function if we lost Elliot. Miss Xander and Dominic even though I was seeing them on an almost daily basis.

The loop of thoughts kept me from doing anything but hesitating when I sat down at my laptop. This wasn't me or how I worked. What was wrong with me?

When my phone rang, I was grateful for the

interruption. When I saw Claire's name on the screen, my brain snagged, sputtered, and stalled.

"Hello?" I answered. At least I could pick up a phone without second-guessing myself.

"Judith? Hi. It's Claire."

My heart sank at the bald panic in her voice. "What's wrong?"

"I'm sorry to call you, but no one else... Can you come get me?"

I'd ask for details like *why* and *what happened* when I had her safe in my car. "Where are you? Home? Are you all right?"

"I'm okay. Cold. I'm at a gas station. Ninth West and Thirteenth South."

What? Why? "I'll be there in ten minutes."

A billion thoughts raced through my suddenly-working-again brain as I headed to the address Claire gave me. The primary two notions were distinct and loud—Dom was right, we shouldn't have let her go, and he needed to end this business relationship.

I should wait to judge until I heard the story from Claire, but it was twenty degrees out, and when I pulled up to the closed convenience store, she was huddled in a lightweight jacket, under the sole working light near the building.

Fucking asshole Dale.

I cranked the heat in the car as I parked, and climbed out. "In the car, now." Opening the trunk, I pulled out the blanket I kept in my emergency kit, and handed it to her.

"Thank you." She sounded so meek.

When I got back in the car, I pointed us toward the nearest late-night coffee drive-thru. "Do you want to tell me why you're out here alone in the cold, miles from home?"

"I don't know."

She didn't know if she wanted to tell me or she didn't know why she was here? If I asked, would she tell me *I don't know* again? I'd try again after her teeth stopped chattering.

I pulled up to a little shack with a large menu next to a small window.

The guy working gave us a warm smile. "What can I get for you ladies?"

"Two large hot chocolates, extra whipped cream." Did I pull a Dale? Fuck me. I shook my head. "Actually, one of those and," I looked at Claire, "What would you like?"

"Can I have coffee?"

At ten at night? To each their own. "Sure. What kind?"

"I don't know."

And now we were back to that. I tucked aside any frustration.

"I'm sorry," Claire said. "I've never had coffee before. But I don't want to go to sleep tonight."

That ought to make things interesting. "Do you like candy bars and nuts?"

"Yes." Claire blew on her fingers and rubbed them together.

I turned back to Coffee Shop guy. "And a small Almond Joy." Which had basically been my gateway drug to coffee twenty years ago.

Xander introduced me. The soft memory pinged hard in my chest.

I had more important things to focus on.

The barista handed over our drinks, and I set mine in the cup holder and gave Claire hers. "Hold onto this to warm your fingers, but don't drink it until we get home. It'll be too hot."

She nodded.

We finished the ride home in silence, while my curiosity screamed in my head to have its questions answered.

When we got back to my condo, I sat us both at the kitchen table, drinks between us. "You don't have to tell me what happened, but I'd prefer it, so I know how to react if Dale is looking for you."

"He won't be." Claire sounded so certain. So wounded. She sipped her drink, and made a bitter face. "It tastes burnt."

"That's the coffee. You don't have to finish it if you don't want to."

She took another taste, and then another. "No. It's okay. It does taste like a candy bar."

One of the reasons I loved it. "Did Dale leave you there or did you get there on your own somehow? Because I don't know if you want to hear this, but he will come looking for you."

Because Claire was his wife. *His.* And boys like that didn't like to lose their toys, even if they tossed them aside sometimes.

I hated thinking that, and I hated even more that it was true.

"He left me there. He told me..." Claire took a long drag off her coffee. "We were driving around for a while, and he was so mad about dinner, and when I finally pushed him to talk... He told me if I wanted so badly to be a whore, I could try it for a night and see what it was really like."

If this were a cartoon, this was where I'd clench my fist so hard, I broke my hot chocolate cup and sent hot drink flying everywhere. The past flashed in my mind, and I was instantly in that moment, more than twenty years ago, when my father said something almost identical to me. Because of my friendship with Xander.

I maintained calm for her sake and my sanity. "You don't deserve that. I'm sorry."

"But what if I do? I was a snot at dinner."

My snort slipped out. I could only be so much fake at a time. "You really weren't. And you were nothing compared to what I would've done."

She hid her smile behind her cup as she took another drink.

"How did you get my number?" I asked.

"I picked up your business card at RinCon."

What? I stared at her, letting my shock show through.

She finally let go of her coffee, and turned to fiddling with her hands instead. "I'm not really a dim-witted little girl, I'm a bit naive. Almost everyone there knows who you are, and when I say I picked up your card, I mean it was lying on a table. Out in the open. Not exactly a secret."

"But you think the game is smutty smut."

Claire fiddled with the paper sleeve on her cup, sliding it up and down before picking at the edges. "I don't know what I think. I know what I'm supposed to think." She looked at me. "But you? I have so much respect for you. For doing that. For owning that. Not everyone at RinCon had nice things to say about you, but people never do with strong women. Everyone there who knew you respected you."

That was true, but I was surprised to hear it from her. "You didn't tell Dale, though." Not that I cared at this point what he did or didn't know about my life. The question was one of curiosity.

"Not my secret to spill." Like that, her cup was fascinating again. "And you saw how he reacted to tonight." Her voice dropped off, and I had to strain to hear the words. "Also, this contract seems really important to your fiancé."

My— Right. She knew what I did for a living, but not that the engagement was a lie.

The instant that little word manifested in my mind, it felt wrong. Bitter.

This was Claire's chance for confession and emotional cleansing, not mine. She wasn't my buddy, even though I'd go out of my way to keep her safe from Dale, and the engagement was a promise I'd made to Dominic, even if that promise wasn't for it to end in marriage. I had to make sure he and I were on the same page before I started telling anyone something new about it.

I can't believe Xander gave his blessing. Cole's whispered words from dinner chose now to pop back into my head.

"You're staying here tonight." I had a task to focus on, and it wasn't *moping about my pretend love life*. "We'll figure out the rest once you've had some sleep. Text anyone who will call the police when Dale decides he wants you back, and tell them you're safe. And I'll show you where the guest room is."

"He won't want me back." She sounded so wounded.

"Maybe not." I knew better. As far as Dale was concerned, Claire belonged to him. He might've been pissed tonight, but tomorrow when he felt like she'd had a chance to learn and be sorry, he'd want his trophy back. I prayed she didn't yield, I'd do what I could to make her see this was a safer option, but the whispers of my past, the ghosts of pain—both mine and that of others I'd seen go through similar things with fathers and husbands—saw this as the start of misery for Claire.

If she was strong, redemption and peace came after. But if she chose otherwise...

I'd cross that bridge when we got there. "Come on, I'll give you the grand tour."

"Okay." She grabbed her coffee and took another sip before following me.

"This is the kitchen and dining room." I gestured to the room we were in, then walked about three feet. "This is the living room. And back here," I kept walking. "My bedroom, and my office-slash-guest-room." My desk was in one corner and there was a full-sized bed in the other. "Make yourself at home while you're here, and I mean it. If it's in the fridge you can eat it. Oh, I guess ask before you borrow my clothes."

"Your condo is so amazing. It's like it's out of a catalog." A bit of brightness had slipped into Claire's voice, and she drank more of her coffee.

Out of a catalog was exactly what it was. I'd let page 72 in the glossy book decide how I'd decorate. Except for the pictures in my room. That was where the important things stayed—photos of my friends. Of my life. That was my space.

"Um… do you have anything I can sleep in?" Claire tugged on her skirt.

Whatever's underneath your clothes? I got it. That wasn't the right answer. Modesty meant being covered even in bed. "Sure. Come on."

Claire followed me back to my room. I grabbed a shirt and pair of shorts for her, and made sure she was set.

Before she left for her temporary room, she gave me a quick hug. "Thank you."

"I'm glad you called me." I meant it as I squeezed back. Better me than the person who would tell her to apologize to Dale and go back.

After she walked into the other bedroom, I sank onto the edge of my bed. This might not be the longest day of my life, but I was pretty sure it ranked in the top five.

My mother's funeral was number one. Longest day of my life. The emotions from that day bubbled to the surface, threatening to choke me. I'd failed her. I'd let that…

I swallowed hard. The same wouldn't happen to Claire, or anyone else, on my watch. No matter what I told myself or Dominic about letting it go unless Claire asked for help.

At a knock, I shoved away the past and looked up to see Claire in my doorway.

"I'm sorry, but I'm too wired to sleep," she said.

I was fucking exhausted, but I wouldn't be drifting off any time soon. Shifting on my bed, I sat cross legged so my back was to the wall. I patted the comforter across from me. "Come on in."

"Thank you." She sat across from me, mimicking my pose.

Silence sank in. She managed to find a loose thread on my comforter. There shouldn't have been any, but she located the one.

And she flicked at it in every way possible, instead of saying anything.

Not that I was carrying the conversation either. When I was in her shoes, Xander's Aunt Rosie let me figure out a lot in my own time, and only stepped in when I was about to be put in a dangerous situation.

Did I have the temperament to do that for Claire? I wasn't sure I did. I wanted to shake her and ask why she didn't get how bad this situation was.

I could keep the thoughts to myself at least for tonight.

"That guy you were with at the con, Xander? He's got kind of a sexy vibe going on." Claire's speaking startled me, and her words rubbed me wrong.

Mine. The thought came out of nowhere. First of all, he was Dominic's.

Only because I share.

Ahem. "He does have that vibe," I said.

"Have you known him a long time?"

"Since we were in high school."

Claire's mouth formed a tiny *O*. "So, like, forever."

A strained chuckle slipped from my throat. "We're not that old."

"No, I know. That's not what I meant." Claire was quick to assure me. "It wasn't yesterday, and keeping high school friends is hard. When he's a guy and you're with someone else, it seems like that would be impossible."

"He's a really understanding guy." The words hit me harder than I expected. *Really* understanding. "He's also married. To a man."

Claire's shock was going to freeze her face in that expression. "*Oh.* So he's gay."

"He's open to all sorts of things." How awkward was it, discussing Xander's sex life and preferences with a random person? With *this* person. "All three of us are." I needed to shut up before I said too much.

The poor loose threads on my comforter might not survive Claire's fiddling if I let her sit there much longer. "Like in your game."

Except that neither Xander or Dominic had a cybernetic dick, and neither needed one.

No reason to scar the poor woman too much tonight. I had time. "Something like that.'"

I didn't realize we'd fallen asleep talking, until my alarm woke me up the next morning.

Somehow Claire slept through the noise, and she looked more like a little girl than I'd ever seen her, breathing gently, curled around one of my extra pillows.

You never deserved anything your dad put you through. Rosie's words to eighteen-year-old me echoed in my thoughts. *Even if you think now that you brought this on yourself, I'll teach you that's not true. You deserve better. You are better.*

Some days I doubted that, even more than twenty years later, and on those days I hated my own thoughts.

But as I watched Claire sleep, I knew I'd do the same for her, so she could make her own decisions like I had.

No matter what men like Dale and my father thought they were fucking owed.

Waking up the next morning was rough, but I was used to long nights followed by mornings that came too soon. Shaking Claire awake made me feel bad though. When her eyelids fluttered open, shock and fear met me first, and then a forced sort of calm sank in.

Was that because she was in a strange place, or was that her every morning with Dale?

"Do you need me to go?" Her voice was lined with sleep and she pushed upright.

What? "No," I assured her quickly. "You stay here as long as you want and need. But I do want to make sure you can get around when I'm at work. I'll probably be there a lot for the next few weeks."

"I don't want you to spend money on me."

"I promise I have it to spare. Besides, Aunt Rosie —Xander's Aunt, not technically mine—owns a garage. She works on and rebuilds classic trucks, but she's also got a few spare cars at any given time. I texted her a little while ago, and she's happy to loan you one."

Claire's eyes grew wide. "Oh, I can't. No."

"You can. You will." I wasn't going to play these *let's be polite and not take anything* games. "This is something that will help you right now, that she and I can give. You'd do the same." A guess on my part, but what little I'd seen of Claire made me believe it was true.

She nodded. "I would."

"Good." I patted a pile of clothes next to her. "I know I'm shorter, but these should fit for now. Get ready, and we can do this before I head into the office."

A short while later, we were heading to Rosie's. I wanted to ask Claire so many questions—was this typical with Dale? Was it worse? Was she struggling with whether or not to go back? And so much more. I also didn't want to scare her off. She could tell me if and when she was ready.

What was I supposed to say to the sweet basically super model next to me instead? Our lives were so different, though mine could've been hers if I'd just made a couple decisions other than the ones that brought me here.

We pulled up in front of Rosie's, and I shut off my car. The place was an old lube station, and she'd kept the original rolling doors and exterior. She owned the station itself, and the house next door.

"Does she know why I need it?" Claire didn't move to open her door.

I shook my head. "That's up to you to tell her. All she needs to know is that there is a need. You don't owe anyone an explanation." It had taken me a long time to figure that out, years ago, but it was one of my favorite lessons Rosie taught me.

Claire nodded and followed me up the path to the house. Rosie answered before I could ring the bell.

For the longest time, I'd wished I could be Rosie. She was almost as tall as Xander, with the kind of muscle that came from a lifetime of work and heavy lifting. She'd gone gray early in life, and embraced it, and at sixty, she still looked incredible. Like if Billy Idol was female and an MMA fighter.

She greeted me warmly. I introduced Claire, who hovered a few feet back from me, gaze cast at the ground.

"I really appreciate this," I said as I took the keys from Rosie.

"Of course. Anytime, you know that. I'm sorry though, I haven't had a chance to fill it up."

"It's fine. I've got it. Hey, I don't know for sure yet, but I may have a guest for Christmas dinner." We always gathered at Rosie's place for lunch.

She looked past me at Claire.

I glanced over my shoulder to see the other woman trying hard to look anywhere but at us, then looked back at Rosie with a nod.

"No worries," Rosie said. "Take care of her and you and my boys."

I smiled. "I always do."

It was as if the classic station wagon had been restored for Claire. She looked both wrong and right sliding behind the wheel. I had her follow me to the nearest service station, and shut down any protests before they could start when I told her to grab some snacks.

My house wasn't exactly stocked for people to eat there.

While I was wandering the aisles, the conversations of various commuters flitted around me. Some grumbled to themselves, others were on the phone—

"It's not that simple." A voice caught my attention. "Yeah, they want you to play, but there's a difference between interesting game content and a dopamine rush designed to program your system to keep coming back for more. It's practically like they're making junkies."

"Don't even joke about that, man. Basement dwellers aren't the same as meth addicts."

What the...? I couldn't help myself. I followed the voices to the coffee station, to find a uniformed police officer talking to a man in a suit.

The officer gave me a quick nod. "Sorry ma'am. Are we in the way?"

"No. Definitely not." The coffee at work was better, because shitty work coffee was an affront to God. "I didn't mean to eavesdrop, but what you were just saying..." Was exactly the kind of conversation I wanted to insert myself into. The Skinner box part of it. I loved discussions like that.

Suit guy rolled his eyes. "Sorry about him. Carl thinks he's going to build the next big game in his basement."

"Really." Now I was intrigued for different reasons. "Are you a programmer, Carl?"

He gave me a dry chuckle and thumbed his badge. "Do I look like one? Nah. This is the best an

Associate's Degree in Computer Science gets a guy like me."

Maybe, but I'd worked with coders who had proved otherwise. I plucked a business card from my purse and handed it to him. "I can't promise anything, but give me a call if you want to find out if there's more to that degree."

Carl took the card and looked between it and me, his eyebrows rising higher with each pass. "Thanks." He pocketed the card.

I told them to enjoy their morning, and found Claire near the register. The random conversation evaporated from my mind as I saw her worrying her bottom lip, glancing everywhere like she might need to bolt at any minute.

"Hey." When I joined her, she jumped. "You okay?"

"Yeah, I'm just... Yeah." She sighed in a way that said she really wasn't.

I nudged her into line, so I could pay. "I know it doesn't seem like it right now, but it's going to be okay." I had no idea how. For her, for Elliot, for any of us. But I'd make sure of it.

That was what I did. I got things right. I made things happen.

And as soon as I figured out what to do about Elliot, how to help Claire, I'd do more of that.

19 /
dominic

I wasn't surprised to wake up to an empty bed—Xander and I rarely woke up at the same time—but I was a little shocked to wander into the kitchen and find him already dressed, ready to go.

"Hey." He gave me one of those warm smiles that made my pulse race after all these years. "I have to drive out to Haddarville this morning, check on things out there, meet Maddox for lunch, and I want to beat traffic."

That made sense. Most of it. "You're meeting Maddox for lunch *there*?" The two of them worked a few blocks apart *here*.

"He's got the day off. His turn in the rotation."

Right. Judith was staggering their days off to make sure everyone got a break, without everyone disappearing at once. "Okay. You be back tonight?"

"As long as my ancestors don't claim my soul

and chain me to the land." Xander seemed to be his normal, joking, handsome self.

A nice change, since last night he'd been as wound up and angry as I was, when I told him about how dinner went. That combined with his request to not bring Judith home, which I was apparently still thinking about, had me on edge.

"Are you all right?" I didn't know where the question came from. "Are *we* all right?"

Xander frowned. "I think so? Aren't we?" His reply was smooth. A little confused.

Except I caught the hitch in his voice. That catch that I doubted anyone else would hear... aside from probably Judith. "I hope we are."

"We are." That sounded more like Xander. He gripped the back of my neck, holding me in place, and pressed his mouth to mine. The kiss was tender, sweet, and stole my breath. There was nothing fake about that. "If you can't reach me, I'll call you back. Good luck with Roger."

"Okay. I love you."

Xander gave me another quick kiss. "I love you too. I wouldn't do any of this if I didn't." With that, he was gone.

Not exactly the sweet note I wanted to end the conversation on.

I finished getting ready for my own day and tried not to replay the conversation as I headed to work.

The lawyer in me was looking for every single double meaning in what Xander said. I was replaying his body language, his tone, his specific word choices.

I needed to stop or it would drive me nuts.

Judith called me when I was on my way to the office. Good. Something new to focus on. I answered and let her come through the car speakers.

"You should know, Claire stayed with me last night," she said.

Nope. I didn't want to focus on this. Though, "That's good news. Isn't it?" It meant Claire was safe. "Is she safe?"

"I don't know. Rather, right now she is, but over-all... Apparently Dale dumped her in the middle of nowhere and told her to whore herself out if she wanted it so badly."

Fury raced through my veins. This wasn't the kind of distraction I wanted, but I certainly wasn't letting it go. I already planned on telling Roger this morning that we were done with Dale, but this was another nail in that coffin.

Something else occurred to me. "Dale doesn't know she's there, does he? At your place?"

"No. I made her promise not to tell anyone where she's staying. And that we'd figure more out after work today."

"Did you ever figure out how she got your number?" I asked.

Judith gave a short, unamused laugh. "She picked up my business card at RinCon."

Of course. Why did we ever think we could hide who Judith was? Why did I think it was acceptable to ask her to? Why did I agree to Roger's plan?

Because I respected him. Because he was like a father to me. Because he should be the one person I could trust aside from my husband.

"But she does believe we're engaged." Judith's comment knocked my thoughts off-track.

For some reason that one little tidbit soothed me. "We should keep it that way for a while."

"I agree."

I liked her compliance a lot more than I should, especially since I couldn't explain why I'd made the request. "Call me if you need *anything*," I said.

"I will. Good luck with Roger today." Her voice softened.

"Good luck without Elliot." I meant it kindly. To be encouragement.

She sighed. "Thanks."

A heavy cloud hung in my mind, fogging my thoughts and insisting this was only the beginning of the storm.

I hoped the feeling was wrong. I needed everything to go back to what it was.

I can't close that door now.

Whatever that meant, I didn't like it.

The office parking lot was mostly empty when I got there. It was early, so that wasn't odd, but Roger's car being here already was. When I got inside, he was waiting at the reception desk, anger splashed across his face.

"I got a call from Dale this morning." Roger's voice was tight. "What the hell were you—"

I held up a hand to silence him. At least I didn't have to figure out how to start this conversation. "I guarantee you don't want to talk about this here. Let's go in your office."

His already expression darkened further. "That's a good idea." He stepped around the front desk and gestured.

His fury didn't matter. Not when it came to this. As a general rule, I didn't like letting Roger down— I respected him. He was my mentor, he was a second father to me. But I wasn't afraid of his wrath.

Besides, once he knew the full story, he'd end this business relationship with Dale.

We stepped into Roger's office, but neither of us sat. He turned to face me again. "Dale called this morning, ready to sign the retainer. Ready to have us process his first invoice. But not until I could explain to him your behavior, your fiancée's, at dinner last night. What's wrong with you?"

Excuse me? "What did he tell you?"

"That Claire was belligerent. That Judith encouraged it. That Claire refused to come home with him last night," Roger said.

Fucking asshole. "And you believed him."

"Judith tends to be—"

"Think carefully about what you're about to say," I cut him off again. "If you wouldn't say it about me in the same tone, swallow that impulse. Dale dropped Claire at a gas station in the middle of nowhere, with nothing but her phone and a light jacket."

Roger's eyes grew wide, but his anger returned in a blink. "Maybe she—"

"*No.* Don't give me any version of *maybe she deserved it.* Dale was the asshole last night. I was worried he was going to hurt her." The longer I talked, the stronger my own anger and frustration grew, and I let it bleed into my voice.

Roger worked his jaw. "In this state—"

"*No.*" I came down hard on the word. "This isn't a conversation about culture or perception or how the majority does things differently and we need to blend in. I will not do business with a man like that. Our firm won't. If he treats his wife that way, how do you think he'll treat a business partner the first time he disagrees with us?" I *hated* having to qualify my argument.

"You're right." Roger's concession was what I

expected when I walked through the front door, but now I wasn't sure how genuine it was. "You're describing unacceptable behavior."

I wasn't going to argue the victory though. "Do you want me to call him, or will you?"

"I'll take care of it," Roger said. "Dominic," he added as I turned to leave. "How do you know what happened to Claire after she and Dale left the restaurant?"

"It turns out we have a friend in common." I fixed him with a hard stare. "I have work to do. This is the right choice for our firm." I walked out without waiting for Roger to reply.

The issue should be resolved, but that lingering cloud made me think it wasn't. In fact, I was questioning everything.

I needed to talk to Xander. The thought hit me abruptly. There wasn't anything specific I wanted to say, but I needed to hear his voice. The impulse gripped me so hard, I ached. I dialed him as I walked into my own office, and stood next to my desk, listening to his phone ring.

The line clicked. "Busy. Leave it." Xander's familiar voicemail greeting made me smile and made my heart hurt at the same time.

"It's me. Call me back when you have a minute. I love you." The words ached to say, because they felt so real and so raw at the same time.

What if I'd made Xander wait too long?

I wasn't sure where the thought came from, but I couldn't shake it. The concern joined the heavy storm lingering at the edge of my thoughts, waiting for its chance to break.

20 /
xander

This was a ridiculous drive to make for lunch. Sure, Gage made great burgers, but not Dante-Larson-is-going-out-of-his-way-for-one burgers.

Maddox wouldn't ask unless he had a reason, though, and I could use the drive to think and clear my head. I also had an investment out here, so this was a good excuse to check in on it. Not that Onyx needed my in-person attention, but doubling down on my reasons made me feel better about making the trip home.

Coffee scalded the roof of my mouth when I sipped from the to-go cup. With the nervous energy thrumming through me, I didn't need caffeine. After Dom told me last night about how dinner went, *pissed off* sank in. It reminded me too much of Judith's past.

Which kept me up half the night with the same

thoughts that lingered today. I was going to need the steady stream of stimulants to stay on my game once I'd been on the road for a little while.

It was more than the encounter with Dale and Claire that had my mind buzzing. I hated seeing Dom and Judith go out, but not because I hated them together. That would be reasonable on my part, right? My husband and my best friend dating like an engaged couple should make me jealous?

But the more I thought about it, the more I liked the idea.

I hated that Dominic and I couldn't do the same, though. I wanted to walk into his firm's fucking Christmas party, Dom on my arm, and kiss him in front of Roger and everyone. To make our marriage official. To have that stupid little slip of paper called a marriage certificate that said we'd made a promise to each other in the eyes of the world.

Yes, the promise was real regardless, but as the months passed, I wanted more and more to show my love to the world.

And I wanted—

No. I wouldn't think that. I refused to think *I wanted Judith on my arm too.*

But I did. I wanted her with us. At the party. At our house at the end of the night. Over and over.

I couldn't have it though. I refused to entertain the thought. She meant more than something frivolous like lust or desire. Her career, her direction, her life, meant more than something as base and primal as *this is mine, hands off.*

More than an hour later, when I pulled onto the state road leading to Haddarville, my head was stuck in the same loop as when I'd left the house.

I drove down Main Street without pause, barely registering the shops. Most of the buildings and businesses had been here for longer than I had, but they'd also been taken over by the next generation of each family. Evie's hardware store, Aubrey's vintage clothing, Sebastian's tea shop, Deacon's antiques.

There were days I wondered why they hadn't gotten out—some of them stayed by choice, like Deacon, and others were here out of a sense of obligation, like Sebastian, but they were all here.

Then again, I was helping Onyx rebuild the diner next to his music shop, and that basically tied me here even without the family name, so who was I to talk?

Onyx had asked if we could meet somewhere besides his building, the same as every time we'd met. He was keeping this a secret from Maddox and most everyone else. Meeting me in front of the city nativity scene didn't seem secret to me, but it also didn't cost me any extra so it was fine with me.

I was early though, so parked at one end of

Main Street, near Gage's Grub, and started a slow stroll to the other.

It was always strange to me, being back in the town we grew up in. Not because once upon a time I thought this tiny place, population 2,000, was a good size, but because I always felt out of sync here. My family founded this town. That was our name on the signs.

But I'd felt like a stranger here as far back as I could remember.

The Christmas decorations would look vibrant and bright at night, but during the day, the grime from melting snow had settled on to any pale surface. I paused in front of the one-third scale nativity scene at the end of the park. Same figures that had been here for years. I didn't remember them ever looking different.

Every few years, some up and comer on the city council would propose replacing the scene with newer figures. Plastic maybe. Something sturdier, or at least easier to repair, that could be made to glow from the inside.

They were always shot down. The original granite pieces came out every year, despite the chips, and a missing piece here or there, they were always repainted and loved as much as was possible.

There was a bitter thought somewhere in the back of my mind about the residents loving a stone camel more than their neighbor, but I wasn't in the mood to chase that thread.

The angel in back caught my attention. Over the years, the pale, heavenly being had been snowed on and covered in exhaust and grime as much as any of the other figures. Rather than celebrating the birth of its savior, the angel always looked so sad.

"I get where it's coming from." Past Judith's voice echoed in my mind. *"You do everything you're told, obey all the rules, and then you realize you're the only one who believes it's necessary."*

That was the night she got kicked out. We stood here in the middle of town for hours, trying to decide what to do. Where she was going to go.

"Hey." Onyx's friendly call yanked me from the past. Somehow he'd stopped next to me without my noticing. Onyx was my brother's best friend, and owned the local music store. Somehow he managed to keep selling physical media relevant—CDs, records, tapes… he had it all. But his obsession was new-in-box 8-tracks. "I hear the town council gets real twitchy if they catch you fucking with their nativity. Mind if I film it for posterity?"

I let the shadows of memory fall away with a shake of my head. "Knock yourself out. Maybe I should've brought this information in an envelope. You could tell them I'm selling you state secrets."

"Meh. They string you up for being a spy."

"Pretty sure the town council would string you

up for dancing, too," I teased. "Speaking of, that's when the secret is out. Dominic did a lot of digging," had a paralegal do it, but close enough, "and there's no way around the fact that you have to get a majority approval before you start construction, and again to sell."

A large portion of the street had been declared a historical district in the last few months, and while that kept the city council from forcing certain changes, it also prevented others without jumping through a lot of hoops. Overall it was better for everyone, but it would make Onyx's desire to keep this a secret as long as possible difficult.

"I can't hide the construction anyway. As long as I can keep the sale secret until I'm ready..."

I clenched my jaw. Maddox was going to be furious when he found out Onyx was selling. Was leaving. I agreed to finance the plan because it was a solid investment, but the only reason I promised to keep it between Onyx and me was to give me time to change Onyx's mind about stealing away in the middle of the night, so to speak.

"Let me show you what Carly came up with, and you can tell me what you like." I pulled out my phone, navigated to the message with the remodel mock-ups, and scrolled through.

An hour later, Onyx had made some decisions, we were moving toward next steps, and I had seen Maddox drive by.

"He's going to ask what we were talking about," I said.

Onyx shrugged. "Tell him to come see me after if he wants answers."

Seemed a bit childish, but I got the impression Onyx missed hanging out with Maddox more than he let on. "Okay."

A glance at my phone confirmed it was early, so I didn't feel bad about the time it took to walk from one end of Main Street to the other.

As I approached, I found my brother sitting in a chair outside Gage's burger place. The table was half covered with snow, and its umbrella was closed. His metal seat had to be icy, but he didn't look like he minded.

Maddox was only nine years younger than me, and it was clear we were related, but our lives had diverged the moment he was born. Dad expected great things from his oldest son, like for me to carry on the family name and make sure the world knew how great we were.

"You freezing that for when you actually need it?" I called when I was within earshot, and nodded at his crotch.

He grabbed his dick through his jeans. "More like putting it on ice after a lifetime of hard use."

Thing was, the Haddar name was Mom's, and she didn't want her boys growing up the way she had, the weight of expectation from this place. She couldn't stop it with me, but she damn well made sure her baby was sheltered.

Not that I blamed Maddox for any of it. I genuinely loved my brother. "Dating your fist doesn't count as *hard use*."

"I learned it from watching you." Maddox winced the instant the words passed his lips, and I did the same. "That came out wrong."

"And now you've made it weird."

"If I remind you *weird* is my thing, does that let me change the subject?"

I pretended to consider the suggestion. "Given I'd rather not talk about your *weird thing*, sure."

"What were you and Onyx talking about?"

There it was. "Baby Jesus. Also, he said go ask him if you want to know."

"Fine. You want lunch?" He nodded at the burger place.

Anything to move past the awkward turn this conversation took. "All right." It was only ten-thirty in the morning, but that meant the place was the perfect level of unoccupied, and I'd skipped breakfast in anticipation of this.

Maddox made it up here more often than I did, mostly visiting Onyx, but neither of us came out here often anymore, and never together. Not since Mom passed away about five years ago.

And the whispers I heard from the kitchen,

wondering why we were both here, amused me rather than surprised me.

But Maddox and I didn't have much catching up to do. We'd seen each other several times last week at RinCon, the same way we saw each other several times every week.

Which was why him asking to meet me up here didn't make any sense.

We took a seat at a table in the back, that gave us the best view of the entire joint. Our food was dropped at our table, and the kid left.

"So, what's with the long-distance meeting spot?" I asked as I grabbed a couple of fries.

He squirted generous amounts of ketchup across both his burger and fries. "I hoped the setting would make you nostalgic."

"When has that ever happened?" Nostalgia made people do stupid things while they chased a high from a life they'd never live again.

Maddox raised an eyebrow. "More often than you let yourself admit."

I was in a contemplative mood, but not enough of one to add another thread of overthinking to the tangle. "Uh-huh."

"Rosie called me."

"Ah." That was the best response I could offer. Aunt Rosie was Mom's sister. When we were growing up, she was the coolest aunt ever. Openly gay, lived in *the big city*, and she took Judith in when things fell apart here.

And the day Judith married Cole, Rosie pulled me aside and gave me some drunken-aunt advice. She told me their wedding was the best thing that could've happened to Judith and me. That Rosie saw our potential and loved us both dearly and we were holding each other back.

I didn't disagree with her, but back then I hadn't cared for hearing the truth spoken out loud. And over the last few decades Rosie and I drifted apart. It was possible I'd ignored all of her messages this year about my and Dominic's plans for Christmas dinner, telling myself I was too busy to think about it.

"What did she want?" I kept my tone cool.

Maddox took a huge bit of burger, after I asked, and stared back at me while he chewed.

Asshole. "You brought me out here for this. I can wait."

"I'm not supposed to tell you," Maddox mumbled through a half-full mouth before taking another bite.

There were days when I swore he was three-something and not thirty-something. "You could've not told me as easily in Salt Lake." And I was as capable of playing this as him, but I liked winning more than Maddox did.

Besides, I was hungry. So I dug into my burger. I

took my time with the intention of letting Maddox finish first.

And when he did, a short while later, that meant I won.

Maddox tried to take his time, sipping soda, using a dozen napkins to wipe away grease and ketchup, and fiddling.

I chewed more slowly.

He finally sighed. "She wants to meet us at the orchard house. At noon. Today. She'll tell you herself."

"Wow." I tried to mask my genuine shock with sarcasm. "Entrapment much?"

"She says she wouldn't have done things this way if you'd taken her calls."

I didn't care about seeing the old house again— it had been vacant for ages, because Mom and Rosie could never agree on what to do with it—but I'd already spent too much time in the past over the last week or so, and seeing Rosie again would remind me of—

Nothing. Remind me of the same things I was already thinking about. Nothing new. Nothing that changed anything. "Fine. Let's go see the orchard house."

We were early, and we spent the next forty-five minutes parked in front of the dilapidated old farm-house. Even if the weather were warmer, I wasn't sure sitting on the porch and waiting was a good idea. We stayed in my car, Maddox refusing to say anything, for fear he'd say the wrong thing.

Rosie finally pulled up in her purple, 1982, Chevy S10.

We all climbed out to meet each other. She was built a lot like me, tall, muscular, and confident. Her hair went silver decades ago, and it was cut short. Honestly, she looked a bit like a well-built Billy Idol.

She wrapped me in a tentative hug. "It's been too long."

"Yeah. You know how it goes." The past was screaming in the back of my mind, hammering at the door I'd locked it behind. It needed to stay there.

"I do." Her smile was tight and didn't reach her eyes. "How are Dominic and Judith?"

I know you lo— I silenced her voice from the past. "Good. Busy. You know."

"Yeah, I do." Rosie frowned. "Saw the game. It's incredible."

"It is."

Maddox's loud cough was as forced as the rest of this conversation. "I didn't say a word."

"Good. Thank you," Rosie said. "Which I suppose brings us to why we're here. I want to sell this place." She gestured to the home. "And I need your help with it, Xander."

I stared at her in disbelief. "I'm a tech investor, not a real estate agent."

"But I want to see it restored. Used as a bed and breakfast or have the orchard producing again or anything that brings it back to life, and you know people."

Mom's dream. That was what she'd wanted for this place, that Rosie argued against for years.

—She'd put all of her energy—

Fucking voice from the past. "You know people too." It didn't matter that Rosie walked away from the family when she was younger. She had been too happy to use their connections and money anyway, to build herself a place in the world.

I didn't have a problem with that, but it did mean there was no reason for me to be here. "If you want my blessing, do what you want with the place, otherwise, you don't need me here." I turned away. "Do you want a lift back to town, Maddox?"

"Lewis." Rosie sounded so much like Mom when she called me by my middle name. The family name. The one Dad wouldn't give me, because damn it, I was his son.

I shook my head, trying to rattle away the thoughts, but I didn't look at her. "What?"

At the stretch of silence, I almost turned to face her again. *Almost.* She wouldn't win.

"I was hoping to do this with you."

—You were selfless in those moments that counted—

I clenched my jaw. "Maddox."

"I'll catch a ride back with Rosie," he said.

Fine. That meant I could get the fuck out of this place now.

I floored it leaving town, but the ten minutes it took for me to hit the interstate were too long. Holding back the voices of the past, Rosie's voice, wasn't an option now.

I know you love her, even if you won't admit it to yourself. That was Rosie from Judith's wedding, drunk and doting on the closest thing to a little girl she'd ever had. *But she's better off this way. She'd put all her energy into you instead of herself, if she ended up with you.*

That was ages ago. The words had faded with time and both Judith's and my successes. Until Mom's funeral. Until that quiet moment when Rosie pulled me aside. The one thing that loosened lips more than alcohol was grief.

I know you worry sometimes about becoming your father. You're not. The words had warmed me before I heard what came next. *You're a far better man, and you were smart, selfless in those moments that counted, to not hold back the woman you love.*

Fuck, I didn't want to be tied to that memory. I didn't want to have it haunting me. It had stayed gone, locked away, silent, for years. It should've died and vanished, not returned louder than ever.

Instead, it played on repeat in my mind the entire drive home, no matter how loud I cranked the radio.

I couldn't go back to the office today, not that anyone expected me to. Most of our clients were busy with holiday and end of year plans, and we were doing a lot of the same.

Arriving at an empty house devoured me, though. I took my time setting my keys by the door, hanging up my jacket. Fishing my wallet and phone from my pocket.

The missed calls and messages caught my attention. Cell reception must've been ultra shitty in Haddarville today, for me to not have heard any of those. I skimmed the text transcripts for most of them to know they weren't important.

But the one from Dominic... Seeing I'd missed his call clenched like a fist around my heart. Odd reaction. Hearing his *I love you. I'll see you tonight*, intensified the ache. The feeling that surged into me, the desperate *need* to hold him, to feel him, threatened to overwhelm me.

I was clinging to a past and questioning decisions that had been the right ones to make. There was no reason for it, especially since I had some-thing—someone—perfect and amazing in my life.

For the next few hours, I distracted myself with work. When I heard Dom's car in the driveway, I dropped what I was doing and strode to the kitchen to meet him.

The instant he walked through the door from the garage, I pulled him in and claimed his mouth in a hard kiss, pressing him into the wall until he was all I could taste or smell.

He gripped my shirt in his fists. His moan mingling with my groan was divinity.

"Not that I'm complaining." His voice was breathless when we broke apart. "But where did that come from?"

"I can't keep us a secret anymore." Desperation drove my words. "I need the world to know you're mine. I can't—won't—keep hiding it."

The way he searched my face, I braced for an argument, but when a soft smile tugged up the corners of his mouth, the tension inside me finally uncoiled.

"All right." Dominic's words made my heart soar. "Let's stop hiding."

This felt so right. The timing. The decision. All of it.

So why did it also feel hollow, like the center had been carved out and misplaced?

21 /
judith

My Tuesday at work was filled figuring out the logistics of a dev team without the best Director in gaming, and making a plan in case Elliot didn't come back.

I'd find someone new, possibly promote from within, but it felt like betrayal to be considering those measures when he was supposed to be returning.

When I got home that night, it was almost nine. Not unusual for me. Claire was on my couch watching TV.

It was good to see someone using both. When did I last have time for that?

She scrambled to her feet as soon as she saw me. "I made myself some dinner, I hope that's okay, there are leftovers in the fridge."

"Of course it's okay. You're not supposed to sit

here and starve." My bigger concern was—"I had the ingredients in my house to make food?"

"I had groceries delivered."

Not what I gave her access to my delivery account for, but it worked. I found a bowl in the fridge with some form of potatoes, eggs, and cheese in it. That'd be a nice change from pizza and Chinese.

I heated some up and joined her in the living room. I still had no idea what to do with her long term. Picking her up was easy, but she'd need work, a place to go...

Or to reconcile with Dale, I supposed, but thinking the words made my gut churn.

"How was your day?" I wasn't used to having someone else around, especially a mostly stranger, but I should probably talk to her instead of myself. That would help with figuring out next steps, too, but I didn't want to scare her off.

"It was okay. I was going to straighten up for you, to thank you for letting me stay here, but... umm..."

Ummm? "Yes?"

"It's already really clean in here, and I can't figure out how, because I couldn't find the cleaning supplies." She sounded sheepish.

Ah. "I spend a lot of time at work. Someone comes in and cleans for me a few times a month."

"Oh. Wow." She sounded genuinely impressed.

Dale didn't have a maid? A cook? "Is Dominic going to be okay with that?"

Right. She thought I was engaged. "He does the same in his place, so I assume."

"It must be nice." Claire tugged her knees to her chest and hugged them.

"Having a maid? These potatoes are really good, by the way." I might consider getting a cook, too.

She sighed and seemed to sink into herself. "I'm thirty. No one wants someone as old as me for a wife, and my mom does all the things I do, so I'm not any good to my parents. If I couldn't cook and clean, I'd be useless. You don't have to worry about that."

Fury raced through my veins, and my food soured in my gut. I set the bowl on the coffee table and turned on the couch so I was facing her. "Hey, look at me."

"Why?"

I covered her foot with my hand, drawing her gaze. "Because I want you to see how much I mean this. Your worth lies with who you are, not what you do for other people. Don't get me wrong, I'm not saying you should be an asshole, but you weren't born to serve."

"But... I was." Her voice was soft.

I got it. I hated that I got it, but I had a decent idea what she was feeling. "You weren't. You're your own person, and life is for figuring out who that is."

"Easy for you to say." She dropped her head into her arms as she spoke, muffling the words. "You already have all the answers."

"I don't, not by a long shot, and it's not easy for me to say, I promise you. I know what you're feeling."

She mumbled something that sounded like *I doubt it*. When she raised her head, her smile was tight, and her eyes dull. "I'm sorry. I didn't mean to dump on you. Forget what I said. I'm going to get some sleep."

"Claire," I called after her retreating back.

She closed the guest room door in response.

I flopped against the couch with a sigh. Was I that difficult when I went to live with Rosie? I'd love to believe *no*. That I'd been reasonable and open and heard her out and never argued.

That didn't sound anything like me.

I'd love to tell Claire everything I'd learned since my dad kicked me out. About faith, about love and sex and relationships, about the world.

But it had taken me years to figure it out, and trying to squash my view of reality on top of hers in a single night would only make her shut me out.

I finished my food, washed my dishes and left them to dry, and headed to bed.

Wednesday at work was like the eye of the

storm. The game was going smoothly, business was getting back to normal, but the tension hung in the air.

Wade had set a meeting for next Monday, to talk through this issue with Elliot and cast a tie-breaking vote. My teams were back to work on the next rounds of content.

I left the office before six that night, and the world felt completely out of whack at that point. The only thing I'd heard from Xander was the news about the meeting with Wade, and a quick *how are you holding up?*

I had a similar conversation with Dom. *How are you holding up? Dale's out, by the way.*

The only thing unusual about either exchange was that I didn't used to talk to either of them on a daily basis. And now it didn't feel like enough.

When I got home, my condo smelled incredible. Like garlic and meat and I wasn't sure what else.

I found Claire at the table, eating a pasta dish in cream sauce that looked as good as it smelled.

Huh. I'd forgotten a table could be used for that.

She scrambled to her feet as soon as she saw me. "I didn't think you'd be home or I would've waited. Let me get you a plate. Sit down."

"You sit down. Now." I used my boss-voice to make her comply.

She flushed red, but did what I told her.

In the kitchen, I found an array of glass dishes,

each with a different portion of the meal in them. This was way better than delivery.

I piled my plate high with food—Xander would be proud of me, eating without prompting—and rejoined Claire in the dining room.

She didn't say anything, and the smell of the food was making my stomach growl, so I dug in. For a short while, the only sound in the room was silverware hitting the dishes as we ate.

"I talked to Dale today." Claire's quiet voice might as well have been a shout.

I swallowed hard as I set my fork down. "How'd that go?"

"He says he's sorry, and that I'd be an idiot to not come home."

Uh-huh. My skepticism was drowned out by a louder voice in my thoughts. One wondering if she'd told him too much. If we were in danger. "What did you tell him?" Cool and collected was my deal. She never saw the spark of fear.

"I didn't tell him anything except that I'd think about it. I didn't want you to be mad at me."

Not the best reason, but it got us the required result.

"But what if he's right?" Claire asked.

"He's not. He's very wrong." I needed to offer more, but I was already telling her the truth.

Claire pushed her food away, a scowl etched on her face. "You don't understand. You're pretty, you're successful, and you have yummy men falling all over you. I'm thirty. No one is interested in me. What if Dale is my last chance at love?

"It doesn't matter if he makes me question a few things about my faith. He reminds me who I am. How important I am. And I'm willing to make concessions for that. I was willing to make myself look like an idiot at dinner, that first night you and I met, to prove to Dale I'm a good, caring housewife who never questions. Tell me you've never played a part, to get something you want."

But you could want so much more. Her micro rant made me ill and filled me with sympathy for her at the same time. I wanted to tell her how dumb this entire thing was, especially why she'd acted that way at dinner, but berating her wouldn't help and technically I'd done the exact same thing that night— faked being a good little trophy-wife-to-be.

"What about how important you are to you?" I asked.

She wouldn't meet my gaze, and while she wasn't eating, she was pushing a lot of food around its dish.

Maybe I was pushing too hard. "Why did you call me Monday night? You have other friends. People in the church. Your parents." Though, she was at RinCon alone… Nope. I wasn't going to make any assumptions. "But you called an almost stranger whose number you got from a business

card. Not that I'm upset. I'm glad you did."
Somehow the reinforcement felt important. "But I
do wonder why."

"Because every other time—" The speed and
ferocity with which Claire snapped her jaw shut
would've severed the fork if it had been in her
mouth. Her panic vanished, and a smile flitted in.

I found myself staring at the vapid woman who
had cheerfully asked me if my first husband was
dead, and if that was why I was childless at my age.

"Your name came to mind," Claire said sweetly.

Nope. "We're not doing this." I didn't have
Rosie's patience. Please, Goddess, don't let this be a
bad idea. "How many other times have there
been?"

"They were all my fault."

I doubted that. "I didn't ask whose fault it was."

"I don't remember."

"Yes you do." Because she replayed every one of
them, asking herself what she could've done
differently.

The chair legs made a horrible squeak when she
pushed back from the table. "I'll put the rest of the
food away."

"It will wait." I grabbed her wrist and pulled her
into the chair next to mine, then turned myself so
my knees touched hers, and I could look her directly
in the eye. "I'm not trying to hurt you. I…"

No one knew this except Xander and Rosie. I'd

never even told Cole, because I hated how weak it made me look. "I've been in a similar place."

"With Cole?" The hesitation in Claire's question was stark.

"No. *Fuck* no. Cole is the sweetest grumpy teddy bear in existence. Growing up..." I didn't want to talk about this, but something told me Claire needed to hear it. This was my past and her now, and I wanted it to become her past too.

"My dad kicked my mom out eleven times, plus three halves." The words didn't ache the way I expected. Speaking them aloud was like a release. "The three halves were when I convinced her we should go, and she was packed and ready, when whichever well-meaning friend she'd told got word back to Dad. There was always a well-meaning friend. A woman from church that Mom would call when it happened, who would convince her she needed to be more understanding. That she needed to be a better wife."

The words soured in my gut. It was probably a good thing I hadn't finished my food.

"Dale doesn't hit me or anything. Please don't think that. He drops me at a corner to give me a few days to realize how I'm acting," Claire said.

I was going to chain Dale to the wall by the balls and make *him* realize how *he* was acting. "Dad never hit Mom, either. I'm almost certain of it. However, his apologies sounded a lot like *if you wouldn't make me so mad* and his declarations of love were more like *you're so lucky I married you. Who else would have?"* And then he'd laugh, and say *just kidding.*

I'd learned from those examples. The first time he kicked me out was also the last. Mom begged him… and I walked out. I called Xander and made him promise not to tell anyone in town…

I closed my eyes and took a deep breath, to brush away some of the emotion, and when I looked again, Claire's fingers were digging into her knees so hard that her knuckles shook.

"Six and a half times," she said softly. "The first time, I left. When Dale blamed me for… He said it was for burning dinner, but I was pretty sure it was because he'd lost a contract at work. I went to my parents' house. Mom told me marriages took work. She let me sleep in my old bed that night, then drove me home in the morning and helped me make the most extravagant and perfect meal for dinner that night. All of Dale's favorites."

I covered her hands until the shaking stopped. "Being with the wrong person, a person who doesn't respect you, is far worse than being single."

"Easy for you to say. You've already landed two hotties in your life, and you get to hang out with a third." Frustration, hurt, and anger bled from Claire's voice. "Do you think someone like me could land a guy like Xander?"

Hello, raging jealousy. Feel free to find the door.

"*Like* Xander? Yes. You're smart, you're talented, and you're super model gorgeous."

"You think so?" Pink spread across Claire's cheeks. "Do you think I could land a woman like you?"

Whoa. Back up.

Snippets of things Claire had said rushed back.

"There's nothing wrong with being with yourself for a while."

She scowled. "I've been *with myself* for thirty years."

"And when you find the right man or woman, they're not going to care how little or much time you've been single." This conversation had shifted in a way I didn't expect. I was both grateful for the change, and worried about overloading her tonight with a world different from her own.

Under my touch, Claire's hands relaxed further, and she turned them so she was holding my hands. "Have you ever been with a girl?" She asked.

"Yes." I might not want to overwhelm her, but I wouldn't lie.

"Is it different?"

"Than being with a man?"

She squeezed my hands. "Aren't you worried about being punished?"

Hell, I'd begged for it on so many occasions. But that wasn't the right answer here. "We were raised our entire lives with the spoken message of *your faith is yours. Find your beliefs. Question. Don't accept others' answers, find them for yourself.* But everything around us said if we didn't accept the answers others had, we were wrong."

Claire pulled away from me and ducked her head.

"I found my own answers," I said. "I stay true to myself first, and myself is attracted to both men and women." And myself never changed herself for a man, especially not for his work.

Especially not for pretend. The words sank into my bones.

But was it really pretend with Dominic?

Not the time for that line of thought.

"Like in your game?"

I nodded. "Like in my game."

"I played it."

The game? My flash of fear wasn't for what she thought, but around if Dale found out. "At home?"

"At RinCon," Claire said. "I, umm..." Her blush was back. "I got a room with a kitty girl NPC. She was really pretty—your artists are really good—and the tingles it gave me down there..."

"Did you have fun?" That was all I cared about. Not which character she picked, or anything else aside from did it make her happy.

"So much fun. I kept expecting it to feel wrong, but it didn't."

I smiled. "Then it wasn't wrong."

Claire leaned in, and when she crushed her lips to mine, shock spilled through me. I kissed back out of instinct, and the entire thing was sloppy and rushed. But it was also as sweet as a kiss could be.

It didn't make my pulse race the way Xander did—and he'd never kissed me. It didn't heat me to the core the way Dominic's kisses did.

But a kiss like that, from her, would make someone else who wasn't me very happy.

Claire was searching my face.

What should I tell her? It had to keep her here but also be a firm *no*.

She pushed to her feet abruptly. "I'm sorry. I shouldn't have… I'm sorry."

"Claire, wait." I grabbed her wrist before she could run away, and stood as well. "I'm with someone. I'm happy with Dominic." I felt guilty about lying.

To myself or her. I wasn't sure.

I didn't let the reaction show. "But I meant everything I said about you. You will find someone incredible for you."

"Okay." She jerked away from me. "It's okay. I get it. I'm okay. I should let you enjoy your night." She scurried to her room faster than a feeling cat.

I sank back into my chair, as the past and present sank back in, heavier and heavier, until they threatened to crush my soul.

22 /
dominic

Xander's fervor on Tuesday night, after he got back from Haddarville, when he declared we were done hiding, was intoxicating and contagious. When he'd kissed me with that intensity, laid down the decision with expansive firmness, I couldn't say *no*.

Not that I wanted to. After the conversation with Roger, I'd been on that cusp anyway.

But since Xander's declaration, there had been nothing. It was Thursday night, and the matter had been dropped. Vanished into the ether.

After so many years of denying it, of being the reason we hid what we were, having a solution so close made me crave it and need it *now*.

By Thursday night I was done waiting for the rest of the conversation, so when Xander got home from work, I met him in the kitchen.

"We haven't talked about this decision to come out," I said.

"At least let a guy put his laptop down first."

I stepped aside, gestured, then followed him into the office. I didn't want to give him a reason to avoid this again.

He set the briefcase with his computer on his desk and paused, back to me. "What do we need to talk about? Hey, world, we're in love. Look, it's that easy."

It should be. I wanted it to be. It wasn't as though I was in the closet. But this still felt like a big deal.

"Oh, right." Xander finally looked at me. "You've been telling a number of your colleagues you're engaged. To Judith. And now you're going to say, *Just kidding. I'm queer as fuck, and this is my husband.*"

Both the edge in his voice, and the reminder of Judith caught me off-guard. Of course I'd end the engagement with her. That was a given when I decided I wouldn't work with Dale, and it should've been my choice much earlier, given how Xander refused to say he felt about it.

But I didn't want that to happen. I wanted to keep her, not just with me, but with us. Xander and I were fraying at the edges and apparently I wanted to tug on one of those very obvious threads and see if it unraveled things.

"I thought we were talking." He met my gaze with a hard stare. "I'll agree some delicacy is needed, but is this really the kind of thing that requires a big plan?"

"No. I suppose not."

He approached me and gave me a quick kiss. "Okay. Then let me help you with your lines. *Welcome home. Missed you.*"

I was certain we'd never greeted each other with *missed you*, and the edge was still in his voice.

Pretending our relationships were something they weren't had gotten us here, and ignoring the fact that we both wanted Judith—we both *needed* her —wasn't going to help now. "I don't want to call off the engagement."

"Really."

"Rather, I don't want things to go back to the way they were. She should be a bigger part of our lives."

Xander frowned. "She's already a massive part of everything we do."

"Exactly. Doesn't that tell you something?"

He shrugged and shook his head. "It tells me we're already all in a good place together."

Fuck. He'd turned this into a contest. He was right, I was wrong. There was nothing overt in his words or actions, but I'd been with him long enough to know. People thought being a lawyer was all about winning, but what I did was negotiation, and that included knowing when I'd slammed into a brick wall.

I didn't want to drop this conversation. I didn't want to walk away with things unresolved. But if I pushed now, I may lose my chance to make my point, and we'd lose Judith.

"Am I right?" Xander asked.

Most definitely not. "You make a great point."

"Spoken like someone practiced in saying one thing that means many things." He closed the distance between us and gripped the back of my neck. "You're not going to drop this, are you?"

"I am for tonight."

Xander pressed his forehead to mine. "Good, because you're right about one thing."

I was right about all of it. "What's that?"

"Telling the world I love you will be easy."

I hadn't said that, he did. As he tilted both our heads and crushed his mouth to mine, I couldn't argue. I didn't want to. Everyone should know how much Xander and I loved each other.

His demand grew more intense as he pushed into me, and my pulse roared in response. This shift in mood, the abrupt intensity, felt off. But did it? This kiss—the need flowing freely between us—was right.

We'd spent so long hiding, and now we could celebrate our love in so many new ways.

Xander pinned me to the wall with his full body,

his hard frame boxing me in. I liked being trapped this way, by him.

I needed to be closer. To make sure he stayed. I gripped the short hairs at the back of his neck, tugging salt and pepper strands with my fists and holding him in place while I tasted every second of this kiss.

He dropped his hand to my half-hard cock, stroking it through fabric. Pulling until I was fully erect, and squeezing hard enough I ached. In the best possible way.

This still wasn't enough. I needed more of him. I reached for Xander to do the same—to cup him and feel his hard length.

He grabbed my wrist with his free hand, never pausing in the way he stroked me, and pinned my arm above my head. He broke the kiss long enough to meet my gaze. "No."

Was he serious? "I don't—"

"And you won't."

That didn't finish my thought or answer my *why*, but he tugged my dick harder, bit my bottom lip in a fresh, hungry kiss, and my questions flitted into the vapor.

Somehow, with only one hand, he managed to undo my belt and trousers. The actions were rough and clumsy, straining the seams on the clothing.

Not that my rock-hard cock wasn't already doing that.

He let my hand go as he freed my dick. His grip was warm and rough around the shaft. *Fuck* that was incredible.

But when he fell to his knees at my feet, my brain skipped. This wasn't like Xander. Not that he was a selfish lover—exactly the opposite—but I was usually the one who—

Oh, God. My mind went blank when he took me in his mouth, and I fell into a long groan. There was no slow-build here. He was sucking my dick like it was a source of life, squeezing my shaft hard. Jerking. Licking.

I didn't have a choice but to fall into sensations that left my entire body tingling. My hips thrust on their own. My body swayed with the attention. I grasped Xander's hair, not caring if I pulled, and fucked his face.

There was no restraint from either of us.

He didn't ease up, and all I knew was him. His mouth. His hands. His grunts as he choked on my cock.

When need tightened in my balls, I'd lost track of where one groan ended and the next began. "I'm going to come." The warning was as much mumble as words.

Words that seemed to spur Xander on.

Orgasm ripped through me, until I was spilling down Xander's throat, my entire body shuddering until I was spent.

Fortunately, the wall was there to fall into. To keep me upright.

Xander stood, leaving my pants around my hips and my cock hanging out. There was a dribble of cum on his chin, and I wiped it away with my shirt cuff.

How was this not enough? I wanted more. Not for me, but for him. I reached for his dick again.

And again, he grabbed my wrist. "I don't want that." The gravel in his voice matched the roughness in my mind. "Not tonight." His kiss was hungry and demanding, our tongues dancing together and the lingering taste of an incredible blowjob mingling with it all.

"This is you and me together," Xander muttered against my mouth. "Always you and me. The way it's meant to be."

His words should be sweet. Reassuring. The kind of promise that came with a sweeping romance. So why did they leave me feeling like we were giving something—someone—up?

23 /
judith

Claire's bedroom door was closed in the morning.

I needed to talk to her, but I couldn't force the conversation. I paused next to the door and knocked softly. "Are you up?"

There was no response, but I heard a faint rustling coming from inside.

"I don't know if you're listening," I said softly. "Everything we talked about last night... I don't tell people those things. Not even my ex-husband knows any of that, and how the night ended doesn't change the rest of it. It doesn't change what you're going through or that I care or that I want you safe, fuck what anyone else says."

An ache grew in my chest as I remembered what I wished anyone would've said to me back then. "This isn't your fault. I'm proud of you for not folding under the pressure. And if I weren't in love with someone else, I'd totally hook up with you."

Where did that…? I wasn't—

"I hope you're here when I get home." *Please don't go back to him.*

I headed to work, and got there before anyone but the on-call developers who'd been in all night. Diving into my tasks was comforting. Keeping the machine running. Pushing ahead. Each new thing checked off my to-do list was another frazzled nerve soothed and settled.

In the hallway, I heard everyone else arriving for the day. I could shut my office door and drown out the noise, but I liked the way the office came alive when everyone was here. The chatter filling the building died down as all my people got settled and started working.

My phone buzzed with a message from Dominic. *You free?*

I'm working, but I'm not in meetings, if that's what you're asking. I could just tell him *no*, but it was impossible to ignore the giddy flutter in my chest at seeing his name.

Meet us out back?

Us. Xander was with him. And now I had a silly grin on my face that I needed to erase between my office and downstairs. *Be right there.*

I told Ivan I'd be back soon, took the stairs to avoid running into anyone while I was in this oddly euphoric kind of mood, and found Xander and Dominic next to Dom's SUV.

"We need to talk." Xander grabbed my hand when I was within reach and tugged me into the back seat, putting me between the two of them, facing Dom.

Okay? "What's up with the location?" And the ominously vague language.

"It's warm. It's cozy. It's private," Dominic said.

I liked the sound of *private*. "So, what's up?"

He reached for my neck, and sparks raced through me when his fingers brushed my skin. He pulled the chain free that I kept his ring on. "Xander and I have decided to stop hiding *us*."

The words drilled through me on a wash of confusion. This was something I'd been waiting to hear for years, and I was so very happy for them. But it was impossible to ignore the disappointment for me.

"That's incredible." I only let my excitement show. I wasn't a selfish twat who couldn't enjoy others' happiness. "Congratulations."

Xander's grip tightened where his hand rested on my hip, and I swore the ghost of doubt flashed across Dominic's face.

"It really is." Xander sounded genuinely excited, and he should be. He'd wanted this, deserved this, for so many years.

I expected Dominic to slip the ring from its

chain and reclaim it. Instead, he traced his thumb along the edge, his brow furrowed.

"It's going to take us a little bit to figure out how to do this. It's not like we flip a switch and tomorrow the world knows we're together," Xander said.

Dominic nodded. "And it's not as though anything else has to change."

The fake engagement does. There was no reason to say it—we all knew it. "Nothing else like what?"

"Well…" Dominic trailed a finger lightly up my arm and sent goosebumps racing over me.

Xander's grip fell away, and Dominic frowned. What just happened? Like that the mood in the vehicle shifted. I glanced over at Xander to see him leaning against the door, as if he couldn't get far enough away from me. He was looking at Dominic, brow furrowed.

"What just happened?" I needed to know as I shifted in my seat so I could see both of them.

Xander opened his mouth, and a ringing noise fell out. Rather, his phone rang, cutting off what he was about to say. He reached for the device without pause. "Should be set to silent," he mumbled.

But none of us completely ignored our phones. His would be set to ring through with multiple calls from the same number, in case of emergencies, just like mine was.

"Yeah." Xander's voice was sharp. As he listened, his gaze fell on me again, and his frown changed to something that made my gut churn. "Don't know. Because you're pushing out the guy who handles these things?"

No.

"I'm sure it's because she's on it." As Xander spoke, he slid from the SUV and tugged me with him. "Let them do their jobs." He hung up and pocketed his phone. "Oliver. Game's down."

What? "Super happy for both of you." I squeezed Xander's arm and waggled my fingers at Dom. "Gotta go. I'll call you." I didn't know if they heard the last bit, because I was already sprinting into the building and up the stairs.

I'd left my phone at my desk. So I could go fuck around with my friends. Who was? Ignoring work. Ignoring my priorities.

As I neared the Dev room, I heard Link's voice, but hard. "Sit the fuck down." The command was followed by him issuing a string of priorities to everyone in the room.

Thank God no one was out here to see me panting like a dog. I paused long enough to catch my breath, smoothed out my hair and clothing, and strode toward the room. "Status update," I said as I walked in.

Chris stood up, his head popping above a cubicle wall, and I glared at him.

"Link?" I walked up to his desk.

He gave me the run-down of what was happening in short, terse words.

I was fine with the tone, as well as the conciseness. "Tell me what you need me to work on." Because yes, I was the boss, but this was their realm of expertise and I trusted them to do their jobs.

That didn't stop me from feeling like I'd failed as I listened to Link's instructions, then headed back to my office. The same drum beat over and over in my head. The one reminding me that I'd been outside fucking around, during the day, while my game was crashing. That I'd been unavailable when I should've been answering a call instantly.

That I was letting my personal life get in the way of what mattered.

This wasn't me. I didn't need other people in order to survive. Sure, I adored Xander and Dominic. I wanted them around. I appreciated our friendship.

But I wasn't a scared little girl who couldn't survive without her man. Especially her fake man.

As my software was loading, to do the work needed, I grabbed my phone. Sure enough, there were more than a dozen texts about down servers, both automated and from the people here.

Elliot must've gotten these same messages, and it had to be killing him the way it was me. I hated what I had to do next, but it was for the greater good. He hadn't followed the rules, and now if he didn't, they weren't going to give him another chance.

I sent him a text telling him we had things under control and to stay away.

And I dove into the kind of coding work I hadn't done in years. Fortunately, unlike the previous crashes, this one didn't take long to recover from. We were wrapped up in just a few hours.

But tension hung in the air. Why now? Why so random? Yes, games crashed, especially new ones, but the causes tended to be obvious.

These were seemingly unrelated and a strange combination of new-to-us and repeats of the past.

Everyone got back to their day, and I was left with my mind whirring in a way I wasn't used to. I didn't know what to do. About anything.

And that wasn't me. I always had a plan. My plans had plans. I always knew what came next. Instead, today I felt lost. When it came to the game and Xander and Dominic and Claire and…

Thanks, life, I hated it.

Working didn't stop my brain from whirring along to other problems. This wasn't right. I should be able to immerse myself in what needed to be done, rather than fiddling with the ring that hung around my neck.

Link called me a few hours after the game crashed. The background noise made it sound like he was in the car. "Chris is sabotaging our game," he said.

Fury spilled through me, hot and bright and carried on a bitter wave that was grateful for a place to focus. If this was true, I'd crucify the asshole. And as Link rattled off his theory, it certainly sounded true.

I'd known people who would intentionally sabotage others' careers to progress their own. Link wasn't one of them.

Chris…

I could see it. Not that I would've said that when I hired him, but over the past year or two… "Are you certain? I have to be positive, one-hundred percent, before we proceed. There are legal repercussions for being wrong." If Link believed it, I did. I needed him to know what he was making a decision about though.

"I'm certain," he said after a pause. "And given what he's put us through… let's execute the fucker."

I should tell him to back off and be professional, but I hated finding out one of our own had turned against us. Had been willing to cost us everything for… I didn't even know what. "Find me in my office when you get back." I'd start the paperwork now. "You can escort him out for me."

"Shame Elliot couldn't be here for this," Link said.

I clenched my jaw and hung up.

Our Human Resources person wasn't happy to have me pushing through an immediate termination, but the instant I told her why, her tone changed. "I'll have you the paperwork in ten minutes," Dana said. "Hang him up."

Link arrived a short while later. He showed me his proof, we had Luna kick Chris off the network, and Link and I made the short walk to the Dev room.

"Is anyone else having trouble logging in?" Chris's question carried into the hallway. "Is the network down?'

I wasn't letting him harass Luna over this. Link and I strode into the room. When Chris saw us, all the color faded from his face.

"Get up," I said. I might be shorter than everyone else in this room, but I knew how to carry myself like I wasn't. "Your employment here is terminated, effective immediately."

Chris opened his mouth, but no sound came out.

"Link will see you to your car," I talked over him.

The rest of the room exploded in an array of chatter, keystrokes, and other indiscernible white noise.

"You can't fire me." Chris scoffed. "I will *sue* you."

Good. He was welcome to fucking try. "The best

fucking contract lawyer in the country owes me a favor." My brain fumbled on the words, but I didn't let it show. "We'll mail you your things."

I stepped aside and let Link and his imposing stature handle making sure that Chris left the building.

"Any questions?" I asked the room. Silence met me, which I wasn't surprised by. Everyone else here was still part of the team. I needed to dial back the empress inside. "You can come to me if you want to talk privately." I softened my voice. "Or HR. Or anyone in management. We'll tell you as much as we can. You're all doing an incredible job. Keep up the great work."

No one said anything, but the clacking of keys told me they were messaging someone.

I wasn't worried about it.

Instead, as I walked to my office, I was worried about my own fuck-ups. I'd been playing house for the last two weeks, and someone in my actual house, *my* company, was fucking with my people.

The conversation with Claire from last night rushed back in vivid, painful detail. I'd sworn when I was younger, when my dad kicked me out, that I'd never lose myself for a relationship.

I'd come close in the last fourteen days. Closer than I should have for Dominic and Xander, and I wasn't even *with* them.

It was time for me to let go of the pretending.

They were moving on with their real relationship, and I was standing in the middle of what mattered the most to me.

Regardless of what the bitter taste in the back of my throat meant, when I thought about putting distance between me, and Xander and Dom.

24 /
dominic

The morning was stuck in my head as I walked into the law office. Judith's panic about the game crashing, about having to hear the news from someone else, was expected.

The way Xander had pulled away from her before that…

Not so much.

I was okay—more than okay—with the idea of sharing his heart with her. I'd always known what they were to each other. The day I met them, I saw their connection as distinctly as if an actual red thread of fate tied them together.

If I didn't love him, if I didn't lo— want her to be part of us, it might be a tougher truth for me to face. But I didn't have a problem admitting I wanted both of them. When I was with the two of them, it was the one time I felt at peace. I was me. I was more than me. I was part of something incredible.

My issues were with asking Judith for the ring back. With telling her the engagement was over. With the way Xander was fighting against her staying in our lives as much as she had been recently.

That she ignored what we were and that he pushed her away.

What was I supposed to do, trapped between the two most stubborn people I knew? And the two people I loved.

"Roger is waiting for you in Conference Room B." The receptionist's comment dragged me back to the now. "With Dale."

What? "Thanks." Now I was on high alert. I strode toward the room in question, knocked on the closed door, and pushed in without waiting for an answer.

Dale was seated at the table across from Roger, who rose with a smile when he saw me.

I didn't like the way this looked, and I certainly wasn't walking into the room without knowing what this was.

"I'm glad you made it back before we finished," Roger said. "Give you a chance to welcome Dale and his firm aboard in person."

Fuck me.

The look on Roger's face was distinctly *play nice*.

You know how this works.

I was so done *playing nice.* "I don't think I will."

"Excuse me?" Roger's pleasant look faltered.

"I won't be welcoming Dale to the firm." I never looked at the man in question.

Roger's chuckle was awkward. Good. "I'll talk to you in your office when I'm done," he said.

"That sounds like a good idea." I turned before he could say anything else.

"I'm sorry about——"

My closing the door cut off Roger's bullshit apology to Dale.

I wouldn't jump to conclusions about what I'd just seen, but there weren't a lot of blanks left for me to fill in. And there was no way I would yield on my refusal to do business with Dale. Somewhere in the past few days I'd reached my lifetime limit of being polite because business required it.

Which also meant Roger was about to find out I was done hiding who I was. What Xander meant to me.

"Again, so happy to have you and your firm aboard." Roger's drifted into my office.

Color me pissed.

A moment later, Roger joined me. Alone. "What was that?" he asked.

"That's what I'd like to know. We agreed not to take him on as a client."

"He's an upstanding member of his community

and church. And he's paying us a nice retainer."

There it was. "Money has never been a reason for us to take a client before."

"It has to be sometimes. By the way, Dale misses his wife."

I doubted that. What Dale missed was having his trophy. *Now* I was making assumptions, and I didn't feel misguided in it at all. "He should've treated her better."

"She should've—"

"I'm gonna stop you right there. Don't say whatever you're about to say." I didn't need to know any more about the situation than what Judith had already told me, and what I'd seen at dinner. She knew what she was doing, letting Claire stay with her. Besides, Claire didn't strike me as the kind of person who would jeopardize a life she wanted for the sake of drama.

Roger's nostrils flared and he clenched his jaw. "Dale is a good client. He'll bring the right kind of focus to this firm, and damn it, I'm tired of struggling. We work hard."

"Yeah, we do. And there are a lot of firms out there who turn that into a cash mill, and we've never been one of them."

Roger raised his brows. "You don't know as much as you think you do. You haven't seen it all."

Now he was just being obtuse. "I won't work with a client like that. Not knowing what I do. If he treats his wife that way, he doesn't treat his business partners any better, he simply hides it behind a wall of *this is how the world works*. Besides, Dale won't work with me. I've decided with Xander that we're done hiding our relationship." *And maybe you should be considering something along the same lines.*

When Roger came out or if he ever did wasn't my place to say.

"Not here you're not."

The longer this conversation went on, the more my anger grew to match my frustration. How much had I overlooked over the past few years? How many things did I pretend didn't bother me, so I could make this man happy? "Whether or not I tell the world who I am is *not* your decision. Just like bringing Dale on without consulting me shouldn't have been your decision."

"This is *my* firm." Roger's voice was tight.

"And I'm your business partner." This back and forth was getting old, and the conversation wasn't going anywhere. "My father had so much respect for you, he spoke so highly of you, and I know why. You are a good person." Or I thought so, anyway.

"Your father was my best friend. My brother."

I shook my head, and the truth sank in. The reality I'd ignored for too long. "This would've disappointed him so deeply. He was so insistent on being true to oneself. Always."

"He also understood that—"

"He died with regrets." The ache in my chest swelled with the memories. "He left things in this life unfinished and he didn't want this for either of us. I won't do that to me. To Xander. I won't be on my deathbed tomorrow or fifty years from now and wondering *why didn't I just...* " I couldn't.

Roger sighed heavily. "I see. Well, I can't have you working for my firm if you can't present a proper front."

His firm? Fuck that. We'd built this place together. We'd...

Nothing. "Acting straight is *proper*? Fuck you." I was done here.

"What are you going to do? Start over? At this point in your life?"

Yeah, I was. "Yes. Because I'm still alive. I'm still breathing, and I'm tired of molding myself to someone else's vision of the world. Yours. Dale's... So, yes, consider this my resignation. My notice of intent to part ways. I'm moving on with the people I love, and if this is what you want from life, you can stay here and collect asshole clients, because you're willing to let a large retainer dictate your ethics."

"You'll regret this." That wasn't the most cliche thing Roger could've said, but it was close.

I shook my head. "No. I'm done regretting things. You, on the other hand, will wonder for the rest of your life what you could've had if you'd stopped hiding."

25 /
judith

Claire was in her room Thursday night, but she'd made dinner again. I tried to draw her out, to thank her, to talk to her…

She wouldn't come out.

But at least she was still here.

Was it odd that I just wanted the company? I'd been coming home to an empty place for years and been fine with it. My friends were the people at work. Xander. Dominic.

Friday morning, she was still there, and still hiding.

Damn it.

I got to the office early. One thing to look forward to—with the root problem of our game crashes solved yesterday, things should run smoothly today. Did I dare hope I wouldn't have to ask the staff to work extra hours over the holidays?

There was a generic meeting on my calendar for

nine, Ivan hadn't gotten back to me yet about who it was with. When Elliot walked into my office at five minutes until, I had an idea, and I was happy to see him, but there was no reason to get all mushy about it.

"I have a meeting," I said.

He dropped into a chair as if I'd invited him to stay for the day. "With me. You get to talk to me for the next hour."

The only thing that sucked about that was when the hour was up, he wasn't going back to his desk. "To do what?" I asked. "I'm already on your side. I'm not the one you need to convince."

"This isn't like you." Elliot's words cut through me. "Standing aside. Not fighting. Pretending this is out of your hands?"

"Do you think I like having lost control of this situation?" The question snapped past my lips. "I don't want you gone and neither does anyone else."

"Then let me stay."

"We're not those kids anymore. Our world has rules and consequences." Not what I meant to say, and the words hit me hard. Was I talking to him or me?

The way he rubbed his wrists, the scars we all pretended we didn't know about, told me I'd struck a nerve in both of us. "Why didn't you and I ever hook up?" he asked.

Because you're like the brother I never had and that

would be weird. "Because you're not ambitious enough for me." Cole hadn't been either.

Xander was. Dominic. They had the kind of drive that was sexy. The kind of push…

… That kept us apart.

"Besides"—I wanted to keep this about Elliot— "You've always been in love with Link."

"Yeah, I have."

It was so weird to hear him admit it, even though I'd known it for ages. It was nice, though. Except in this case, "him or the job. Pick, or the board picks for you. Don't take things that far." The words came out with more pleading than I intended.

Elliot scrubbed his face. "I can't. AcesPlayed is my baby as much as it is yours. This game… it's my everything."

"But it's not." This was something I knew. Because I wouldn't be torn. I would pick the company. Again and again. "I'm not telling you to give up Link. If you have the perfect guy, that's longer term than any game. No one could've pulled this off besides us. We breathed life into it." And I was so proud of that. Of my team. Of his. "That will never change, regardless of what you choose next. What if…"

I lost the thought before I could grasp it.

"Yes?" Elliot asked.

I shook my head. "I don't know." That had been

my answer too often lately. It wasn't right. I should always know.

"What if I moved into a consulting position? Like a contractor? Put someone else in charge, so I'm not the guy who determines Link's future." Elliot's suggestion had a lot of merit. "Let me have a say still. Let me keep my stake in the company."

I almost succeeded in hiding my smile. It was a simple suggestion. Elegant. "Could you do that?"

"I don't know. But give Link my old job and that'll make it easier."

Bad idea. I promoted Link, and it made it look like he was being rewarded for breaking the rules. But Link had stepped into the role while Elliot was gone, and he knew this product better than anyone else.

Besides, if Elliot made this decision, we took that option away from the board. They couldn't vote to push him out if he wasn't in, and I could keep a fantastic part of the company, just with a little twist to how we approached things. "All right. Let's do it," I said.

Telling Link, seeing his disbelief, was incredible, and telling the rest of the team and seeing their reactions was just as good. But watching Elliot kiss Link in front of the room...

That hit me wrong. As happy as I was for them, the moment tasted bitter.

I needed to keep this ball in motion now that

we'd started it rolling. Call Xander. Call the rest of the board. Tell them the issue was resolved.

Why did it feel like my feet dragged as I headed back to my office?

I wanted to tell Xander the great news, but his name made my brain stall.

No, the image of him pulling away from me yesterday in Dom's SUV, overlapping with that kiss between Elliot and Link, that was what hung me up.

This was ridiculous. Not losing myself in a relationship included not projecting misplaced feelings on my best friend. I didn't bow to anyone. I didn't hesitate over emotional bullshit.

When I reached my office, I called Xander.

"Hey." Was his tone off as he answered or was that me?

I was happy about this, and there was no reason to hide that. "Hey yourself. I have what I can only describe as fantastic news."

"Yeah?" There was the lilt to his voice.

I told him about the conversation with Elliot. "So there's no reason to hold the vote. Nothing to push him out for."

"That's a loophole Dom's going to be proud of," Xander said. "I'll tell Wade and Grant?"

No. This was my news. My company. My job. "I'll call Grant and Scott, and you can tell me if Oliver turns several shades of red when he finds out." The longer we talked, the better I felt.

Xander chuckled. "I'll definitely tell you that."

This was fantastic. After days of stress and the unknown, things were going right and I simply hadn't been prepared for that. Now that I'd processed, now that I'd shared the news with Xander, I felt good.

I needed to wrap things up before my traitor brain came in with more bullshit doubt. "Okay, I have to make a couple more calls. We'll talk soon."

"Definitely." And there was that hitch in Xander's voice again.

Nope. I was making things out to be more than they were.

We said quick goodbyes and hung up.

I called Scott and he cheered. We chatted for a few minutes about the games—his and ours— before we both agreed we should get back to work.

"Thank you," I said. "For giving me my start. For putting me on the path to get here."

His laugh surprised me. "You would've done this, or something equally as great, with or without me. Thank you for letting me be a part of that."

"You're welcome." I was feeling the warm fuzzies to the max as I called Grant. He didn't answer, so I left him a quick message telling him what happened.

And then I wanted to call Xander back. To suggest he and Dom and I celebrate. Which was a perfectly normal thing for us to do.

But that ache inside was back that I hated and couldn't define. I wanted that to be gone. I wanted...

To never be the scared girl from my past again. To never be my mother, yielding to the people who insisted they knew what was best for me, especially when they were wrong.

I wanted to get over whatever the fuck this was that felt uncomfortable and made me so fucking weak.

26 /
xander

She should be a bigger part of our lives. Dominic's voice echoed in my head.

She's already a massive part of everything we do. And I meant it. What more did he want?

The same thing I did.

I needed to get over my hang-ups of the past. Once she gave Dom back his ring, once that stupid farce was officially over, I could relax. The three of us could go back to life like it was.

The thoughts had been circling for hours, and I was walking into a meeting with Kandace. I needed to knock this the fuck off and get to work.

My phone rang, and Judith's name and picture flashed on my screen.

Nope. I wasn't tumbling down that rabbit hole. Judith and I as friends were supportive. Powerful. Made to conquer the world.

Judith and me as anything else? Bad. Idea. Rosie

had been right about that since the first time she said it.

"Hey." The instant I answered, I knew I sounded off.

"Hey, yourself." So did she. "I have what I can only describe as fantastic news."

I liked the sound of that. As she launched into the news about Elliot, I liked the hype that bled into her voice even more. Though, the hitch I still heard had to be that this didn't go exactly the way she wanted.

Having Elliot shift to part time, putting someone else in charge, wasn't ideal. Though this was probably the best possible outcome besides *nothing changes at all*.

Why couldn't *nothing changes at all ever* be life?

I almost asked if she wanted to celebrate tonight. The offer lingered on the tip of my tongue, and it would be a normal thing for us to do. Find any excuse we could to have dinner with her.

Instead, I promised to let her know how badly this news pissed off Oliver, and hung up.

"Do you need to reschedule?" Kandace's voice cut through my wandering thoughts.

I was standing to the side of the hallway, looking like a first-class space cadet, and drowning in my own thoughts. "Nope. I'm good now." With one caveat. "Actually, two seconds." I sent Wade a quick note telling him we needed to talk. I'd head down to his office right this second, but he'd been in non-stop meetings since he got back. "*Now* I'm ready." I followed Kandace into her office.

As a tech investment firm, we were inundated with pitches on an ongoing basis. There were several levels of filters in place, to make sure the partners didn't spend all our time just reading incoming ideas. For instance, the messages that simply said *I have a million-dollar proposal. When can we meet?* Were weeded out at a base level.

What Kandace and I were doing was further along in the process. Some of the better ideas didn't grab the attention of every partner, but still caught some of our eyes. She and I were looking over those that we were considering, but no one else was interested in.

The thing I disliked about this part of the process was that it was unlikely we'd invest in 99% of these, not because they were bad ideas, but it took more than a great concept to skyrocket to success. The odds said most of these didn't have the kind of support behind them—business plan, charisma, platform, or something else—to make them a reality.

She started with the first idea on the list—a gaming company. No surprise there. We were tech investors, and every other Joe Developer had the *Hottest Idea Ever* (TM) for a new game.

Judith's idea hadn't been unique on the surface,

but the way she planned to execute it, the industry support she gathered, her experience and drive, all made it one of a kind.

Because she was brilliant. Had vision. Was a vision.

If the timing in our lives had been different, she would've been mine years ago. It was a thought I rarely let myself put into words, and it ached now.

Because she and I being involved romantically was like these pitches—on the surface it was a solid concept.

But in practice...

"Pass," I said as Kandace was halfway through reading a bullet point aloud.

She looked at me, brows raised. "Excuse me?"

I shouldn't have talked over her. "It's not working for me."

"Same." She sighed, made a mark on the page, and set it aside.

Why not?

That was the same thing I kept asking myself about Judith. Why couldn't she and I—

Because Rosie was right. I'd hold her back. Judith should be mine, she should've been from the start, and she never could be, because—

"Are you sure this is a good time?" Kandace's question cut through the rambling thoughts.

"Yes. Why wouldn't it be?"

"Besides the fact that you're not listening to me?" She nodded at the paper in my hand.

I looked down to see the edges frayed and tattered. A print-out that had been fresh off the printer when I walked in here.

"Is it about the phone call?" Kandace asked.

Good excuse. "It is. I'm hoping to talk to Wade before I spread the news far and wide, but there's a solution for the AcesPlayed issue."

"Yeah?" Kandace grinned. "No wonder you're off in Xander Land."

What the...? "The fuck is Xander Land?"

"I assume it's where you go when your mind isn't here, and that it's next door to Dominicberg and Judithville."

Clever. They did tend to be the source of my distractions, but I wasn't sure I liked being that obvious. "Maybe I'm thinking about porn." Inappropriate thing to say at the office? Without question. I wouldn't say it to anyone but Kandace, and only because she saw the term as a business word more than a sexual one.

Which was why her blush surprised me.

"Maybe, but unlikely." Was that a hint of shyness in her voice?

Perfect excuse to take the attention off me. "You've been different since you got back from Italy." An honest observation, but not at all relevant to the conversation.

Her face went redder. Her Italy trip was months ago. Fascinating. "I'm not. The allure of that stunning place has faded."

"Maybe. But something else is lingering. Are you daydreaming about the perfect sandwich shop?"

"The perfect sausage." She was almost tomato-colored. "I mean... That sounded... You're trying to take the focus off you and what has you detached from *this* meeting."

One hundred percent busted. "I'm not the one talking about sausage. You've already taken the focus off me."

"Which you want me to do because...?"

A knock interrupted our back and forth, thank fuck, and I looked over my shoulder to see Wade in the doorway. "You wanted to talk?" he said. "I've got five minutes."

"You're welcome to stay in here," Kandace offered. "I'm not sure I want to see the darker side of this conversation, but I do want to see it play out."

She'd definitely changed.

Because while my news was good, I had to tell Wade his brother was being an asshole about this, asking for something that was a bad idea for the firm and defied the votes of the other partners. Judith and Elliot reaching an agreement didn't change Oliver's opinion that AcesPlayed was a bad investment.

I jerked my thumb at the open seat next to me, but Wade was already sitting down.

He perched on the edge of the chair, one knee bouncing. He'd always been a *go go go* kind of high energy.

"By the way, I wanted to thank you both for the flowers and notes," Wade said. "This has been really hard on Paige. She and her father were close, and we didn't hear from many people in the firm. Not that I expect it, but the consideration was nice."

"How's she doing?" Kandace asked.

"It's been tough on her." Wade's laugh was tight, like he knew he was repeating himself.

I felt bad for Wade and his family. "I'm sorry."

"Yeah. You wanted to talk? You have news?"

Right. *Good* news. At least, I thought so. "Judith has reached an agreement with Elliot. We don't need to push through with the board's vote for AcesPlayed."

Wade's knee bounced faster. "Vote is still happening. Oliver has raised some good points with me."

"He's wrong." I could be more tactful, but that wasn't what needed to happen here.

Kandace and Wade both looked surprised.

"You're talking about m—"

"Our business partner." I didn't want to give Wade a chance to play the *he's my brother* card. "If I was making this kind of mistake, I'd expect one of you to call me on it, regardless of our friendships."

"We all would," Kandace said. "This firm works not only because we each bring different insights to the table, but because we can be honest about them, and no one voice holds more weight than any other. If Oliver believes AcesPlayed is a mistake, he's welcome to pull out, but he doesn't get to decide that for the rest of us."

I knew she'd have my back, but unfortunately, this situation ran deeper than that. "This isn't just about him trying to pull us out of a single solid thing."

"Isn't it?" Wade's fidgeting stopped and he held my gaze. "Speaking of relationships and favoritism. He disagrees with your closest friend, and now he's wrong? That's not what's going on here?"

It was absolutely what was happening in my head. I wanted to hurt him in a way that would probably land me in jail. "This decision might be personal, but that doesn't mean he's right. And this isn't the first time he's done this recently, it's just the biggest."

"Xander's right. Three of the four investments Oliver's dumped in the last year have soared in valuation since we pulled out, and the fourth didn't crash. It's remained steady." Kandace was ready with the details. Bless her.

Wade clenched his jaw. "We've all made bad

calls before. This is a risky business and that's part of why we play the game—we like the gamble."

He had me there. I didn't just love the risk, I all-but got off on the win. "Still doesn't make me wrong about this. I know family matters. I get that. But sometimes we have to choose—"

"What do you want me to do here?" Wade asked. "Do you think firing Oliver is appropriate? Would you fire your brother?"

"I love Maddox. I'd do anything to shelter him, even now." No reason to lie about that.

Wade raised his eyebrows. "So… no."

I hadn't been talking about letting Oliver go, but now that we were talking about it, I had a hard time thinking of an argument against it. "If he was making these kinds of emotionally charged decisions and hurting the group, yes. I'd hate it, but I'd do it. Ignoring the issue will crash you and everyone around you, and it won't do Oliver any good either."

"Backing out of one game won't crush me, just like none of the other sell offs did," Wade said.

"Not financially and not instantly. What happens when a year from now you're at twice as many? If you personally want out of AcesPlayed, if Oliver does, I'll buy you out." It would be a strain, but I'd do it. "Every other partner has said we stay, and we're built on allowing those decisions."

Did Wade just growl? "You're lecturing me

about not making this personal, but you're pushing to keep Aces because of Judith."

"It's always personal, and we always invest in the person as much as the idea. But this isn't about my friendship with her, it's because she's worth investing in. Her numbers are solid. Any other company doing what hers is right now? We'd be scrambling to keep them, and you know that. Anyone else with her numbers and you'd be kissing their asses." There was no more direct way for me to put this.

Wade shook his head. "I don't know that I agree with you. I do think you need to walk away for the rest of the day and think about whether or not this is a hill you want to die on."

Excuse me? "I don't have to think about it, I know. I've made my decision."

"He's not wrong about this, Wade." Kandace's support would help. The only stake she had in this was, well, her stake.

"Both of you, then, take an early weekend." Wade pushed to his feet. "I have another meeting."

My fury and disappointment soared as he walked from the room.

27 /
judith

I didn't know if I was in the mood to celebrate. Yes, we figured out a solid resolution, but it wasn't the one I wanted. I hated that we'd been forced to choose from the lesser of two evils, rather than taking the path that made the most sense overall.

It was also weird that Xander picked a new place for us to all meet. A little bar on the other side of the valley. And that he'd had Dominic extend the offer.

When Dom called, he'd sounded as high strung as I felt, and it took a little nudging to get him to tell me he'd walked away from his firm, and Xander was close to doing the same.

Today was definitely not a win.

The men were waiting for me out front when I arrived, and none of us said much of anything as we headed inside and grabbed a table at the back of the room. Not that we'd hear each other if we did talk—the noise levels in here were off the charts for such a small space.

Xander flagged down a waitress and grabbed us three beers.

"Maybe we should call this a commiseration party instead of a celebration?" I tried to joke, but I wasn't feeling it.

Dominic shrugged. "Sounds accurate."

As long as the mood was already flat. "How about I break up with you?" Nope, that didn't sound playful either. I unhooked the chain from around my neck. "This can be an anti-engagement party." I handed Dominic the ring on the necklace.

I hated the pit that formed in my chest at the action, but what else was I supposed to do?

Dominic's frown was impossible to miss, and so was the way Xander's expression turned blank.

"I guess today is a day of endings," Dominic said.

No. Really. Xander looked like he was carved from stone. "Or revived beginnings, depending on how you look at it."

"I like the positive spin, but that's not really you." Okay, I was done trying to tease. It was all coming out flat.

"Why not?" Xander asked. "It's not like I'm an eternal pessimist."

Where did the edge in his voice come from?

Same place as the rest of the mood in here, I supposed. "You're a realist. Like all of us."

Dominic held up the chain, the ring still dangling from it, and let it dance in the dim light. He took my hand, turned it up, and dropped both ring and necklace into my palm. "Here's something positive. Hold onto this for a while longer."

Oh. I loved the idea. I hated the idea. I hated that I loved the idea.

"Are you kidding me right now?" Xander had gone from exuding nothing to radiating anger in a blink.

And he was right to be pissed. I dropped the ring on the table. It lay there between us, the most mocking inanimate object I'd ever seen.

"We agreed—"

"Nothing." Xander talked over Dom. "We agreed to nothing. You talked, and I never thought it was a good idea."

"Talked about what?" I had a feeling I already knew, but I couldn't admit it, not even to myself.

Dom focused on Xander. "Why isn't it a good idea?"

"You have to ask? After all this time?" Xander scoffed. "Then again, given how quickly you two slid into this fake engagement…"

The noise level in here no longer mattered. Their voices had risen to carry easily across our table, and probably to the neighboring ones as well.

"That sounded uncharacteristically passive aggressive. What the fuck is going on?"

"There's nothing passive here. This is flat out aggression," Xander said.

"It's bullshit is what it is." Dominic's voice rose another couple decibels. "I've watched you two for seven years as you pretended you weren't head over heels for each other."

We weren't. We never had been. Xander and I didn't do love. We didn't…

"And you're going to get upset over a few kisses and a ring?" Dominic continued, unaware that the war raging in my head was building to the same proportions as the argument at our table. "Everyone but the two of you sees that you belong together."

This wasn't what I was here for tonight. I wanted the company of friends. I wanted to either cheer or jeer. I didn't need yet another person, the last person who should be doing this, deciding that he knew better about my relationship with Xander than Xander and I did.

"I'm not with her because I love you." Xander focused on Dom. "I'm with *you*, Dominic."

Exactly. I was the friend. The wing woman. So why did Xander's words feel like a slap? "Except that you're not." I needed to keep my mouth shut, but that had never been me. I had thoughts, and I was going to share them. "The two of you—"

"Had an agreement," Xander said.

Right. The *agreement*. "Even though it's killed you to keep things quiet."

"Yes, if fucking killed me. I want to tell the world we're together, and now we can. *We're in love*," Xander shouted the three words. "I want to hold Dom's hand in public. And kiss you and sometimes I just want to pin you to the wall by the throat and make sure the world knows you're mine."

"Okay." Like that, Dominic backed off.

The words were sweet. Touching. A conversation I'd been waiting for them to have for years. And tonight it pissed me off. It dug under my skin and gouged my heart from beneath my ribs. "*Okay?* Just like that? After all this time? After making Xander wait for so long?"

Dominic scowled. "No. Not *just like that*."

"We had a mutual agreement, and I hated it, but I understood." Xander doubled down on a narrative he'd been fighting for so long. "Gossip destroys people."

"Is that why the two of you aren't together?" Dom asked.

And now we were back to this? He'd just gotten a shouted confession of love from his fucking husband and he wanted to bring me back into the conversation? "This isn't about us."

The laugh Dominic let out was harsh. "But it is. Because Judith isn't the outlier in this relationship, I am. It's always been about the two of you. And I've always been okay with that, except that you fight it so fucking hard. Don't you dare come down on me if you're not willing to admit to yourselves, out loud, why you're not together."

Because—

"Because I don't want to ruin her." Xander slammed a fist into the table. "Is that what you're looking for? We're not together because Judith deserves the world, and I won't be what stands in her way."

Oh. Fuck me. That was a little sweet and a little infuriating. "Excuse me? You won't stand in my way by being with me?" Correction—it was a *lot* infuriating. "Who the fuck are you to think... I'm single because I choose it, not because some person—*any* person—decided that for me. Not even you, Alexander Lewis Haddar. You don't decide who I fuck, or who I date, or whether or not I'm successful. Your dick isn't so magical that it can stop me from being me."

"That's not—"

"What you meant? That's exactly what you meant. Fuck you both, we're done. Period. Don't call me. Don't drop by. Don't forget your ring, Dom."

As I stormed from the bar, I was so furious that red ate at the edges of my vision. Xander thought the two of us hooking up...

He thought my loving him...

He'd been full of shit this entire time about how much he believed in me. Of all the people in the world to pull something like that, to think they could stand in my way, he was the last one I thought...

But I'd been wrong.

"Judith." Xander grabbed my arm, yanking me to a stop.

Heat roared inside, mingling with anger. I whirled on him, not trying to hide how upset I was. "What?"

I'm sorry. I know you earned this. We earned it. You're my best friend. Come back and we'll figure this out and finish conquering the world together.

That was what I wanted him to say. I didn't need him to declare his lo— Nothing more. Simple enough, right?

"Understand where I'm coming from," he said. "It's not that I think you're weak or that I have some magical influence over you. You don't need anyone —you've never made me doubt that."

"You're right, I don't." At least, I didn't need them in the way he meant. I needed my team—my people—but I didn't need love or a man who thought that loving me would make me less. "Good-bye, Xander."

When I got home, I found Claire in the living room. She shut the TV off the instant she saw me. I hadn't seen her in days, not since the kiss, and I had the sudden urge to tell her everything. An ache to spill my guts; to have someone I could just talk to.

I was supposed to be helping and protecting her. Supposed to be the strong one, showing her how to not need anyone else. Caving now wouldn't help that message.

"I'm glad you came back before I went to bed," she said meekly. "Can we talk?"

I took a seat next to her on the couch. "Of course."

"I want to apologize for the other night. For the kiss. I didn't mean…"

When she trailed off, I waited for a moment to see if she was going to finish the thought. There was no reason for her to go into life thinking any part of it was a mistake. Sure, she and I weren't going anywhere romantically, but she wouldn't have known if she didn't ask. "Don't apologize." I kept my voice kind. "You hoped I was interested?"

"Yes."

"And you liked it?"

"Yes." Pink flooded her cheeks. "And I get it, that you and I aren't… You've been a really good friend to me. I don't think anyone else I know would've done for me what you have."

"You needed it."

Claire smiled. "I did, but that doesn't mean anyone else would've… Thank you. And we're still friends, right?"

"Of course we are." For some reason that was the most comforting thing she could've asked me tonight.

She clapped. "*Yay*. What are you doing tonight?"

Same thing I did every night… "Working."

"Nope. Not on a Friday night." The shock in her voice was exaggerated as she grabbed my arm. "You're taking a break and watching *A Muppet Christmas Carol* with me."

I… What?

"Stay there." She nudged me into the cushions. "I'll be right back." She walked into the kitchen, and a moment later I heard the microwave start. Then the smell of popcorn filled the house. When was the last time I had microwave popcorn?

Claire returned with a giant bowl of popcorn, and a six pack of Dr. Pepper. She settled next to me again, started the movie, and let it run.

For the next little while, we watched a ridiculous movie with puppets and a person, a man who loved money more than the people around him, and was haunted by his past, present, and looming future.

Claire seemed to know most of the script by heart and said more than half the lines, along with voices, along with the characters.

By the end of the movie, though, she had curled up with her head on my leg and fallen asleep.

I couldn't bring myself to wake her. This was

peaceful, friendly, and made me miss what I had with Xander and Dom.

What I'd thought I had.

Because I'd assumed we had friendship and sex, and Xander was hiding more from me because…

If I entertained those thoughts I'd wonder if he was the only one lying to himself and love was weakness. Instead, I let the TV play its next suggested movie, *Miracle on 34th Street*, and tried to lose myself in the sugary old sweetness.

I didn't remember ever believing in Santa, but I used to believe in—

It didn't matter, because I'd been wrong, and now I knew better.

Why did Xander have to do this? Why didn't I see it coming? Why did it hurt so much?

Why did I want to make things right with him anyway, and tell him I loved him and he loved me and that he could never leave me again?

Why wasn't I strong enough to ignore all of that?

28 /
dominic

The things Xander said to Judith didn't come as a surprise to me—it was everything I'd assumed from what he'd said over the years—but I'd hoped if he said it out loud, if he heard the words himself, he'd realize he needed a shift in perspective.

But I understood where they were both coming from. I got why he felt that way and I knew exactly why Judith was furious.

They needed to talk, not clash and shatter the way they just had, but they also needed to admit how much in love they were.

Neither seemed likely.

The drive home with Xander was quiet, and the returned ring from Judith sat like a weight in my front shirt pocket. It wasn't the heaviest thing weighing on me though—the silence was oppressive and my heart should've dropped through the floor of the car by now.

When we reached home, the moment we stepped into the house, Xander gripped my face between his hands and pressed his mouth to mine in a long kiss. The kind of searing lip lock that scorched my soul.

I loved the affection, the same way I always had, but—

"That's not because of her." Xander pressed his forehead to mine. Why did saying Judith's name out loud make things worse, not better? "That's because of us. Because the one good thing about tonight was shouting to that entire bar that I love you. *Fuck* that felt good."

He'd get no arguments from me. "It sounded incredible. I never should've asked you to wait so long. I should have… I'm going to make it right."

"You already are." The way he held me, the heat that flowed between us, was one of those bonds I didn't think anything could break.

But that didn't mean it was as strong as it could be. I would think that it sucked, feeling like something was missing, but it was a very specific someone and I couldn't regret wanting her or knowing that he did too.

Silence stretched between us, and the tension running through Xander's grip, the tightness that kept us locked together, faded into comfort.

I both hated to say what I was about to, and knew I had to. "Judith belongs in our lives too."

"She is in our lives." Xander's tension was back, springing him upright, and seeming to make his body hum.

She may not be anymore. Not after tonight. Not if they couldn't make things up to each other. "That's not what I mean," I said.

"Are you saying I'm wrong?" The challenge in Xander's question was unmistakable.

And yes, that was absolutely what I was saying. Fortunately, I was better at argument than saying so outright. There were better ways to approach this that still let me tell him the truth without him shutting me out in the process. "Judith thinks you are."

"And you?"

"I love you," I said. "I love her, and I'd told her that before what happened today, but our lives are complicated. I hope I still get the chance to tell her." And that my words mattered if she and Xander kept not speaking to each other. Yes, I wanted them both with me, but it wouldn't be the same if they weren't both with each other as well. "What you two tell each other, that's not up to me. But if you said to me what you said to her, I'd be pissed off too."

Xander clenched his jaw and his nostrils flared. "Think about it a little longer and maybe you'll understand."

"I've been thinking about it for years—the fact that you think you have to protect her from you—and I still don't get it."

"I can't help that." Like that, Xander pushed the tension away.

And that meant he wasn't going to hear a word I said. "I suppose you can't." Not any more than I could make him listen to me. It frustrated the hell out of me, but I couldn't force him and Judith to do anything they didn't want to, including admit they loved each other. I also wasn't willing to give Xander up. Yeah, I wanted Judith to be a part of that, but I was holding onto the love I had for all it was worth.

The less-than-satisfying end to our *discussion* bled into a night of saying very little to each other, and going to bed.

The muted mood led into the next morning. We'd been together long enough that silence was comfortable for us, but what lay underneath this particular lack of conversation... I didn't care for it.

"We should go out to breakfast." As I said the words, I wasn't sure if they were brilliant or idiotic, but they were *something*. "Near the law office. As a couple."

Xander's smirk told me I'd picked correctly. "We should, yes."

A giddy kind of anticipation hummed under my skin as we drove to one of our favorite breakfast places, a block or so away from where I worked.

Where I used to work. With everything else, I hadn't even dealt with the details of my walking away from the law firm. I'd start later today, making calls to current clients. Reese. Sonya. Others who worked directly and exclusively with me.

When Xander and I stepped from his car, it was both foreign and familiar to slide my hand into his. We'd been *out* the entire time with our friends, but we kept the public displays of affection to those places we knew were *safe*.

The spark when Xander brushed his lips over mine was potent, even though the kiss lasted less than a second.

I liked this. A lot.

The waitress was one we saw a lot, and she greeted us with a warm smile. Her gaze dropped to our intertwined hands, and a pause hung in the air. And then her smile was back, looking as genuine as ever. "Your table's free." She nodded toward the booth in the back.

"Thanks, Maribel," Xander said before leading me in that direction.

We still sat across from each other. I'd rather look him in the eye while we talked and ate than one of us claim the other the same way someone might claim a suitcase.

"Y'all want your usuals?" Maribel asked.

Xander and I exchanged looks, and both nodded. "Yeah. That sounds great."

"Perfect. I'll be back with coffee." She turned away. There was another pause, and she glanced over her shoulder at us. "It's about time." She walked toward the kitchen.

My cheeks heated and I let out a light laugh. "Did we ever really fool anyone?"

"Ourselves, maybe." Xander winked.

The same way you're fooling yourself about Judith. The thought was real. Valid. But this wasn't the time for it. He and I deserved moments that were ours, as much as she did with each of us.

We came here all the time, yet, as we ate, I found myself examining every little movement. It was like watching a witness in a courtroom, or studying someone during a contract negotiation. Except that *someone* was me.

Had Xander always poured my coffee when the waitress brought us a carafe? Did his hand really brush mine that many times during a meal? Was any of this normal? Was any of it abnormal?

"Hey." Xander reached across the table to tilt my chin up with his finger. His arms were long, but he still had to half-rise from his seat to do so. "Are you here?"

"Of course."

He brushed his fingertips over my lips before sitting again. "You sure? I don't need to crawl under the table and suck you off to get your attention?"

It was such an absurd-but-arousing question, it shattered the shell that had formed around my brain. "Don't let me stop you, but you've got my attention anyway."

"Good." Xander's grin was sexy. Confident. Exactly what I expected from the man I'd fallen for.

As we finished our meal, my doubt was gone. This was what it should be. What we always should've had. I was overthinking things because I'd done so for so long, but there was no need now.

We were together and we were out.

As we headed home my heart was soaring. Xander and I had waited for so long, because of me, and we finally got to have this thing I'd denied him for so long. This open, public love.

It was incredible.

So why was there a hollow pit inside that insisted it wasn't enough?

Because Judith wasn't here. Because this wasn't all three of us telling the world how we felt about each other.

29 /
xander

Breakfast with Dom was incredible. It was like being able to stroll naked through the center of the city without anyone caring. Exposed. Free.

I'd waited so long to tell the world I loved Dominic that doing so should be an all-consuming joy.

It was close. The part of my heart that belonged to him was shouting.

But part of me was distracted and that didn't seem fair to either of us.

I needed to talk to Judith and straighten things out. To make her see… Every time I got to that part of the thought, my brain ground to a halt and froze. It didn't matter, because I'd figure it out as soon as I spoke to her.

I'd tried to call, the words would come to me if she was on the line, but she didn't answer. Leaving a message wasn't the same. She always took my calls, so if she wasn't picking up she was in crisis mode.

Or screening me.

Anything I had to say wasn't going in a message. And it would be something along the lines of *understand where I'm coming from. I wanted to protect you. You can't be upset about that.*

That was exactly what I needed to say. Why didn't it feel right?

When Aunt Rosie showed up at our place early afternoon, I wasn't in the mood. "This is a bad time. I need you to call first."

She stepped into the house, keeping me from closing her out. "I've been calling for weeks. I need you to talk to me."

"I don't care what you do with the orchard house."

"Really?"

I turned away from her with a growl of frustration. This wasn't what I wanted to be dealing with right now. I wanted to be talking to Judith and for her to realize we shouldn't be fighting. Hearing people question my intentions was getting so old.

The thought surged in on a wave, and I didn't try to hold the feeling back. I faced Rosie again. "Of course I fucking care. You've sat on that property for years, ignoring what Mom wanted to do with it until she wasn't here to have a voice in the decision anymore. Until she passed that choice on to

Maddox and me. Now what? You expect us to yield where she didn't? Or maybe you want us to talk you into what she never could? You've turned this into a no-win situation, and I don't play those."

Rosie closed the front door behind her, but stayed in the foyer. "No. You never have."

Except for Judith. That was a loathsome thought. She wasn't a game. *So why did I...*

"If you're not going to budge, it won't hurt to hear me out," Rosie said.

That was horrible logic, and I'd said similar things on more than one occasion. "Fine. Come on in." I led her into the living room.

Dom was waiting for us. "Do you need anything? Drinks or anything?" he asked.

"I'm fine." Rosie waved him off as she settled onto the couch.

"Thanks." I squeezed his hand. He would know there was a lot in that single word. *Nothing for me, thanks. Knowing you're nearby and listening is a comfort, thanks. Thanks for standing by me.*

Dominic kissed me on the cheek. "I'll be in the kitchen."

Thanks.

"The two of you are good together," Rosie said when he was gone.

"Yeah, we are." Resentment tinged my reply. She'd never once said that about Judith.

But she was right about Dominic, and it wasn't

as though I wanted my relationship with him to change. Not after we'd made it this far. Not now that I got to tell the world over and over that he was mine. "The orchard house?" I wanted the conversation away from me and my relationships.

"Your mom was right. I want to turn it into the safe haven she always envisioned."

"Oh." This was where I should hide my surprise and pull out the poker face. Too late. This was something we'd pushed her on for a while. I could dig in and remind her of that, but I'd hate to have her back down. What she was suggesting... There was no better way I could think of to honor Mom's memory. I still needed answers, though. "Why? After all this time?"

Rosie raked her fingers through her hair, leaving the short, platinum strands sticking up in every direction. "I was scared that I wasn't enough for it. That I wasn't the right person for the job. What do I know about saving people?"

Why did those words hit hard? "You saved Judith." In a way I never would. Never could. I sank into the chair next to Rosie and rested my elbows on my knees.

She shook her head. "No. She saved herself, I just gave her a safe place to do so, and that's what I want for others as well."

That was what Mom had wanted, too.

"Maddox is on board," Rosie said. "He's

agreed to sign anything he needs to, but you know I can't move forward unless you both give me permission."

After all this time, was it really so simple? I was tempted to put up a fight, simply because I'd expected one.

"Xander will sign too." Dominic's voice came from behind me.

I looked over my shoulder to see him standing in the kitchen doorway, arms crossed.

"But the contract goes through me," he added.

Fuck I loved him. "You heard my attorney."

"That went better than I expected." The smile that slipped onto Rosie's face was subtle and relieved. "Do I dare bring up the second thing I've been asking you about?"

Which was...? "Might as well."

"Are the three of you coming for Christmas dinner?"

Right. That. "Dom and I will bet there."

"Judith?"

Other people, I might assume they'd make things right in the next week or so. She and I... No telling which of us was more stubborn. I hated the idea of not talking to her for so long, but at this point, "She's not speaking to me."

Rosie's joy vanished behind a frown. "Why not?"

"It's complicated." But was it really? I knew she

was too good for most anyone, and I had her back for those times when she didn't realize that.

Which she didn't appreciate.

You know that's not it.

That was exactly it.

So why did my heart put up a more painful resistance every time my brain doubled down on the truth?

"I've been thinking a lot about the two of you lately. You and Judith." Rosie ducked her head in a way that was uncharacteristic of her. "You may not want to hear this." She looked at Dom.

He probably wanted to hear it more than I did.

"I'm good." He moved further into the room and settled on the arm of my chair.

Rosie nodded and turned her attention back to her clasped hands. "It goes with the work, I suppose. Making a decision like this, I can't help but think of that day you called me. That night she came to live with me."

"And?" I should've brushed the words off. Told her *that's good*, or something equally as generic. I shouldn't be prompting the conversation to move forward. But I'd spent so much time living mentally in that same space for the last few weeks, I had to hear how her thoughts were different than mine.

How melodramatic was I to think my reality depended on it?

Too melodramatic. I needed to stop.

"I projected a lot of my fears onto her—onto you—while she was staying with me." There was a heavy regret in her voice. "And even years later, at your mother's funeral I said some things— I doubt you remember, but those words have haunted me."

"Hmm." I didn't do *haunted*. I did practical. Realistic. I learned from the past and never made those mistakes again.

Dom squeezed my shoulder, and I swore something cracked inside, but I didn't know what.

Rosie searched my face. For what? The way she looked away made me think she didn't find it.

"I don't want to say something like that to someone else," she said. "So few people are as strong as you. As Judith... You've become an incredible man."

Of course I had. I never would have been anything less. "But?"

"And she's an amazing woman. But you and Judith together"—

Are dangerous. Are toxic.

—"You make each other even better, in a way that shouldn't be possible." Rosie looked at Dom. "Not that you don't..."

Dom chuckled. "I'm not going to argue. I think the same thing."

"I'm sorry I ever said otherwise." Rosie stood. "Even if you don't remember, I do, and I'm sorry."

I wasn't sorry. "I'm glad you stopped by." I gave

her a quick hug. "Dom and I will be there on Christmas. Send him the house paperwork when you have it." My phone chimed as we pulled apart.

Judith?

"All right." Rosie's smile was tight. "I'll talk to you soon."

"I'll see you out." Dominic to the rescue.

Tension cranked through me as I reached for my phone, and disappointment crashed around me when I saw Wade's name on the screen. I wasn't in the mood for this right now, and if he thought I was blunt before, he was about to feel the mallet's flat end of my mood.

"Yeah," I answered.

"Do you have a few minutes?"

"I have an entire afternoon to tell you all the ways you're wrong."

Wade's chuckle was dry. "No need. I've already figured that out. You know how much it hurts me to say you were right and I was wrong."

Apparently my day was going to be full of *what the fuck* moments that were good. This was good, wasn't it? "I do know. So why are you saying it?"

"Because it's true." Wade sighed. "I've been going over Oliver's decisions recently. Not just my gut, but the hard data, and yeah, it's been costing us. It sucks to say, but sometimes even the people we love can be wrong."

Couldn't say I'd been there.

Uh-huh.

"So thank you for sticking to your guns," Wade said. "I'm going to save the *we need to part ways* conversation with Oliver until after Christmas, but I won't let him do anything before then that makes a difference."

"I'm sorry you have to do that." Finally, my brain was working well enough to sound intelligent. "But you're making the right choice. And yeah, I'd be bummed too if I was in your shoes."

"You and Judith are lucky to have each other." Wade's comment seemed to come out of nowhere.

Right now we didn't have anything. "Okay?"

"You have the kind of faith in her that few people ever find, and as far as I can tell, she deserves it."

"Thanks. See you on Monday?"

"Yeah." Wade sounded lighter.

I was jealous of that. I wanted to feel this heavy weight lifted. But Wade was wrong about one thing —I didn't have Judith. I'd pushed her away for so long…

The thought hurt. It ached everywhere. I needed her back, and I was already dialing her number as Dominic walked back into the room. Fuck, I needed her. I loved her. I had to tell her.

Her voicemail picked up again.

She was screening me. I had no doubt now. I wouldn't tell her I loved her in a recording. This was something I was only saying to her face, and I'd make sure she knew how much I meant it.

And if I couldn't have her back...

I didn't know, but I'd never lost anything this important before, and the feeling was the worst.

30 /
judith

I ignored Xander's calls on Saturday. If he thought he had some magical penis that could keep me from succeeding, I didn't need to talk to him.

But I missed both him and Dominic. Why did Xander have to go and be an idiot about this? Why did I have to want that he could give me a good reason to forgive him?

I picked up when Cole called on Sunday morning, and it almost felt traitorous to talk to him but not Xander. Which it shouldn't, and I was being ridiculous. Though, if he was calling to congratulate me on my bullshit engagement, I didn't want to listen.

"I would've called last week, after we ran into you at dinner" he said after we exchanged *hellos*. "But I figured you'd be busy, and that meant you'd blow me off."

"I would never." I feigned hurt.

He laughed. "You would frequently. But I learned a long time ago not to resent you for that. Are you really engaged? Should my congratulations be sincere?"

It figured, the one friend I had in this world, the one person who knew me this well, was my ex-husband. Dominic probably came close, but he had a bias. Toward Xander, who I'd be having this conversation with in any other circumstance. "Are you free today? Have lunch with me?"

"Name the place, I'll meet you there."

"Thank you." I didn't want to be alone today, and Claire was sweet, but I suspected this wasn't a situation she'd understand.

A short while later, I met Cole at a little hole in the wall diner halfway between his place and mine. A spot that didn't have memories of Xander associated with it. We grabbed a table, and ordered coffee.

"Are you really engaged?" Cole asked again.

I was grateful he didn't do small talk, but today at least a little would've been nice. "No." Not anymore. *Never again* would be best. "Thank you for playing along."

Cole was a big man. Imposing. He demanded attention just by walking in a room. It was easy to see now why I'd fallen into his arms back then, when Xander was so out of reach.

I never should've done that to him, but we'd hashed that out before.

Except the Xander part.

"You probably won't tell me, but what's up?" Cole's question overlapped my thoughts.

I shrugged. "Why would anything be up?"

"I realize I'm not the most perceptive person in the world, but Luna has worn off on me, or something. And I know you. Something is up."

Yeah, it was. I hated this weakness. This *need* to not be alone. I was supposed to be strong and independent, not needy and looking to others for answers. "Why are you the only person left in my life I can talk to?"

The waitress came back with coffee and water. Cole drank his black, and way too hot. I made sure mine was sweet enough to give me a sugar high even without the caffeine. At least some things never changed.

"You have Xander. You've *always* had Xander." The way Cole said his name, casually as if it were just another word, made an ache grow inside.

I didn't have Xander at all. Had I ever? He thought he was being my knight, which I never asked for, and I thought…

What? That we were enlightened because we could be friends and have sex and not need more? And I missed him. I missed Dominic. Despite what Xander had done. What he'd assumed.

"Be honest." I needed to climb out of my own head. "Was he ever a problem between us?"

Cole studied me. "We had an open marriage. We were both always seeing other people. The only problem I had was you never admitted what you were."

Because we were just friends.

I didn't believe that. I didn't want that. "I can't talk to him about this." Because it's about him.

"That's why you need to." Did Cole know what I wasn't saying? Luna really had rubbed off on him.

"You mean the world won't mend itself magically?" I meant to joke. It didn't feel funny.

He shook his head. "Why can't you talk to him? Details, not vagaries."

"Because we are who we are." I wasn't sure I could recap the fight, and I didn't know a better way to explain the situation otherwise.

"That says so much more than it should." Waving down the waitress, Cole had her bring us more coffee.

"And fries too. Lots of cheese." This sucked. "I used to be friends with the guys at work. Why can't I talk to them?"

As if it was taunting me, the scratchy speaker playing Christmas music started to push out *All I Want for Christmas is You* by Mariah Carey.

Cole sipped his coffee slowly, setting it down when

our waitress returned with the pot, and drinking more as soon as she was gone. "You mean the men you've spent twenty years reminding you're in charge?" he finally said. "You hold their futures in your hand."

But we were all friends. "I really don't. Not them. I run the company, but they're my equals." Except I didn't believe that. I never had. They were all skilled. The best at what they did, but...

"They're not your equals. You're one in a million and no one can stand next to you."

My breath caught at the sincerity in Cole's words, but I was also surprised to hear *him* say it. "What about Luna? Graham?"

"They're also one in a million, and you don't come close to what they are." Like that, he took the moment away. "But they're their own people, and they would never have succeeded the way you have."

"Do you think I've made the wrong choices?" I didn't know where the question came from. I *knew* my decisions were the right ones, and I didn't need anyone else to confirm that for me.

"For you or for me?" Cole asked. "Because I'd be miserable in your life, but you're exactly where you've always wanted to be. Where you're meant to be."

I should take the observation for what it was and move on. "Then why does it feel like something's missing?" Nope. Not where I needed this conversation to go.

"Why are you and Xander really not speaking?"

The fries arrived. Greasy. Salty. With way too much cheese. Perfect for giving me a minute to collect my thoughts. I shoved a bite in my mouth, and ignored that it scalded me on the way down.

When I finished the bite, Cole still hadn't said anything.

"This engagement bullshit, the last few weeks, so many things have gone wrong." The words tumbled out without my permission, and I couldn't rein them back in. "There was the way this Elliot bullshit spiraled, the board is collapsing, Chris was sabotaging the game—he's been with us from the start and he— I was playing house instead of taking care of business." I snapped my mouth shut around another bite of fries before I could say more.

Cole took another long sip of coffee, as if he was going to wait me out, then set the mug down. "Everything you just described would've happened regardless. None of it was because you dared to care about something other than the company. And you handled it regardless, because you've put this structure in place to do so.

"Yes, it sucks to lose people, to have people betray you, I'm sorry. But you always plan for these things. Even if the people working for you aren't your BFFs, you're not doing things alone, because you made sure of it. You're allowed to have a life outside of the company and it doesn't mean you love AcesPlayed any less."

I... No. How did that all make so much sense? It shouldn't, because it meant I'd missed something crucial, and it was still just out of my grasp.

"You don't have to put AcesPlayed on hold to love Xander," Cole said. "You didn't have to set aside your career for me, either, but he understands your drive. Xander gets you in a way I never could, and he always has. Honestly, for the longest time I didn't think anyone else could compete with what the two of you are, but Dominic... He proved me wrong. All three of you together."

"I don't remember you being this insightful when we were married." I liked the sound of what he had to say, and I was tired of fighting it, but Cole's words didn't solve my biggest issue.

Cole almost looked sheepish. "I didn't know Luna when we were married." He was so smitten for the people he loved. It was adorable and rare and I loved seeing it for him. For them. Was I just the teensiest bit jealous, too? Maybe.

"Speaking of impenetrable bonds," I teased.

"Too easy. But also, you could have that with them."

But I couldn't. "If Xander feels the way he said he did. If he thinks I need..." I couldn't even say the words to repeat what he'd told me. "I can't."

"I've never seen you give up on something you're passionate about."

Though the conversation moved to less angsty things, Cole's words lingered through the rest of the coffee. Through us finishing off the fries, and me heading home.

I was surprised to find Claire gone when I stepped inside. As far as I knew, she hadn't left since I brought her home almost a week ago. Not that I was trying to keep her here, she had the car, but she didn't feel she could go to most of her friends. Based on how they'd *helped* her in the past, I was inclined to agree.

There was a note on the table that said *went to my mom's.*

I wanted that to be a good thing—Claire shouldn't have to surrender her life because of Dale —but I couldn't help the worry that bubbled up inside. I was about to call, just to check in with her, when a key rattled in the lock.

Claire stepped into the condo, smile on her rosy cheeks. "Hey, you're back. How'd it go?"

"It was… good." I meant that. The conversation with Cole had my head spinning, but it also had me feeling better. "How about you?" *Did your mom tell you to stop being a bad wife? To go back home to your asshole husband like a good girl?*

"It was good." Claire's smile grew. "I thought she might be mad, you know, about this whole Dale thing, but she was really understanding. She said she was just happy I was safe."

There was a whisper of jealousy that her mom *got it*, but that was drowned out by my relief.

"Plus, I snagged some extra decorations." Claire held up two large Christmas gift bags.

"Yay." I tried to find some enthusiasm, but couldn't grasp what I needed.

Stepping past me, Claire moved into the living room and set the bags down. "I promise it's not a lot, and we'll have fun." She sounded undeterred by my response. "I have lights, tinsel, and icicles." As she talked, she pulled things from each bag, and set them in distinct stacks on the coffee table.

None of them looked too brash or obnoxious. They were all tasteful, gold or silver, and simple. Was that a hint of disappointment inside that she didn't want to hang bright, garish colors around my condo?

No. But I did suddenly want the feeling of warmth and cheer in here. For the longest time, I let Xander be a driving force in how much I decorated for Christmas. It was all part of a kind of twisted and unofficial tradition. He'd remind me I needed to decorate and not be a Scrooge, I'd sigh and make a big production out of *again, this year?* And he'd be here.

Even the first few years after he and Dominic got together, it was the same.

Why did we stop?

Because I found reasons not to. Year after year, work was too much, I put the guys off, there were more important things to do.

Because I couldn't see them together, especially this time of year. I couldn't look at Xander, at Christmas, with someone like Dom.

Someone who had Xander's heart in a way I never could.

God, that hurt. The truth was a bitch sometimes. Why did he have to say to me what he did?

"Are you okay?" Claire looked concerned.

No. My heart was broken. Was that stupid? How else was I supposed to describe this ache in my chest? There was nothing I couldn't fix... except this.

I was startled when Claire threw her arms around me and squeezed tight.

"What are you...?" I didn't have a choice but to hug back. My body wouldn't let me ignore this.

"I don't know what's making you look like that, and you probably don't want to talk to someone silly and inexperienced like me, but I'm here."

The longer she squeezed, the more the weight on my chest lifted. The frustration and pain didn't go away, but they no longer felt overpowering. "Thank you." I took a deep breath, lingered a little longer, and gently broke away. "I'll grab a step ladder. How do we attach these things to the wall?"

"I have hooks." Claire said.

This would be fun. "Perfect. Let's do this."

We dove into decorating. The longer we worked, the more Claire's holiday cheer buoyed me. There was no reason to talk about work, and she didn't seem any more interested in small talk than I was, so we flitted from one topic to the next.

"We should watch more Christmas movies when we're done." She handed me three plastic icicles with hooks.

I positioned them on the strand of tinsel I was next to. "You really like those. The world isn't always rainbows and butterflies and happily ever after." I wasn't trying to be cruel, but I did want to understand.

Hopping down, I moved the step ladder over a few feet, and climbed again to hang more ornaments.

"I realize that," Claire slipped hooks into plastic with practiced efficiency. "Not sure if you noticed, but everything around us spends a lot of time trying to remind us how much the world sucks. Pain sells. And people pay a lot of money to escape it."

That was one of the most profound things I'd heard in a long time. "Denying it doesn't make it go away."

"I'm not denying anything. I may work to make bad situations good..." She trailed off.

When Claire didn't finish her thought, I glanced

at her. She was thinking about Dale, I was certain of it. Before I could reassure her, she gave a quick shake of her head. "But that doesn't mean I ignore the bad," she said. "And sometimes, most of the time, enjoying genuinely kind things feels like its own sort of defiance. You know? Like giving the world the finger and telling it I can feel good despite its attempts to the contrary."

I'd never heard happy endings described as defiance before. "I like it. You pick the movies and I'll watch."

"*Yay.*" Claire clapped.

My phone rang. *Xander?* I reached for the device without thought.

No. Grant's name was on the screen.

"I have to get this," I said to Claire, and hopped the few steps to the floor. "This is Judith," I answered.

"It's Grant Lent."

I know. Thanks for the update though. "What can I do for you?"

"I got your call Friday, about Elliot. You're making a mistake." Of course he didn't apologize for waiting to call me back, for doing so on a Sunday, or for shitting on my resolution.

And I wouldn't back down. "I disagree. This is one of the best possible solutions, given the circumstances."

The sigh Grant let out was one I'd heard too

many times in my life. I didn't used to interpret it as *silly woman, you don't get it,* but over time that became all I heard in a noise like that.

"If you run this business based on emotions, on *friendship* you will fail," Grant said.

"No." My reply came easily. "Compassion, reason, instinct all have their place when they're used right. This isn't about any of that—it's about not burning a bridge with one of the brightest minds in the industry. The numbers say that."

Another sigh from Grant. How many until I set a personal record? "Call it what you will, but I won't be involved with a company that runs itself this way."

Was that a threat? I didn't know if he was bluffing, hoping for me to yield, or if he was just pulling out, period.

That was fine. I'd pick my interpretation and make the final decision. "I'm sorry to hear that, but I understand. I'll have a buy-out offer to you by Wednesday, that's based on the terms of our contract."

"You're making a mistake," he repeated.

And if he didn't have anything new to say, this conversation was over.

"No, you are. AcesPlayed is about to take off in ways I don't think you can wrap your brain around. We will be one of the biggest game companies in the world. People will know our name, and not just because we make a game with sex and nudity. But your opportunity with us has passed. You'll have a buy-out offer by Wednesday. Happy holidays, Mr. Lent."

I hung up in the middle of his sputter-sigh.

He was wrong about something else, too. The same thing I'd been wrong about for a long time. AcesPlayed *was* personal, and I could mix that with business and still be successful. I had up to this point, and there was no reason to cut myself off now from a good thing.

I just needed Xander to realize that us admitting how we felt about each other didn't mean the world ended. It didn't stop me from being more for him, and that maybe us loving each other, loving Dom, was the best possible way to give the world the finger.

I dialed his number, and after several rings, went to voicemail.

Please, Xander, for once in your life don't be an unyielding ass about this.

31 /
dominic

X ander and I decided to spend Sunday afternoon cleaning out my office. I'd still be on long enough to transition clients and any outstanding work, but I wanted my personal items out of there now. I was ready to make a clean break.

The books were the easiest to box up, and the heaviest to haul out, so we took care of those first. When the back of my SUV was stacked with a few rows of books, we returned to my office for the trinkets.

I pulled my framed degree off the wall, and an ache pinged in my chest. "I thought I'd be here until I retired," I said softly.

"I know." Xander pressed into my back. "But what's ahead of you is even better."

Right. A fresh start. A place I didn't have to hide me. Us.

Xander pressed his lips to my cheek, took the

diploma from me, and set it carefully in a box. "Besides, you still have me, and I'm incredible."

"True." My chuckle dropped off as a new thought slid in. Was I a failure as a lawyer that I hadn't seen such an obvious counter sooner? "Why are you good for me and not Judith?" I didn't want to pick a fight, but I had to know.

Xander frowned and leaned his weight against the edge of the desk. "I was hoping you wouldn't ask that until I figured out the answer myself. It's the same question that's been nagging me since Rosie left this morning."

I took the spot next to him, our arms pressed together. "Sorry-not-sorry. Why does your loving her mean she won't succeed, but it doesn't mean the same for you and me?"

"Because..." Xander cleared his throat with a cough. "She doesn't need me. She never has."

I wanted to say *that's not true*. Anyone could see they needed each other. That assurance had to come from her, and I was afraid if I said anything, he'd stop talking.

"You and I, we make each other more," Xander said. "Since that first night, I saw something in you... We make each other better."

I felt like we were close to the truth but not quite there. "So do you and Judith. Look, I don't care if you think she's perfect and can do no wrong."

"I don't—"

He did. "And I don't care if you want to keep her on a pedestal," I talked over him. "My point is, she may not want to be up there, and if you're going to put her there, you belong up there with her."

"That doesn't make sense."

I rested my head on his shoulder. "Neither do your reasons for refusing to admit how you feel about her. I love you, but sometimes you're as stubborn as a rock."

"That doesn't—" Xander let out a noise exhale. "Do you want to make a detour when we're done here?"

To Judith's. The unspoken part of the question was as loud and clear as the rest of it. "Yeah. I do."

"What is this? Where are all your books?" Roger's voice cut through the somber-sweet mood.

I stood and turned to find him standing in the doorway. "It's what it looks like. I'm cleaning out the bulk of my things."

"Why?" Roger's laugh was tight.

I stared at him for a moment. Was he joking? "Because we agreed it was best for both of us if I moved on. Away from the firm. I wasn't planning on sneaking out in the middle of the weekend, but I do want to get a start on moving my stuff."

"That wasn't... We weren't... That was a disagreement. It happens," Roger said.

What? "This wasn't a lovers' quarrel. You and I

have a different opinion about how this firm should be run, and I'm moving on."

Xander straightened up and turned to stand by me. I loved knowing he had my back.

Roger raised his brows. "There's always compromise in business. We refine contracts for a living, you know that better than anyone."

"Yes, there are times when compromise is appropriate, for me, this isn't one of them. If you're going to work with Dale Monson, I'm not going to work with you." I didn't want to have the exact argument we'd already had, but if Roger needed to hear it again...

"Speaking of Dale," Roger said. "I just got off the phone with him as I was driving in."

Why did every alarm in my brain just go off? "Okay."

"He wanted to let me know he'd found his wife, and he was heading over to pick her up."

Fuck.

Xander was sprinting toward the exit, and I was right on his heels. Maybe nothing was wrong. Maybe it would be fine.

I wasn't willing to take that chance.

I slammed the tailgate shut on my SUV, as Xander slid into the driver's seat. I was barely inside before he was pulling out of the parking lot.

"Call her," he said.

I'd already dialed, but her phone rang again and again before it went to voicemail.

We were overreacting, and this was fine.

My gut said otherwise. Why did we have to be downtown, the weekend before Christmas, when we needed to be there, at her place?

I dialed again. "Dale knows where to find Claire. Call me back the minute you get this," I said, then hung up and sent the same thing in a text.

Please let us be overreacting.

32 /
judith

The sound of someone hammering on my door made me frown. When the noise got louder, and Dale's shouted, "I know you're in there," reached Claire and me, the air all rushed from my lungs.

I knew how this went. I'd seen my mother go through it, and in this moment, my memories were as fresh as if it happened yesterday. "How did he know…?" I was asking myself more than Claire.

"I swear, I only told my mom." Her voice was tiny. Terrified. "And she promised just between us. Oh my gosh, I didn't… what do we do?"

Two things we wouldn't do were cower or cave. "Do you want to go home with him?"

Claire's hesitation was another reason for my heart to drop. "No," she said. "I really don't."

"Okay." That was enough for me. "Call 911.

Tell them you're separated from him and you don't want him here. Stay out of sight."

With wide eyes and her phone clenched in her hand, Claire nodded and scurried from the living room.

Time to do this.

I kept my exterior calm, despite the fact that my heart was hammering against my ribs so hard, it might break free at any minute, and I opened the door enough to see Dale. "May I help you?"

"Let me see Claire." His command was firm, and his face bright red, but we were still at the *I'm going to intimidate you with my presence, to get my way* part of things.

"She's not here. Please go." The shorter my answers, the less room there was for misinterpretation. I nudged the door shut.

Dale jammed his foot in the way. He used his body to shove both the door and me back a few inches. "I'll wait."

"No. You won't." It didn't matter that I was several inches shorter than Dale, I raised myself to full height and stepped in his path. "Leave."

For a heartbeat, his face twisted into something ugly, but his imposing blankness returned quickly. "You don't need to be involved in this. Tell me where my wife is."

"I don't know." I had no guilt about lying. Not

to him. Not now. At least, unlike the non-existent engagement to Dom, this was a worthy mistruth.

"*He's in the house.*" Claire's timid voice filtered into the room.

Fuck. I planted my feet firmly and stood between Dale and the rest of my home. "Leave. Now."

"*Claire,*" he shouted. "I just want to talk to you."

Please don't come out. Please don't come out. "Leave. Now."

"What did you say to her to make her do this?" Dale asked.

My inner little girl was whimpering and backing into a corner, but she wasn't me. I wasn't her. I didn't dare look at anything but him. I didn't dare take my attention off him or break eye contact or give any indication I was backing down. "Nothing. Get. Out."

"I just want to talk to my wife." Dale reached for me.

"Don't touch her." Someone grabbed his wrist, and Xander's low growl almost made me whimper in relief.

Dale jerked away from the touch and whirled. When his gaze landed on Xander, his entire body went rigid. "Who the hell are you?"

In response, Xander took a step toward him.

Dale backed up.

I was aware of Dominic moving deeper into the

house, presumably to check on Claire, But I was fixated on the scene in front of me. As Xander advanced, angling his body with each step, Dale retreated, until his back hit the wall.

"If you lay another hand on me, you'll find yourself in civil lawsuit hell for the rest of your life." Dale's voice wavered.

Xander held up his hands and stopped a short distance away.

I couldn't help but notice it was within Xander's reach, but not Dale's. "I'd rather not touch you," Xander said.

Any other situation and I might snicker at that.

"Good." Some of Dale's confidence seemed to return and he moved to step around Xander.

"You do want to hear me out, though." A low, threatening current ran through Xander's words.

Dale stalled. "I doubt that."

Xander dipped his head close to Dale, as if to share a secret. "If you come near Claire again without her initiating, now, ever, your reputation in this state, in your church, will look far worse than what I'd do to your face with my fist." Xander's voice carried clearly through the whole room.

Now Dale's expression had shifted to fury. There was no more blank, neutral mask. "Do you know who I am?"

Did he really just say that? Why was I surprised?

"I do." Xander nodded. "Do you know who *I* am?"

This was fascinating and terrifying and did I mention fascinating? Also, I was swooning a bit. A big bit.

"Nobody," Dale said.

I wished I could see Xander's face right now, for a variety of reasons, but because I pictured a slow, threatening smile sliding into place. "I'm Lewis Haddar's oldest grandson." Holy shit, he'd pulled out the family name. "Do you know what a man like that could do to your standing?"

"That's an empty threat." The way Dale chuckled, he wasn't convinced. "You're the family black sheep. You've all-but been disowned."

"It doesn't matter. I still wear my family name, and if you know my grandfather, you know that legacy is everything. He may not like me, but I mean a hell of a lot more to him than some random abusive prick who wields their god and faith like a shield. Walk out of this house now. Never come near Claire again. Or Judith. Or Dominic. Never let me find out that you've talked to anyone I care about."

I was a strong, smart, independent woman who probably could've handled this myself, but was I turning into a swoony puddle at how Xander was doing it? Definitely.

He turned away from Dale, and the world

slowed to a crawl. I watched, stunned, as Dale swung a wild punch at the back of Xander's head.

And missed, clipping his shoulder instead.

Now I could see Xander's expression, and the way his eyes narrowed was sexy in a terrifying kind of way. "Now I'm going to hit you." He drove his elbow into Dale's gut.

"Sir, step back please." That was a new voice, and the way he said *please* told me it wasn't a request.

The police were here. That was a good thing, wasn't it?

Xander held up his hands and put a few feet between him and Dale.

"Elder Monson?" Officer One hovered his hand over his taser. "Are you all right?"

Fuck.

"This man just assaulted me." Dale's calm, authoritative mask was back.

No. Uh-uh. He wasn't doing that here. "This is *my* home. *Elder Monson* forced his way in." My heart plummeted when Officer Two faced me, expression tight. Holy shit, I recognized him.

"It's you." Carl smiled. "From the gas station."

Was this for real?

"Who else is in the house?" Officer One barked.

"My roommate, and my friend." Out of the corner of my eye, I saw Claire and Dominic step into the room.

Dale clenched his jaw. "Roommate? That's my wife. You took her. You've kept her here."

Was he serious right now? Of course he was. "You dropped her at a gas station and she called me for a ride," I said.

"Enough." Officer One didn't look happy to be surrounded by so many unknown variables. "Nobody move while we sort this out."

"I just want to take my wife home." Dale didn't move.

He wasn't taking her anywhere. "She doesn't want to go with you." I turned to Officer Two. "You never called me."

"I didn't think you were serious."

Xander's fingers twitched, but he kept still.

"I don't joke about handing my business card out." Could I pull off sweet and in control at the same time? We were about to find out. "Please. This man forced his way into my home. He threatened my roommate, and he tried to hit my friends. Please take him out of here."

Office One gestured with one hand, still keeping the other near his holster. "You three, over there." He waved at Claire, Xander, and Dominic.

They complied.

He stepped closer to Dale.

"My ID is in my purse, near the door." I nodded. "You have my permission to check it. This is the address on it."

Officer two kept half an eye on the room while he grabbed my purse. I guided him verbally to my wallet. He showed my driver's license to his partner, who scowled.

"Sir, you'll need to step outside, please," Officer Two said.

Dale was bright red, but there was no *Do you know who I am* this time.

After what felt like an eternity of giving our side of the story to Officer Two, he promised they would escort Dale from the condo property and tell him not to come back.

I would've preferred they take him to jail, but apparently he'd sweet-talked Officer One while we were giving our own statements.

As the police left, I watched to make sure Dale did as well. My pulse hammered in my ears. My head felt like it might explode from the tension.

But the way Xander and Dominic had stormed in here was possibly the sexiest thing I'd ever seen.

I turned to Claire. "He may come back. Do you remember the place where we picked up the car?"

She nodded.

"Go there. Tell Rosie I sent you and she should text me when you arrive. It's up to you how much you tell her, but let her know we're all right."

Xander pocketed his phone. "I just texted her. She knows you're on your way."

God I loved him. It both ached and soothed to think those words.

Claire grabbed some things, and gave me a huge hug. "Thank you."

"I'll walk you to your car," Dominic said to Claire. "And you're not staying here either." He looked at me.

I'd tell him not to boss me around, but I loved his worry. That he was here. That they both were.

The instant they walked out the door, Xander turned to me. The look in his eyes was terrifying and enticing. He backed me to the wall, hands on either side of my head, and stood close enough I felt his heat.

"I would've torn him apart if he hurt you." Xander's voice was jagged. "I don't care how improper or unprofessional or illegal that is. If he'd touched you…"

We were still fighting, weren't we? I was still upset that he thought he had some magical presence in my life that determined my fate. Because at this moment, all I cared about was that he was here. That he was close. That he came for *me*. "He didn't."

"Good." Xander moved a hand to my face, and tingles spilled through me. "I'm sorry I said what I did. I don't have the right words to explain, because my mind is on other things, but we'll talk about it. The thing is, I'll never stop wanting to protect you. I can't—won't—change how I feel about you. But I do know you succeed because of you. Because you're incredible and one of a kind."

I know probably wasn't an appropriate answer. His intensity had me so tongue-tied I wasn't sure I could speak anyway. "So are you."

He smirked. "How long has it been since I kissed you?"

"Never." We both knew that. He had to be as intensely aware of it as I was.

Xander dipped his head and brushed his lips over mine. It was a soft, painfully tender kiss.

That grew hard in a flash when he slid his hand to grip the back of my neck, and crushed into me. His mouth was hard on mine. His body. The primal growls that rolled from his chest.

I could crawl up inside this feeling forever, and let it—him—consume me. Clenching his shirt tightly in my fists, I held on for all I was worth. This was better than breathing.

How did I think I was living without this connection?

33 /
xander

I'd been an idiot to pretend I didn't want Judith wholly and completely. To try to convince myself she was *just a friend*.

And now that I had her pressed to the wall, this woman who was a perfect blend of softness and strength, I didn't ever want to let her go. I couldn't stop kissing her. Tasting her. Even when we broke apart, I had to keep her face captured between my palms.

I pressed my forehead to hers, loving the way our jagged breathing blended musically. "I was so jealous when I saw that kiss between you and Dominic, that night at the *engagement* celebration. Jealous of him. Jealous of you." I was rambling. I didn't care.

"But you know what was worse?" I nipped her bottom lip. "What I never got over?" Another kiss. Another sigh. "That you let Cole take your virginity at one of those fucking orgies, in front of a room of coders."

"Virginity is a construct——"

I crushed my mouth to hers, letting desire mingle with and wash away regret. "It should've been mine. *You* should've been mine. Even though it took me this long to admit it, I've loved you since the day I met you, and you always should've been mine. If you want to be fucked in front of a room of horny programmers, if you want me to worship you with my mouth, where no one in the world can see, if you want something in between, I'll give it to you. Anything." I kissed her again and again. Tiny, short pecks... Hard nips... Anything that let me experience her.

"What if I want Dom, too?" Her question was soft, but there was no hesitation in her voice.

I smiled against her mouth and dragged a thumb along her cheek. "He's the only person I'll share your heart with, and I'm not letting him go either. I'll tell anyone and everyone that you're both mine. I'm tired of hiding it from the world and myself. I'd burn the world down for you, but that doesn't make me want him any less."

"I love you too." The way she said the words, breathless but with all the confidence I expected from her, was one of the hottest things I'd ever heard. "I love you so much it aches."

I kissed her on the nose. "You do like pain."

Her laugh was a masterpiece in art. "Touché."

"You two are terrifying when you work together." Dominic's voice wove its way into the moment. "And sexy as fuck."

I forced myself to pull away from the kiss enough to face Dominic, but I didn't let go of Judith.

"Don't stop on my account. I was enjoying the show," Dominic said.

Judith tangled her fingers with mine. "How long have you been back?"

"Long enough to hear everything we said about him." I wasn't sure, but I was pretty close.

The shock on Dominic's face was ridiculously exaggerated. "You were talking about me, and not just making out? I hope everything you said was good."

"It always is." Reaching out her other hand, Judith wiggled her fingers.

Dominic grasped her fingertips.

This was close to perfect, and I needed it to be completely there. "I propose we continue this somewhere safer." I kissed Judith on the forehead. "Pack a bag, you're coming home with us."

"Bossy much?" Like she had room to talk.

"Always." I let go of her hand to grip her chin. "It's an order, not a request."

Her smile was playful and mischief danced in her eyes, and if I hadn't still been hard from all the kissing, that look would've made my cock strain against my jeans.

"Yes, sir." Her compliance would've been hot, except that even if she was willing to yield in the bedroom, she never called anyone *sir* seriously.

Rather than call her on it, I smacked her ass as she walked away.

As she vanished into her bedroom, Dominic pressed into my back and wrapped his arms around my waist. He pressed his lips to my cheek. "It's about fucking time."

"That doesn't sound like positive reinforcement to me," I teased.

"The way you had your lips glued to hers was plenty positive. Enough charge in the fucking air to power this entire block of condos."

I smirked and faced him. "You know I still love you too, right?"

"I was here for that part."

"You deserve to hear me say it to your face. To see me... To..." Fuck it. "You're still my husband. I don't plan on what we have changing."

"It won't." He furrowed his brow. "Okay, it will. But not in a bad way."

That was fair. "You figured this out a long time ago, didn't you?"

"I did. But sometimes you're slow."

"I prefer *stubborn*," I corrected him.

"Toe-may-toe, toe-mah-toe," Judith said from behind me. "Sometimes you're slow."

This was still the same as it had been since we met Dom. The three of us riffing off each other. The easy teasing and conversation. I'd argue with their phrasing, but I already knew they were wrong. I took Judith's bag. "You're telling me you figured things out so much faster than I did?"

"As far as you know."

I rolled my eyes, and we headed out to Dominic's SUV. I put Judith's bag in the back, with his boxes. Something caught my eye and I slipped it into my inside front pocket.

"You're riding up here with me." I tugged Judith toward the front passenger seat.

She paused rather than climbing into my lap. "Pretty sure that's not legal."

"Fuck legal. I'm not letting go of you for a while." I offered her my hand.

She shrugged and hopped up. It took her longer than it probably should to get settled, and her squirming had my dick aching for more.

As we headed toward the house, there was so much I wanted to say, but I didn't want to do it here. It would wait until we were home, safe and warm, with the people I loved.

"You know…" Judith's tone had shifted to something more demure. More somber. "When I saw

Dale at my front door, when I heard him shouting, my entire past came back."

"I know what you mean." At least, from my perspective. I wrapped my arms around her, and she leaned her head on my chest.

Dominic navigated city streets with practiced ease. "You both handled it brilliantly."

"He's right," I said. "You were brilliant."

"I know. I never said I wasn't." Like that, Judith sounded like herself again.

I smirked and leaned my cheek against her head.

A short while later, Dominic parked in the garage, and we headed inside. The instant we were through the door, the urge to pin Judith to the wall was back. That *need* to claim her and fuck her until none of us could think or walk.

But the desire was tempered with the fresh thoughts of the encounter with Dale.

Besides, I'd never romanced her. It was either friendly fun or hard fast sex. And I had the perfect idea to change the tone of the evening. "Have you eaten yet?" I asked her.

"I had lunch with Cole, but that was hours ago."

Like that my jealousy was back, roaring with distaste.

She smacked me playfully on the chest. "Knock it off."

"What?"

"Being a jealous prick," Dominic said.

"I—"

Judith stared at me, challenge in her gaze. "You totally were." She draped her arms around my neck. "You shouldn't be jealous because Cole and I talked about you almost the entire time." She rose on her toes. "And how you and Dom own my heart."

I liked the sound of that. I gripped her waist and kissed her hard.

"Is that what I have to watch from now on?" Dominic's tone was playful.

Judith glanced over her shoulder. "You like to watch."

The way he twisted his face, he was considering the comment. "That's true."

She pulled away from me to face him. "And participate, I know." She gave him a quick kiss.

Inspiration struck. I knew how we were spending the next little bit. "Go put your bag in the bedroom." I'd do it for her, but she'd want to do things her own way.

She nodded and walked further into the house. I moved into the living room and Dominic followed. I grabbed the throw off the back of the couch, spread it in front of the fireplace, and flipped the switch to turn on the gas fire.

"Picnic. I love it." Dominic was already heading back to the kitchen. "I'll throw some food together. Keep your princess occupied."

Judith returned a moment later, and paused when she saw me near the blanket. "Picnic?"

"One of the single most romantic dates there is." I tried to repeat what she'd said a few weeks ago.

She joined me in front of the fire and wrapped her arms around my waist. "I love it."

Dom returned a short while later as well, with a tray of fruit, meat, and cheese. He'd managed to make cold cuts, Swiss, blueberries, and canned pineapple look like a delicate-but-casual meal for three. The beer in champagne glasses was the perfect finishing touch.

As the three of us settled on the blanket together, gratitude and love flowed through me. This was more perfect than I ever thought my life would be. A kind of serene love I'd never dared admit that I wanted.

The way Judith laughed when Dom tried to feed her. The way Dominic wrinkled his nose in amusement when Judith teased him about how delicate his meat looked on a platter. That instead of a past full of regrets, I saw a future of possibility stretching out ahead of us, with all three of us, set to conquer anything that stood in our way.

34 /
judith

Shortly after we started eating, all three of us got the same text from Rosie that Claire had arrived and was safe.

I knew the feeling.

Xander thanked Rosie and promised to call her later, and we went back to one of the sweetest gestures I'd ever been gifted—a picnic by the fire.

If someone had asked me a month ago if my life was complete, with RinCon and the game release looming, I would've said *of course*. But I would've done so ignoring the little pit inside that said I was lying.

Now I knew it was okay to need other people. To want Xander and Dominic, their love and adoration, in addition to the things I'd achieved. That loving them didn't make me weak or somehow lessen who I was.

We finished eating, and cleared off the blanket.

None of us drank much considering Dom had split a single beer between three glasses.

This was nearly perfect.

Nearly.

"Don't get me wrong," I said. "I love your company, and the gesture was super sweet."

"But...?" Xander asked.

I shrugged and tried to keep a serious expression, but the corners of my mouth tugged up. "I was pretty sure I was going to be fucked silly when we got here. All signs pointed to *yes, please.*"

"I thought we should wine and dine you first." Xander almost looked offended.

Dominic held up an empty can. "Beer and endear you?"

I loved how easy this was with them. "Consider me seduced." The casual banter was fun, but adrenaline and lust lingered. I wanted the result of those kisses Xander gave me earlier. I wanted to give myself to them and surrender control.

Xander shifted his weight to his hands and knees and crawled toward me. I leaned back on my arms and pressed my foot to his chest, holding him back, while I looked at Dom. "Are you going to get in on this?"

"No." Dom shook his head. "The two of you might combust, and I definitely want to watch, but I'm not sure I trust myself too close to the flames."

Xander pushed against my foot with a growl,

sending goosebumps racing over my skin. I'd yield soon, but they made me wait and this was fair in return. I extracted the novelty candy cane from where I'd tucked it into the waistband of my pants when I stole it from Xander's coat pocket.

"Where did you get that?" He had the nerve to look surprised.

"Where did you?"

"Dominic's desk. Someone gave it to him for Christmas."

Did they have any idea they were gifting their boss with a peppermint flavored dildo, or did they just think it was clever and festive? "And you thought *oh, hey, I should carry that in my coat pocket?*" I asked.

With a shrug, Xander nodded. "Well, yeah. That and I planned on using it on you."

Great minds. We thought a lot so often, how were we out of sync about each other for so long?

Denial sucked. But we were better now. "I was thinking the same thing." I tried to push him away with my foot. "Maybe you should join Dom in the watching." I didn't really want that, though.

Xander grabbed my ankle. "Maybe not." He shifted my leg out of his way, lunged, and grabbed the candy cane from me.

"Oh no." I exaggerated the distress in my voice. "Now what are you going to do with me?"

Xander continued the path up my body, until he

covered me enough to push me back with his entire frame. He used enough weight to pin me to the floor. "Whatever the fuck I want." His growl was enough to make my panties damp.

I loved this playfulness mixed with intensity. It was like what we'd had before, years ago, but more. As if a wall between us had come down. He crushed his mouth to mine, and my desire spiked at the heat that flowed between us. That feeling was never going to get old.

He deepened the kiss, plunging his tongue into my mouth to dance with mine. I couldn't get close enough to him, no matter how hard I tried, but that didn't stop me from pushing. From grinding.

He glided his hand over my sweater and underneath. His touch started on top of my bra, as he started rounding the bases. Were we really making out on a blanket in front of a fire like a couple of kids?

Yes. And I loved every second of it. I'd felt all of him before, but not like this. As I glided my hands over his shirt, this wasn't a quick fuck, it was an exploration, and I was going to memorize every inch of his body against mine.

But the longer we kissed and groped, the more I needed. He pushed my top and bra out of the way, and I stripped off his shirt. When I lowered my mouth to his nipple, to tease with my teeth, he let out another growl.

Apparently one of my boyfriends was going feral for me.

Boyfriend. I fucking loved it.

I glanced past Xander to find Dom watching us with an intensity that matched ours, while he stroked his erection through his trousers.

That was pretty hot too.

Xander dropped his hands to my pants, to undo the button and yank open the zipper, while I kicked off my shoes and undid his belt.

Now that the frantic need had sunk in, it seemed we couldn't get each other's clothes off fast enough. I was pretty sure we tore at least one thing, and I didn't care. Lying naked next to him, fleece on my bare skin and his gaze devouring me, was incredible.

Xander grabbed the candy cane and ripped the plastic with his teeth. When he had it more than half unwrapped, he pressed it to my mouth. I let him in without much resistance, holding his gaze as I dragged my tongue around the peppermint stick.

I wanted this to be a good show for both of them. Their attention as I did things to the candy that I usually reserved for their cocks was incredible. Like dozens of invisible fingers dancing over my body.

Sugary drool dribbled down my chin in my enthusiasm, and Xander and Dominic both groaned. The chill that raced over me was pure anticipation.

Xander drew the candy cane out and teased it over my nipples, leaving a sticky trail behind. The cool rush was similar to the ice, but not identical. When Xander pressed his mouth to my skin, to lick away the candy and suck on my nipples, the icy feeling lingered, mixing with warmth.

Need pulsed between my thighs, hot and slick, and I squeezed my legs together. The action intensified my want rather than muting it, but Xander kept up his attention on my breasts, nibbling and licking until I thought I might come just from his teasing and my anticipation.

He glided the candy down my body, leaving a sticky trail and licking along the same path. Over my stomach. Around my clit.

And when he penetrated me with peppermint, the cool both heated and chilled me. It was uncomfortable in the best possible way.

He dropped his face between my legs too, fucking me with the candy cane while he sucked on my clit. I'd never been eaten like this. *Fuck.* I clenched the blanket in my fists and pressed into his face. Climax was *right there.*

Xander pulled back, both candy and his mouth, right as I neared that peak, and disbelief rocked over me.

He gave me the most wicked smirk, and joined Dominic instead. I would've been disappointed, except they were sharing the candy cane. Licking it clean. Kissing each other while they sucked my juices off the stick.

"Clothes off," Xander said to Dominic, and dropped the peppermint toy on an empty plate. Xander turned back to me while Dom stripped.

I would've enjoyed the show a little longer, but Xander had his face between my legs again. He dove his tongue inside me, and I arched into the incredible sensation. He licked my inner walls with a hungry intensity that had my pulse racing and pushed me toward orgasm again.

But that release was just out of reach this time, having been snatched from me moments ago. I hung on that edge, grinding against his face, gasping and whimpering prayers in Xander's name.

When he pressed his fingers to my clit, it was like he'd found that button. The one that sent me tumbling into pleasure. I came hard, orgasm filling every inch of me, and making my toes and fingers curl.

When he pulled away, I was spent, but still wanted more.

Xander moved up my body again and captured my mouth with his. He tasted like peppermint and me, and I couldn't get enough. I couldn't stop kissing him. Tasting us. I was lost in the kiss when he slipped his cock inside me.

This was better. This was… I was a part of him. He was part of me. We were sticky and sugary and slick and joined. I gripped the back of his neck, loving the way the short hairs tickled my fingertips, and wrapped my body around his.

Dominic's grunts mixed with ours, making the entire thing even more delicious. He was jerking off to the sight of us.

I would be too.

Xander slammed into me hard and fast. Like fucking me just became an Olympic sport. Like there was no better contest to win. He mumbled against my lips. Words that barely made sense. That I felt so good. That he couldn't hold back.

The sounds Dominic made said he was close. He was coming.

God that sounded incredible.

I wrapped my legs tighter around Xander, pulling him deeper inside me. "I swear to God if you hold *anything* back"—I pushed the words out between desperate kisses and nips on his lips—"if you don't come inside me, I will never forgive you."

Xander's laugh was strained, and he hammered me harder.

The intensity, the sensation of being one with him, jerked another orgasm from me. I clenched around him, milking him, yanking him over the edge with me. I knew those thrusts. Those grunts. The way he stuttered and groaned when he spilled inside me.

I knew it because I dreamed about it, even when

I wouldn't admit it to myself. Because this was where we were always meant to be.

As the edge faded away, we slowed, then fell back onto the blanket together.

I didn't realize Dominic had joined us until he teased his fingers over my pussy. He dipped inside me, making me shudder, and pulled out quickly.

Then he pressed his mouth to mine, his fingers trapped between us. His tongue flicking over mine, over the taste of Xander. Me. Peppermint.

And then he gently pressed me back into Xander, who wrapped an arm around me and held me tight.

I remembered every time I'd lain wrapped up with Xander, and Dominic, after sex. None of them even ranked in the same class as this.

"I've been thinking…" Xander's words rumbled through my back.

Propping himself up, Dominic studied us. "When did you have time for thinking?"

"I'm talented."

I leaned more weight into Xander. "I'll say. What were you thinking?"

"I don't want you to go home. Or rather, I'd rather you call this *home*."

Oh. Should that terrify me? "Don't you two need to discuss this first? Before you ask me?" I should hesitate, shouldn't I? This wasn't the kind of thing to rush into, because it wasn't part of any plan I had.

"No," Dominic said. "At the risk of sounding cheesy, anywhere the two of you are is home."

I should keep questioning this. Diving into every detail and making sure it was the right decision.

But I knew this was where I wanted to be. Who I wanted to be with. "Okay."

Xander wrapped an arm tighter around me and kissed my shoulder. Dominic pressed into both of us.

He was right. *This* was home. Wherever they were. I'd spent so long believing that to rely on anyone completely besides me, to give all my faith to anyone else, made me weak.

But every day I needed the people around me. The people who worked for me. Claire's friendship. Cole's.

And Dominic and Xander's love.

It all made me better. More complete.

There was nowhere else I wanted to be than here, and no one else I wanted to be with than them.

35 /
dominic

"That coffee smells like heaven." Judith wandered into the kitchen, wearing one of Xander's T-shirts and rubbing sleep from her eyes. "Or Christmas. Is that today? Christmas day? Did Santa come?"

I poured her a cup of fresh coffee as she crossed the room. When she reached me, I swiped a kiss from her then handed her the mug. "In order of your questions," I said, " Yes, yes it is, and you'd have to ask Mrs. Clause."

"He said as if I remembered what I asked." She took a long sip of the drink, eyes half closed, and let out a contented sigh when she was done. "What were we talking about?"

"Were you talking about why my shirt is missing?" Xander joined us. His hair was mussed and his gray sweats hung low on his hips.

Fuck, I loved waking up to the sight of both of them. This was better than any Christmas present.

Judith glanced at him, then returned her attention to her drink. "You have an entire closet full of shirts."

"So do you. You're probably the reason I can't find my phone, too." The second part of his grumble was soft. He joined us, and refused the coffee I tried to hand him, taking a quick kiss from me instead. He also pressed his lips to the top of Judith's head.

We'd moved in most of her clothing over the last few days, and we'd spend the next week slowly bringing over anything else she wanted. But today I was making them both celebrate Christmas and pretend they knew how to take a day off.

Judith shrugged. "But I'd argue that this way is really a win for all of us." This time her gaze lingered on him longer, sweeping up his frame. A smirk played on her lips.

"I should've bought you shirts for Christmas." Xander's grumbling was light. He took her coffee and took a sip.

Perfect segue. I was trying not to be like a kid on Christmas, waiting for the whole family to wake up, but I'd been waiting on them for almost an hour. It was a good thing none of us tended to sleep in. "Speaking of, we should open presents."

"That suggestion's not up for debate," I said

before either of them could come up with a witty reason to be contrary.

Putting the side of her hand to her forehead, Judith gave me a sloppy salute. "Yes, sir."

Having her here the last few mornings, waking up with her in our bed and not having to send her home at night, had been amazing. It was as if she was always meant to be here. As if all three of us were.

I ushered them into the living room to sit by the tree, then grabbed two shoe box sized packages and handed one to each of them. I'd been tempted to go all-out and buy all the presents, but the three of us agreed those gifts were better served with people who couldn't buy whatever they wanted.

"Ooh, new Converse?" Judith asked as she slipped a finger under one edge of the paper and carefully pulled it up.

I'd never seen her wear a pair of Converse in her life. "No." The boxes were the size they were to keep the two of them from guessing what was inside. Their actual gifts were too distinctly shaped to wrap directly.

She managed to take off the entire piece of wrapping paper without a single tear, though I had no idea how or why. When she had the box uncovered, she raised an eyebrow. "I don't wear a size 13 men's shoe."

"Just open it." I rolled my eyes but I was amused.

She took just as much care pulling out the crumpled paper stuffed inside, and the way Xander fidgeted, it was clear he wanted to make the process go faster. Then she was finally at the small velvet box nestled on the bottom of it all. She worked her jaw and her eyes were wide as she lifted it out, and there was a moment of hesitation before she opened the lid.

"Oh. Dominic." Her voice was breathy when she exposed the ring inside. It was my grandmother's ring.

"This isn't a proposal or an engagement ring," I said as I slipped the jeweled band from its box. "But it's always been meant for the woman I love, and that's you. It belongs with you."

Holding out her hand, a smile flitted on to her face. "I love it. It's stunning. Thank you." She let me slip the ring on her finger, then she leaned in and pressed her lips to my cheek. "I love you too."

I would never get tired of hearing that.

When we turned to Xander, a whisper of a scowl vanished from his face. He wasn't as delicate tearing off the paper, and within seconds he was surrounded by shredded, colorful wrapping and crumpled kraft paper.

He stared at the smaller box in his hand with a furrowed brow. "I'm not going to look good in a delicate jeweled ring." Though there was a catch in his voice.

"Open it," I prompted. It was possible I was more excited about this than they were, but I knew what was inside.

When Xander lifted the lid, he grunted and his jaw dropped. "Is this…?"

"Yeah, it is." My father's wedding band. Simple gold inlaid with polished oak. There was no family tradition associated with this ring, but traditions had to start somewhere and it belonged on the man I loved.

Watching him slip it on, seeing that promise on his ring finger, clenched around my heart in the best possible way. And his kiss after, the kisses all three of us shared, were incredible. Full of promise and future.

Xander's gifts were next. A short, diamond cut gold chain for Judith with a delicate lock hanging from it, that coincidentally—or not—matched the ring.

"A lock? As in, you own me?" She didn't sound upset.

He hooked the necklace on her. "Yes."

Thumbing the chain up, and holding out her left hand, she let the light catch both pieces. "You know you're both already my favorite accessories," she teased.

When I unwrapped Xander's present, my heart

leaped into my throat. It was an engraved sign, the kind that hung next to a door, like a business. Pewter on wood. It said *Dominic Mancini, Esq.*

"For the new firm, once you find the right place," he said.

It was perfect.

"Best for last." This wasn't the cool, collected Judith that the world saw. This was the carefree woman only we really got to know.

She grabbed two identical boxes from under the tree and started to hand us each one. She paused, seemed to weigh them in her hands, then swapped who she was giving them to.

Weird. The box was neatly wrapped so that it could be opened without tearing in paper. I slipped off the top, and stared in confusion at what I saw inside. "Is this—"

"—my phone?" Xander pulled his out, the confusion on his face matching mine.

"Yup." Judith looked pleased.

I didn't get it. "Um… thanks?"

"I knew you took it," Xander said.

"I had to make sure neither of you checked your emails before it was time." She settled onto the couch, playful smile on her face.

Why would we? "It's Christmas. Who checks their phone first thing Christmas morning?" But I already knew the answer.

"Me." Xander wiggled the device, then

unlocked the screen.

I did the same, and found a new email waiting from Judith.

"Seven years ago, we marked the start of something new, and we made sure we'd always remember it," she said as I opened the message. "I love that everyone else who matters has done the same, but this is just for us."

In the message was an address and a name—the same tattoo parlor Xander frequently got inked at—plus a date and time. The attachment was an intricate Celtic knot, sketched out in fine ink lines. On closer inspection, not easy to do on the tiny screen, I saw our initials were woven into each of the three sides.

"It's perfect." This entire morning, everything about it, was amazing. "How did we go without this for so long?" I didn't mean to say that out loud.

"Because you're dim." Judith winked.

Xander grabbed her, pulled her into him, and half-fell onto me. "Takes one to know one." They were both laughing.

This was definitely perfect.

This was the family I'd tried to convince myself I already had, but it had never been this real. I'd never felt this whole. I could trust Xander and Judith. I loved them. I was happy and grateful to dedicate the rest of my life to them, and I knew they would be the same for me.

epilogue 1

onyx

Anyone who didn't know better might think this was *John Hughes the Class Reunion*, gathered in Aunt Rosie's dining room. She wasn't my aunt, but she was Maddox's and we'd all called her that for years.

Judith was Molly Ringwald—duh. Xander was Judd Nelson, and Dominic was Emilio Estevez. Alys was Ally Sheedy, but way cuter and currently sporting fuchsia hair, and Maddox was Anthony Michael Hall, but sexy on top of brainy.

"Hey, Cat. Pass the potatoes?" Maddox's voice and use of my nickname jarred me from the flashback to the eighties.

"Don't do it," Xander warned. "You give him too many potatoes and he starts to do things."

But they were only *The Breakfast Club* on the surface.

Claire grabbed the bowl of mashed potatoes from its spot between us at the dining room table. "What kind of weird things? Like... obscene things?" She was new to this group, and pretty in a Joanna-Eberhart-doesn't-fit-in-with-the-other-Stepford-Wives kind of way. And as far as I could tell she was Judith's new best friend, which was taking some getting used to, but was nice.

I wasn't sure I wanted to picture Maddox fucking mashed potatoes. Or maybe I did.

The look Alys gave Claire was confused-but-amused. "Like sculpting them."

"Doesn't matter how many times you build the obelisk, it still doesn't mean anything, and they still won't come," Xander teased.

Maddox rolled his eyes. "Fuck. Build a mashed potato shrine to our alien overlords once when you're twelve and the world never lets you forget about it."

"In a world with the internet, everything is forever," Judith said.

Rosie shivered. "Horrible thought."

These people had a lot more depth than anyone in a movie.

The teasing and playful conversation continued as the meal did. I loved this tradition, all of us gathering here, but this year it was tinted with a different lens.

Or maybe this was the first year I'd taken off the rose-colored glasses.

A clanging rang through the room, and Rosie stood as she tapped her fork against the crystal goblet in her hand. "A toast," she said. "To everyone in the room, and the amazing things you've accomplished. This year and overall."

Everyone raised their glasses, and drank.

I'd always felt like I was part of this group. For as long as I'd been friends with Maddox, he'd drawn me into this weird little circle of people. But today I was on the outside looking in.

It was different and disconcerting, but the feeling had been growing for a while.

I was going to swallow it today though, and enjoy this holiday with everyone.

Through the meal and after, everyone's phones kept chiming. Rosie grumbled about it a few times, but she allowed it, because they were holiday greetings from other people. Judith and Xander especially were getting hit with the notes.

As we all eventually pushed away from the table, I struggled to fight my moodiness. Everyone helped clean up the table and stack dishes in the kitchen. Claire tried to stay and wash, but Rosie wouldn't let her. It would wait a few hours.

We moved into the living room as a group, and I grabbed a chair at the edge of the room. I couldn't shake this feeling of being an observer. Maybe one of the aliens Maddox had built his mashed potato sculpture to so many years ago.

"Hey." Maddox startled me when he dropped into my lap and draped an arm around my neck. "Why did the cat ask for a drum set?"

Fucking... Maddox and his bad jokes. I didn't know if I wanted to be sucked into this or stay on the perimeter.

"Why?" Alys asked.

Maddox was watching me, amusement dancing in his eyes, and his smile threatening to burst out.

Behind him, Claire waved her arm. "Oh, I know this one. Because he wanted to make some mewsic."

"Get it. *Mew*-sic." Maddox repeated. He and Claire both burst into giggles.

The joke wasn't funny, but their amusement was contagious.

"Holy fu—" Xander's sigh was exaggerated. "This is why we didn't have kids."

"Sorry, *grandpa*." Maddox glanced over his shoulder. "Do you need your walker to hobble to your car? I didn't know old people couldn't have fun."

I laughed along with everyone else, as the bad jokes and teasing continued. I was going to miss this next year, and no one here knew yet that I'd be gone, so I'd better memorize the fuck out of it now. Even though I was leaving, these people were my friends, and I'd remember them when I was on the other side of the country.

epilogue 2

fourteen months later

xander

The midday sunlight glinted off the hood of my Impala. As I parked in Elliot's driveway and shut off the engine, my cell phone rang. The screen just said *Joker*.

Good. Maybe I could finally put an issue to rest that had gone unresolved for far too long.

I swiped *Answer*, but before I could say anything I heard, "You sent my kid a drum set? Were you high?"

Always a joy to hear from Roger *Joker* Simms. I chuckled as I climbed from the car and closed the door behind me. "I'm assured they're top of the line drums. Maddox promised."

"I'd tell you that's not the issue, but I think you already know that." I could practically hear Roger's eyeroll. "If this is your way of getting me to work faster, you can't rush these kinds of results."

"I sent the drums because the kid asked for drums, and who am I to impede future greatness?" I'd also done it because Joker thought it would be fun to send a sexy soldier stripper to Judith's office for her birthday, and claim it was from me. As if I'd pick any theme other than sexy Viking. "But now that you mention the job…"

It never sat well with me that we couldn't pursue more serious actions against Chris and Bryce. I wanted them to suffer for what they'd done to Aces-Played, and Simms had access to *resources* Dom and I didn't.

"I should have the Old Man charge you double, solely because of the drums." Joker groused.

I'd pay a thousand times the quoted price to have this matter dealt with, but he didn't need to know that. "I don't think I heard you right. Did you say your girl needs a cymbal to go with that drum set?"

"For the love of God, no. But your little matter has been handled."

I knew I'd gone to the right place. The firm Joker worked for in Virginia operated in that gray area of the law that I couldn't touch, and I was grateful for it. "Do I dare ask for details?"

"Probably best you don't. Let's just say the evidence we provided to an overseas ally was enough to get Dumb and Dumber extradited. They'll be taken into custody as soon as their government-sponsored flight lands on sovereign soil."

One thing Simms had already told me—Bryce and Chris had expanded their operation beyond AcesPlayed. Nothing local, they thought they were being smart by keeping their crimes international.

Nope.

"Thank you." I was sincere with my words. Knowing that cloud no longer hung over us…

"I did it for Judith." Joker raised his voice as a cacophony of enthusiastic drumming sounded in the background. "And you're dead to me, Xander," he shouted.

I chuckled. "As if. I owe you, though." One of those important lessons I'd learned from Judith— favors were the most valuable currency there was, whether they were good favors or bad.

I rang Elliot's doorbell and Mrs. Ria answered. She greeted me with a warm smile, and gestured behind her. "He's expecting you. You know the way."

I did. I'd been here several times in the last few months. Sometimes it was because Judith, Dom, and I were hanging out with Elliot, Link, and Fallyn. Most of the time it was because I was listening to pitches from people in Elliot's incubator.

My grandfather had a house like this, positioned at the edge of Haddarville, up on a hill like he was overlooking his entire fucking legacy. Elliot was putting his home to much better use. It felt alive in here, the way a home should.

Elliot screened the projects of everyone who lived here, on an intense level, before letting them sign on. All of their projects were solid at least in concept, and he felt they had the skills to make them happen.

I came in a little later in the process. As people were nearing completion, they got to do a trial run of their pitch with me. As far as they were concerned, I was doing Elliot a favor. He told them he had a friend in investment who would give them tips and pointers before they started the real deal of finding investors.

But it served me too. It gave me first pick of any project that caught my attention. We didn't tell them that though, not to be deceptive, but because we didn't want the knowledge adding extra stress to what they were doing.

As I headed toward the drawing room at the rear of the house, voices caught my attention as they floated out from the kitchen.

"It's built-in, the developers put it there." That was Landon. He and Nigel spent a bit off time over here, especially those weekends where Megan was working. For some reason they all made excuses like *they're helping people learn industry standards for coding*, and it was probably true, but I didn't know why Elliot and Nigel didn't just own their friendship.

"That means it's not an exploit," Nigel said.

I had to hear this. I stopped in the kitchen doorway in time to see Fallyn huff with exasperation.

"Of course you're taking each other's side, you're fucking." She sat across from them at the table in the breakfast nook. King was at her feet, looking happy to be around people.

Nigel shook his head. "Go ask Elliot. He'll agree with us."

"Which is my point," Fallyn said.

I could see it.

Landon furrowed his brow. "That's the opposite of your point."

I didn't have a stake in this conversation, but I was tempted to pick a side just to see where things went. If I had time, I might consider it.

"No." Fallyn could hold her own anyway, without my help. "My point is, one—fucking someone is a bad reason to take their side, and two —it makes the game overpowered."

Fucking someone?

"You called it a hack," Nigel said.

I was curious what they were talking about.

"I called it an exploit. It's there so you can hit a secret handshake combination of buttons, get all your health and stats back, regardless of the situation, and walk through an otherwise difficult game. That's an exploit whether or not it's built-in. Especially if you're telling people you're badass because you beat the game on its highest level."

Nigel shrugged. "But you did. The game says those are the rules for winning, and you won."

Ah. They were talking about the latest *Ninja Manifesto* game. I moved further into the room to grab their attention. "I think you're missing the real point."

Three pairs of curious gazes looked at me. "What's that?" Landon asked.

"Why the fuck are you playing a DM game?" Why take a side when I could make my own? "Did you get bored with originality?"

The way Nigel rolled his eyes, I thought they might fall out of his head. "No one asked you." He wadded up a paper napkin and tossed it. It bounced off my arm and landed on the floor.

King's tail wagged harder, thumping against the floor, and Fallyn gripped his collar. "Puppy, sit." She glared at me. Did she want me to sit too? "Don't you have a meeting to be in?"

I doubted she was upset with me. I'd never had a problem with Fallyn before. All of this was in good fun.

"Maybe." I grabbed the makeshift projectile off the floor and tossed it back toward the group. King jumped up and snagged the paper ball out of the air, then deposited it at Fallyn's feet, waiting for her to throw it again.

I turned away. "She's right, you know," I called over my shoulder.

Fallyn's *ha* reached me as I walked away, as did Nigel's grunt of disagreement.

I found Elliot in the drawing room with my actual meeting. He introduced me to Brigham, we made some small talk, and Brigham dove into his presentation.

I gave him my full attention, making mental notes as he talked about what worked and what didn't in his presentation. This wasn't going to be a project for me, but some of the other partners may be interested, and when he was done I'd give him my feedback and maybe Jonathan's name.

He got to a stat about coffee shops in the lower forty-eight, and I stopped him. "Is that number real? It can't be."

"I can cite sources." Brigham looked offended that I'd question his numbers. "And yes."

I let out a long whistle, impressed with the data.

"Don't…" Elliot winced."

"Puppy, *no*." Fallyn's shout came from the other room, accompanying the sound of running.

"Don't whistle." Elliot sighed as King ran into

the room and jumped up on him. He was laughing, where Fallyn looked exasperated when she ran into the room.

Elliot scratched behind King's ears and nodded at me. "His fault."

"You were my favorite for about five minutes, Xander." Fallyn huffed.

I laughed. This place was the same madhouse as always, and that was fantastic. I loved that seeing this was an extension of my world with Judith and Dominic. That she and I came from what we did—a small town with its head up its ass and families that were the same—to be a part of this. A world that was having fun. Creating. Living.

I couldn't have planned something more perfect, though knowing Judith, this had been part of her master scheme the entire time.

---

dominic

I sat in the conference room of my law office, next to Sonya and across from the people whose contract she was signing. Misa was the representative for the Japanese distributor who was purchasing the manga rights to Sonya's bestselling series.

My firm wasn't big, it was me and a few staff members, but thanks to contracts like Sonya's and

Plaid Peanut Butter, we were surviving, and growing with a client base I was comfortable with.

I'd been going back and forth for weeks with Misa's attorney, who sat next to her, making sure no one got screwed over in this deal. The contract was finally in a good place.

Misa's English was flawless, with a light accent, as she asked a few final questions. Her attorney's English wasn't as good, but given that my Japanese was limited to about three words I'd picked up at the AcesPlayed offices, that I probably didn't pronounce correctly, I wasn't one to judge.

I highlighted a few places in the contract that had been sticking points, to make sure everyone still agreed with the final wording. When we were all solid, Misa and Sonya both signed.

We wrapped up the meeting with bows and handshakes, and saw our guests to the front door. Misa turned to Sonya. "I hear you have a restaurant here that's…" Misa flushed, and ducked her head.

"Yes?" Sonya asked.

"Joystick's?"

I hid my amusement behind a mask of serious-ness. *Joystick's* was a geeky-themed place with a tattooed waitstaff who were mostly male. It was like Hooters, but for geeks who liked sexy men.

Sonya nodded. "We do. Would you like to cele-brate tonight?"

Misa nodded.

"I'll text you details," Sonya said.

Misa and her lawyer were on their way.

After they were gone, I nodded toward the hallway. "Are you going to do this?" I asked Sonya. I'd been trying to get her to commemorate a contract with me for months. Reese loved the ritual, because it meant photos of her success, but Sonya avoided it for the same reason.

But she'd wanted her books in manga form for a long time, and Jeremy and Quentin had pushed hard to make this happen. This was a bigger deal than most.

"Fine." Sonya huffed, but she was mailing. "But only this once, and only because it's Japan."

I pulled her up next to me, in front of the plaque that hung by my front door, and took a selfie of both of us. All these photos hunt in my office, marking milestones. Reminding me of how incredible this was.

And dotted with so many photos of Xander, Judith, and me.

Speaking of, they were walking toward us.

"Is it done?" Judith asked Sonya with a grin.

Sonya nodded. "But I'm going to leave you all to whatever you're up to. I need to get back to work.

"You really should," Judith said. "I heard one of the new writers say Spock and Uhura were a way better ship than Spock and Kirk."

Sonya scowled. "I thought I screened them better than that," she joked, and walked away.

As Xander, Judith, and I headed out to lunch, I couldn't help but think about how perfect This all was. This was what life should be.

---

judith

I'd been to the Video Games Award Ceremony many times in my career, but this was the first time I was here representing AcesPlayed, and it was an incredible feeling. Especially since the game had been nominated in a couple of categories.

The ballroom at The Howard was filled with large tables, and a temporary stage and podium sat at the front of the room. I was seated near the edge with Xander and Dom, and we shared a table with Scott, Kenzie, and Brienne. AcesPlayed hadn't won any awards yet, and neither had Rinslet, but I was still enjoying the show.

Yes, taking home an official trophy of recognition would be nice, and I was pretty sure it would be enough to make Xander come in his seat... Or at least drag Dom and I into the nearest coat closet to fuck. But I didn't expect a win tonight. The industry didn't quite understand what an incredible thing I and my team had done.

I was trying to keep a pleasant mask in place while someone on stage fumbled through their acceptance speech, when my phone buzzed with a new text.

It's a girl, the message from Phillip read. Like that, my smile was genuine. I flipped through a series of pictures of their new baby, with Adrienne, with him, with Dustin. This was their second child, and the entire family looked so happy.

Currently, Phillip's text was much better news than what I was getting here. I shared the pictures with our small group, and sent back a *Congratulations* from everyone.

A short while later, Scott excused himself. He was presenting the final award of the night, for Player's Voice—the one category that players picked rather than a panel of industry representatives.

When he stepped onto the stage, he spit out what was probably supposed to be a joke, but landed flat with his emotionless delivery. He sighed. "Really? We're going to make *another* joke about how some of us are older than dial-up? Who writes this shit, the executive staff at DM?"

A wave of laughter rippled through the crowd, and he smirked. A glance at Kenzie showed her hiding behind her hand, but after more than ten years with him, she expected it.

"Let's skip the script and get down to the list,"

Scott said. He read through the nominees for Player's Choice, including AcesPlayed.

I liked hearing our name called, but expected that would be the last time tonight.

Scott tore into the envelope like Xander opening Christmas presents, pulled out the card inside and frowned.

What was that?

He beckoned to someone at the edge of the stage, and after a little back and forth, a young man joined him at the podium.

"Am I allowed to do this?" Scott asked. His question was whispered, but he hadn't pulled away from the microphone. Most likely on purpose.

A tiny voice inside me knew what this was, but I didn't dare listen. That was the path to disappointment.

Whatever the award show representative said was much quieter and didn't reach the audience.

"Because conflict of interest," Scott said.

They exchanged a few more muttered words.

"And I'm single-handedly responsible for her greatness." Scott's voice was clear and distinct in an otherwise deadly still room.

Kenzie slipped lower in her seat. "Oh my Gawd," she muttered.

Xander clenched his fist.

I couldn't hear anything else over the sound of

my pulse hammering in my ears. Had Scott read the card yet?

He faced the audience again. "The winner is— and I was kidding by the way, I'm lucky to call her a friend, but she earned this on her own—The winner is Judith Walsh and AcesPlayed with their debut MMORPG."

Did I hear him right? Was I dreaming? The way Xander and Dom were kissing me, the hugs from Kenzie and Brienne, said this was real. People cheered and clapped, and I was being pushed toward the stage.

When I got up there, Scott handed me the trophy and gave me a huge hug.

"I always knew you'd make it up here," he whispered in my ear. This time the words were just meant for me.

I had a speech prepared, and I recited it. At least, I was pretty sure I did. This all felt like a dream. An incredible, vivid, once-in-a-lifetime dream. I walked on clouds back to my seat, and remained floating as the ceremony wound down.

There were after parties, and everyone wanted to talk to us. To congratulate me.

And we'd join them soon enough. Xander was already tugging me and Dom toward an empty room that was near enough to hear the crowds, but far enough away we probably wouldn't be walked in on.

Probably.

We were going to celebrate in our own way now, and then join the rest of the world when we were done.

I loved this. All of it. It turned out I could really have it all.

Thank you for reading Judith, Xander, and Dominic's story. For taking this incredible journey with them, and me. through the entire AcesPlayed series.

Though this series is done, the characters will be back in a brand new series, where we'll go to Haddarville and some small town poly romance.

Onyx, Alys, and Maddox will open the Third and Main series, with DEV GIRL.

Alys has wanted more than friendship from her best friends for years, but men like them don't go for women like her—the shy, dorky dev girl they see as one of the guys.

Onyx suggests a road trip with the three of them, to get their friendship back to where it used to be. Two weeks driving cross country with her two favorite people? She's going, and she's bringing her master plan to seduce them both.

But the confined quarters and long hours together reveal deeper, darker secrets than

how much Alys wants the guys, and by the time the trip is over they may not even have friendship, let alone something more.